THE THIEF DOVE ON THE NET. Whirled. Plopped it over Kenzie's head and spun her, locking her arms at her sides.

No. No. No.

From behind her, furious hands wound the long line from her chest down to her knees. Cursing and spitting, Kenzie was knocked blindly to the ground. Shoved and rolled into the trees, screeching monstrous words. Trapped in the growing darkness like a fly in a spider's web.

She screamed with rage—until something snatched and sliced at the nylon mesh over her face—and crammed a bag into her mouth.

A filthy, suffocating plastic bag.

STAKE OUT

Bonnie J. Doerr

Bonnie J. Doerr

Stakeout

Contact Information: info@leapbks.com

Cover Art by *Leap Books*

Interior Illustrations by *Laurie Edwards* and *Joanna Britt* (pgs. 14, 31, 89, 176, 214, 302-3)

Leap Books
Powell, WY
www.leapbks.com

Publishing History
First Leap Edition 2011

ISBN: 978-1-61603-007-0
Library of Congress Control Number: 2011922384

Published in the United States of America

Acknowledgements

Sea turtle conservationists and environmental stewards throughout the country have guided me throughout the long process of creating this book. They will never know how a simple word or expression of encouragement spurred *Stakeout* to its completion. I wish I could personally thank them one and all.

I owe a special debt of gratitude to the following individuals who went above and beyond to ensure completion of *Stakeout*:

Ryan Butts – Administrator Turtle Hospital, Marathon, Florida

Bernadette Hearne – Fellow writer and keen-eyed reader/editor to whom I owe eternal gratitude

Joan Langley – Historian, friend, provider of warm, supportive retreat for writing and research

Meriwynn Mansori – Most generous Spanish reader

Richie Moretti – Founder/Director Turtle Hospital, Marathon, Florida

Maggie Moe – Fellow writer who kept me going during difficult periods

Sue Schaf – Florida Fish and Wildlife Conservation Commission/former Administrator of Turtle Hospital, who kindly provided a guided personal tour of the hospital in its days as a private institution

Pamela Schill, DVM – Offered expertise on dealing with Salty's illness (Any errors concerning diagnosis and treatment are purely the result of literary license or author error and should not to be taken as medical advice.)

Elaine Sweet of Sav-a-Turtle – Read and approved Protect-a-Turtle information for its credibility

Finally, endless gratitude to my editor Kat O'Shea for her gentle, wise edits

DO NOT DISTURB

SEA TURTLE
NEST

VIOLATORS SUBJECT TO FINES AND IMPRISONMENT

**FLORIDA LAW
CHAPTER 370**

**U.S. ENDANGERED
SPECIES ACT OF 1973**

No person may take, possess, disturb, mutilate, destroy, cause to be destroyed, sell, offer for sale, transfer, molest or harass any marine turtle or its nest or eggs at any time.

Upon conviction, a person may be imprisoned for a period of up to 60 days or fined up to $500, or both, plus an additional penalty of $100 for each sea turtle egg destroyed or taken.

No person may take, harm, pursue, hunt, shoot, wound, kill, trap, capture any marine turtle, turtle nest, and/or eggs, or attempt to engage in any such conduct.

Any person who knowingly violates any provision of this act may be assessed a civil penalty up to $25,000 or a criminal penalty up to $100,000 and/or one year imprisonment.

SHOULD YOU WITNESS A VIOLATION, OBSERVE AN INJURED OR STRANDED TURTLE, OR MISORIENTED HATCHLINGS, PLEASE CONTACT FWC AT

1-888-404-FWCC OR **＊FWC** MOBILE PHONE

FLORIDA FISH AND WILDLIFE CONSERVATION COMMISSION
MARINE TURTLE PROTECTION PROGRAM

Praise for Island Sting

Stakeout is the second book in the highly acclaimed, fast-paced eco-mystery series by Bonnie J. Doerr. Here's what reviewers are saying about the first book in her series, *Island Sting.*

An exciting adventure, highly recommended

~Midwest Book Review

Action-packed...exciting...vivid descriptions of setting add to its appeal

~*Winston-Salem Journal*

Environmentalism leaps to the fore in this absolute page-turner...Island Sting is a fantastic adventure with far more meaning than most.

~The Long and the Short of It Reviews, 5 stars

Island Sting is an un-put-downable book

~Book of the Week, Middle Grade Ninja

Finalist Epic Award 2010

Nominee YALSA 2011 Popular Paperbacks

***Winston-Salem Journal*'s Crossover Charm Best Book List of 2010**

Most people called it theft. Kenzie called it murder.

Theft. Like some lame crook had made off with a computer or TV. But raiding sea turtle nests was mass murder, and Kenzie vowed to end the slaughter.

She'd keep her promise to Old Turtle, if she could ever get this dead-in-the-water boat moving again.

Taking Angelo's boat was her *first* mistake. She'd moved to Big Pine Key, Florida, when summer vacation began. Only a few weeks ago. Yet from day one it was clear Angelo obsessed over this runabout. He'd spent hours customizing it. Even if she had a drivers' license, he'd never trust her to handle it safely—no matter how many times she'd ridden in it. But how could she resist such temptation? Ten yards from her house. The perfect transportation. The only transportation.

She'd asked over and over for a ride to Turtle Beach.

Mom?

Too busy.

New job.

New boyfriend.

Angelo?

Lobster season.

His dad needed him.

All day.

Every day.

Then this morning—*wham*. She'd heard the *Turtle-News* report, freaked, and took off—without checking the gas. Her *second* mistake.

She'd focused on one thing only. Get to Turtle Beach. That's where she'd find evidence to snare the creep stealing sea turtle eggs. Island police were clueless. No evidence. No suspects. No theory. *Bee boogers*. Law enforcement may have surrendered, but she'd just begun to fight.

Kenzie kicked the empty gas can. The boat rocked. Her puppy cringed. "I'm not angry at you, Salty. I'm angry at me." She wrapped all twenty-two pounds of the pup in her arms, calculating the distance to the beach. Not far. Swimming was second nature to her. She could make it. But what about Salty?

Thunder rumbled. *Great*. A storm brewed. Where? Kenzie searched the sky. There. Just beyond the island.

She ruffled Salty's yellow fur and scanned the thin white line of sand. No visible help there. "It's you and me, Salty. Just you and me."

Wait. Behind the beach in the treetops—a large rectangle shone. A metal roof? Ana lived on the beach. Could that be her house? Ana had told Kenzie about the loggerheads when they'd met last month. Ana could help find the nests *and* fuel.

Kenzie hadn't planned to look for Ana's house, only the turtle nests. Problem was, she really didn't have a plan. Mistake number *three*.

So, what now? *Muscle power.* How hard could it be to row a fourteen-foot boat? She'd seen Angelo do it. She turned backwards on the seat, lifted the oars, then dropped each oarlock in place.

"Maybe we'll get lucky, Salty. Maybe it'll be you and me, plus Ana."

Swinging the wooden handles, she glanced behind her, dug the oars into the sea, and aimed the bow at the roof. Kenzie pulled hard against the water.

Row, glide.

Drift back.

Row, glide.

Drift back.

The strong current surprised her. The shore appeared no nearer.

How close was the storm? Hard to tell now that the rumbling had stopped. She leaned out from under the canvas top for a larger view. Minutes ago the blinding-blue sky perched on a horizon of white, puffy clouds. Clouds that now billowed with gray. Above the island, charcoal clouds swelled and piled. No soaring seabirds. No blue. Vast silence.

Creepy.

Salty curled at Kenzie's feet. His dark eyes shifted, and his nose twitched.

Move it, girl. Arms aching, she rowed on. Only a few months off the swim team and already weak.

The sky and sea darkened. Reflected sunlight no longer threatened to burn her pale, freckled skin. Good, right? Howling winds gusted longer and harder, driving her farther from land. Not good. New York weather never changed this fast. She rested her head on the oar handles. *I'm doomed.*

Thump.

Kenzie jerked upright.

Thump. Thump.

What the—?

Salty scrambled to the bow, propped his forepaws on the edge, and then barked. Nonstop.

Kenzie stowed the oars. "Okay. Okay. I get it." Balancing on the gunwale, she moved forward, knelt, and peered over the side.

A sea turtle. She pictured her science project's identification chart. Yellow and brown, tie-dye patterned shell—hawksbill. Shell bigger than a bicycle tire, small tail—mature female. *Awesome.*

More than a threatened species. An *endangered* species. Big news. Turtle Beach: nest site for loggerheads *and* hawksbills. Kenzie swore at the unknown thief. "You're in *double* trouble now, you creep."

Kenzie glanced toward the beach. A steely curtain of rain charged across the island. Its target? Girl and dog. Goose bumps prickled her skin.

The turtle bumped the boat again. Why wasn't it diving? "Dive, turtle. Dive."

The wall of rain marched closer. The boat rocked harder. Up. Down. *Splash*. Kenzie hung on. What could she do about the turtle now except push it away? Protect it from the battering boat. She reached over the side. *Splat*. Salt water burned her eyes. She shoved. The turtle spun. Faced her. There, caught in its beak-like mouth. A plastic grocery bag. The hawksbill was choking, struggling for air.

On a downward dip, she leaned over the gunwale to grab the bag. No luck.

The boat rocked up.

She steadied herself and waited.

The boat rocked down.

She stretched her arm.

Not even close.

Again and again she tried. Waves rushed one after the other, each pitching her high above the turtle. She'd have to jump in. The boat lifted and slammed down. *Bam*. Her hat flew off as she crashed to the floorboards.

Whining, Salty nosed her leg. If she dove after the turtle, the puppy would follow. Too risky. They'd be battered like the turtle, and how could they climb back on this wildly rocking boat? Kenzie's heart sank as she stumbled to her seat.

Salty climbed onto her lap. Shivering, he clutched her soggy hat between his teeth.

"Good catch, Salty. Good puppy. I can still see the shore. We'll make it. We'll be okay." If only she believed her words. "Get down, now."

Salty crouched in the bow. Kenzie stowed her hat and retied her flapping hair. The temperature plummeted. Stinging rain slashed sideways under the Bimini top. The leading wind roared, building waves and forcing the turtle farther from the boat. *Keep it together, Kenzie.* She was here to save turtles. No squall would stop her. *I can do this.* She wiped the salt grit off her face, then grabbed the oars.

She shuddered, exposed and defenseless against the dark wall of rain. The shore disappeared. The hawksbill vanished. Which way were they drifting?

Think.

Drop anchor.

Wait it out.

At least there's no lightning.

Kenzie dropped the oars, reached forward, and found the slippery anchor line. She heaved the anchor overboard. Panicked as the rope slithered off the bow.

No. She'd forgotten to tie it off. She lunged for the vanishing rope. *Thump.* Dip. The boat lurched on a taut line—already fastened to the cleat. *Thank you, Angelo.*

Once anchored, the boat rocked worse than ever. But better than drifting out to sea. What would happen to the hawksbill in this storm?

Waves sloshed over the sides. Seawater swirled around Kenzie's feet. Something banged her ankle. Kenzie fished under her seat. Angelo's milk-jug bail. She could work with this.

Scoop. Toss.

Splat.

Scoop. Toss.

Splat.

By the time she'd reduced water on board by half, light pierced the clouds. The torrent retreated as swiftly as it had attacked. The wind and the sea calmed. The sun blazed.

Salty shook. Water drops flew. Kenzie hugged the stinky puppy. Her stomach relaxed. "I told you we'd be okay." Salty wriggled loose and barked an alarm across the water.

A few yards away, the hawksbill floated. The bag still trapped in its mouth.

Kenzie pulled anchor. She swung the oars into the settling sea. A few yards from the turtle, she anchored once more. The turtle didn't move. Not a flipper.

Kenzie stripped to her swimsuit, grabbed the loose end of a towline, and leaped overboard.

Be alive. Be alive, turtle. Be alive.

KENIZE COULDN'T TELL if the turtle's flippers moved at will or by wave action. It didn't matter. She wouldn't abandon it, dead or alive. Carefully avoiding its sharp claws, she wrapped the line behind the turtle's thick front flippers, said a quick, intense prayer, climbed back onboard, and lifted the oars.

Forward, dip.

Pull back.

Umph.

Forward, dip.

Pull back.

Umph.

Kenzie towed the heavy hawksbill behind the boat. With every pull, the poor turtle surged forward—a helpless passenger on an unwelcome ride. In spite of a favoring current, her muscles burned. After endless pulls on the oars, her nose twitched at the familiar rotten-egg odor of seaweed—beached and decaying. *Finally.* She neared land.

Hang in there, turtle. Almost there.

She anchored a few boat lengths from the rocky shore, then slipped on her soaked T-shirt. Having experienced the pain of blisters and peeling skin, she positioned her hat tight and low on her forehead. She moved to the transom, pulled on her water shoes, then lowered herself into the quiet, knee-deep water. Salty jettisoned off the boat, then belly-flopped beside her.

The turtle turned its head toward the brief disturbance. *Yes. A physical reaction.*

Kenzie waded to the hawksbill. The plastic bag in its mouth swayed on the surface. Could she pull it out? Apprehensive, she eyed the turtle's hard, sharp beak. Nothing to worry about. She'd never read anything about turtles biting, even if they were strong and healthy. *Go for it.* She grasped the bag inches from the hawksbill's mouth and tugged. No luck. The turtle's jaws locked. Its sharp beak ripped a hole in the plastic.

The turtle was alive, so even if it had swallowed other trash, its air passage remained partially open. Small comfort. Turtles could hang on a long time after swallowing plastic bags, suffocating little by little.

Kenzie sank to her knees. "Mama hawksbill, we'll save you first. Then figure out what to do about the loggerhead nests." She patted its head. "Don't worry. Your nest too."

"Stay away, Salty." For once the puppy obeyed, paddling in distant circles while Kenzie freed the turtle from the towline.

Easy now. Loosening the line, she inspected

19

the turtle's skin. *Excellent.* No damage from the thick rope. After untying the knots, she slipped the line over the turtle's head, then tossed the rope into the boat.

"Mama Hawksbill, you are about to become a kickboard for the captain of St. Joe's swim team. Former captain, that is." She checked for barnacle-free handholds, grabbed the turtle's slippery, algae-covered shell on either side of its small tail, and flutter-kicked it toward the beach. One, two, three kicks. That wasn't so tough. Her legs were nowhere near as tired as her arms.

Salty swam beside them—a proud naval escort.

Floating the turtle took little effort thanks to the buoyant salt water. And now that the storm had passed, the protective barrier reef seven miles off shore restricted waves to their usual gentle lap

But how and where do you secure a turtle this size on a rocky beach? *Tide pools.*

Off to the left. A large outcropping of stones. If she could get the hawksbill into a tide pool, it couldn't drift away. At the water's edge, Kenzie propped the listless turtle against a large, flat rock. She stretched, waiting for her heartbeat to ease.

Already on shore, Salty paced and practiced his hurry-up bark.

Timing her pushes to catch the gentle waves, Kenzie maneuvered the turtle onto the stones. The water lifted. She shoved.

With one last *oomph*, Kenzie forced the immobile turtle onto a table-sized flat rock. When the next wave floated the turtle, she guided it to a shallow stone-ringed pool, then released it to rest. The hawksbill would be safe until high tide.

Exhausted, she plopped backward into the shallows. Weightless relief. She closed her eyes and floated, surrendering to the rhythmic lap of gentle waves and the soft cocoon of warm water. A blurry image of a different turtle—Old Turtle—floated into view.

Months before, as she stood alone at the New York Aquarium's ocean exhibit, Old Turtle floated toward her. Tapped the glass with its giant head. One, two, three times. Its wise, forlorn expression begged for help. One by one, other sea turtles congregated. The weight of their sorrow weakened and dizzied her. Palms flat on the glass, she steadied herself and responded with a plea of her own: *What do you want? What can I do?*

Sister Bernadette's reflection had appeared in the glass. Poof. The spell broke.

"Kenzie," Sister said. "Please, stay with the class."

As Kenzie moved away, she maintained eye contact with Old Turtle and telepathed a promise: *I'll figure it out. I will. And I'll do it—whatever it takes.*

She opened her eyes and blinked away the saltwater burn. The aquarium vanished. Reality rested in plain sight: a hawksbill in extreme distress. She lived in the Florida Keys now. *I got it, Old Turtle. I'll save the hatchlings.* But saving the adult turtle came first. What a way to launch her plan.

Kenzie captured her floating hat, then staggered to her feet. She waded forward and clambered over the slippery rocks to the beach. A beach not much wider than a few lanes of St. Joe's pool.

Branches cracked. There, near the trees. Someone in a purple plaid shirt. Salty bolted. "Salty, no!" Too late. Genetics ruled. Purple Shirt fled into the thick scrub. Salty chased, startling a squawking flock of chickens out of the bushes. *Chickens? On a beach?* Salty ignored the birds and trailed Purple Shirt deep into the brush. Seemed his genetic jumble didn't include bird dog.

Purple Shirt had watched them without offering to help. Suspicious. And why run? Like a puppy's so scary... *Purple Shirt could be the creep destroying turtle nests.*

Kenzie raced across the debris-covered beach, then charged into the woods. She followed the jingling tags and playful barks until the puppy noises faded. She stopped. Twigs crunched. Heavy footsteps. Where? That way. She stumbled through the maze of buttonwoods and mangroves, unable to keep up.

Maybe Salty had given up and returned to the beach. She turned back. Walked a while. Stopped and called. No answer. Walked some more. Stopped and listened. Nothing. A few more yards and she'd be out of the trees. Finally. The clink of dog tags. She scanned the immediate area. There—under the cabbage palmettos. Salty lay in the sand, seriously licking his right front paw.

"Salty, what happened?" Kenzie rolled him over and examined the backside of his right leg. The weird, tiny toe above his foot dripped blood. "Your dewclaw. Poor puppy."

She gripped the hem of her well-worn T-shirt between her back teeth. Biting and yanking the thin fabric, Kenzie ripped a ragged strip of cotton off the bottom, wrapped it around Salty's paw, and tied it high on his leg. Cradling one arm under his chest and the other around his rump, she picked him up. Salty lathered her cheek with licks.

"Let's go find Ana, puppy."

With a squirming, whimpering dog in her arms, she didn't see the pile of fishnet until she stumbled over it. Plastic bottles, cans, and glass littered the sand. What a mess. No wonder Salty cut his paw. This beach topped anything on the list of must-do litter cleanup assignments for the Teens Care team. Careful to avoid debris, she zigzagged along the tree line until she spied a brown stilt house tucked back among the scrub. A high wooden fence hid everything on ground level. Who or what could the owner of this desolate place be trying to keep out? Searching for an entrance, she plodded along the weathered gray fence. An earthy animal smell permeated the air.

"Hello. Is anybody home?"

Nothing.

She turned the corner and came to a rusty-hinged gate plastered with multiple *Keep Out* notices. One small sign displayed a picture of a gun and the warning: *If you can read this, you're in my sights. Get out!*

This unwelcoming house couldn't be Ana's.

Kenzie shifted Salty in her arms. He grew heavier by the minute. "I need help. Is anybody here?" She leaned to peek between the boards, squeezing Salty. He yelped. Above her, a sliding door screeched open.

"Go away. If I see you or that dog around here again you'll both have something to yelp about." A purple blur retreated into the shadows.

Purple. Could that person be—

"Please, wait. Do you know where the Muñoz family lives?"

"Yellow house. Keep on past the point." The gruff voice fired from the dark. "Now git."

The door scraped shut.

Git? *No problem. We're out of here.*

Kenzie returned to the beach and trudged over the littered sand. Her arms, already aching from wielding the oars, now trembled from Salty's weight. She rounded the narrow piece of land that stuck out into the water and—there it was—a yellow stilt house reflecting sun and sea in its wall of massive windows. She'd survived the wicked forest and discovered a golden treasure. A sign proclaiming *Bienvenido* marked a path leading to the property. As she followed the neatly raked trail, she matched her pace to the silly yellow-brick-road song.

This was more like it. No fence. A clear line of sight under the house to the gravel drive and the large burgundy van parked there. A van she'd seen at church. Mr. Muñoz's van.

A ship's bell hung on the stair rail beside

an open-air elevator. Kenzie jerked the bell's knotted rope back and forth.

A door creaked open. Ana's cheery voice responded, "*Momentito.*"

"Ana. I found you."

Ana's wheelchair rolled onto the porch above. "Kenzie, *Hola.*" She smiled down through the railing. "I am surprised to see you here. This morning the weather is not so good to visit the beach."

"No kidding," Kenzie shifted Salty up on her shoulder. "Ana, I need help."

Kenzie hadn't known Ana long. Yet she believed Mom would welcome and trust Ana. Like a healthy bowl of oatmeal. Kenzie, however, sensed Ana would shamelessly sneak chocolate chips and tons of sugar into that wholesome cereal. Ana was the perfect friend. *The perfect alibi.*

"Please, come up."

At the top of the stairs, Kenzie sank into the nearest chair. She rested a panting Salty on her thighs, hung her arms, and shook off their quivering fatigue.

"Oh no. Your little dog is hurt."

Salty nosed his bandage.

"*Pobrecito.* Poor baby. There is blood." Ana stroked Salty's head. "I will get some medicine and water." Ana spun her chair to go inside.

"Ana, wait. There's a turtle on the beach that's in a lot more trouble than Salty. We have to get help. It's choking."

"*¡Dios mío!*" Ana turned around. "It must have washed up during that squall."

25

"Not exactly. I'll explain later. Do you know who to call?"

"*Claro*. Of course. The Turtle Hospital."

"There's a turtle hospital?"

"*Sí, chica*. Across the Seven Mile Bridge. I will call now."

When Ana returned she held a tray on her lap. "In one half hour they will come." She handed a soda to Kenzie, then placed a bowl of water on the floor.

"Thanks, Ana. A turtle hospital. Awesome."

While Salty lapped, the bulky wrap slipped down his leg.

"Now we take care of your puppy." Ana returned to the kitchen.

"Ana," Kenzie called, "there's another problem besides the turtle."

"Okay..." Ana wheeled out with peroxide, a roll of gauze, and liquid soap. She poured the soap into the remaining water. "This other problem, what is it?"

"Does your dad have any gas? My boat ran out."

"Always *Papi* keeps spare fuel in the storage room. *Pero*, I did not know you have a boat."

Kenzie twirled a strand of hair around her finger. "Actually, I don't."

Ana's eyes widened. "You came in Angelo's."

Kenzie slid down in her chair.

"Kenzie, you and Angelo... You are good friends. Still I cannot believe he permitted you to borrow it."

"It's unbelievable all right." She lowered herself to the floorboards beside Salty. "Like you said, unbelievable beach day too."

"You did not come to swim at the beach. You came because of turtles. Yes?"

"Busted." Kenzie removed Salty's makeshift bandage.

"That day at church. I remember. You were so interested when I told you about the turtles. How did you find my home?"

Kenzie glanced toward the point. "I went to that wooden house down there, but—"

"Ancient Angry Edna frightened you away."

"Edna? That was a woman?"

"She is what Mamá calls a 'character.' Only one time have I seen her. She does not like dogs."

"No kidding."

"She fears them, I think."

Purple Shirt—Edna—ran from the beach because she feared dogs? That tough lady? Kenzie stroked Salty's soft ears. No way.

Ana cleaned Salty's cut. "You should have called me. *Papi* would be happy to bring you here."

"It was kind of a spur-of-the-moment thing."

"Today I planned to visit *Abuela*. It is good I am not finished my summer reading assignments, or I would be with grandmother in Miami."

"Good for me. Not for you."

"*Verdad.*" Ana handed the gauze to Kenzie. "You bandage Salty. I will get towels to cover the turtle. Wet towels will protect and cool it."

Kenzie bit her lip. *If it's not too late.*

SALTY FOLLOWED ANA AND KENZIE onto the small, enclosed platform next to the stairs. Ana fastened the gate behind them, then hit the power switch.

"Mom would love to have one of these," Kenzie said, as the elevator rattled to the ground. "She hates carrying groceries up seventeen steps."

"It is useful." Ana handed the towels to Kenzie. "I must get Doonie."

Anna switched off the elevator's power, and Kenzie opened the gate. "Doonie?"

"My beach buggy. Grandmother bought him last year for me. See?" Ana rolled toward a storage shed across the concrete floor under the stilt house. Inside the open door sat a yellow beach chair mounted on fat, oversized tires.

"I'll get it." Kenzie moved to pass Ana.

"No." Ana wheeled in front of her. "I can do it." The chair grazed Kenzie's toe.

"Hey." Kenzie jumped back. "You need a horn on that thing."

"Oh, no. *Lo siento mucho.*" Ana looked as if she'd flattened a kitten. "I am so sorry. I just...I do not want people to feel—"

"I get it, Ana. It's okay." After wiggling her toes, Kenzie danced a few steps. "See, no problem. Get your chair."

Ana worked the yellow beach buggy through the doorway and backed it against the doorjamb. She set her metal chair's brakes, pushed up off its arms, then switched her right hand to Doonie's arm. She pivoted and plopped onto the buggy's higher seat.

"On the beach, my wheelchair is not so good." She patted her buggy. "It is easy for Doonie to go over sand."

"Nice. But how's Doonie at climbing trash mounds?"

"Trash? Our beach is clean."

"When's the last time you went around the point?"

"It has been too long."

"Then let's roll."

On the way to the beach, Salty leaped and nipped at the towels, showing no sign of a limp.

"Quit it, Salty." Kenzie lifted the towels high. "We don't have time to play tug now."

They made easy progress until they rounded the point, where the aftermath of a human hurricane littered the sand. Ana struggled to keep her balance as she maneuvered Doonie over and around piles of debris.

"This stinks." Kenzie kicked a discarded water jug. "And I don't mean the seaweed."

Ana stopped rolling. She surveyed the sand

around her and the beach beyond. "So much trash here." She rubbed her hands on her slacks as if wiping them free of soil. "I did not realize."

They slogged on, avoiding a mound of cans and bottles entangled in seaweed, only to arrive at a pile of wood—broken lobster traps.

"More junk." Kenzie flung wooden slats into the trees, scattering a hen and its chicks. "What's with the chickens? It's weird to see them on the beach."

"People bring chickens here, *Papi* says, to move them out of neighborhoods. They make a mess in his garden. He plans to call a lady who will take them away."

Kenzie jerked another wooden plank out of the sand. "Too bad that lady can't take this mess away with the chickens. It's impossible for you to wheel Doonie on this beach without hurting yourself, and I don't see how turtles could safely nest *anywhere* around here." She whacked a soda can with the board before hurling it, too, out of the way.

"Please stop worrying, Kenzie. I am fine and turtles often nest nearby. I will show you another time." Ana touched Kenzie's arm. "You go on. I will return to wait for the ambulance. They will find the turtle a little past Ancient Angry Edna's house, *sí*?"

"That's where I left her."

"I will tell them."

Salty scampered ahead of Kenzie, weaving and snuffling the rocky shoreline. When he reached the hawksbill, he stood guard, barking nonstop until Kenzie joined them in the tide pool.

"I'm back, mama turtle." She stooped and touched the turtle's head. "Help is on the way."

The hawksbill showed no response. Its sorrowful, droopy eyes were so much like Old Turtle's that Kenzie's own eyes filled. "Don't be scared. I'm going to cover you to keep the sun off. Look at you. Even the algae on your back dried out."

After saturating all the towels with seawater, she draped one end of the bath towel over the turtle's head, then smoothed the cloth down its thin, wrinkled neck. The hawksbill's front flippers twitched.

"Good girl. Hang in there." Kenzie covered its barnacle-and-salt-crusted shell with the larger beach towels.

The temperature, in typical hot-air-balloon style, had been rising all morning. Now, an hour before noon, the sun's rays scorched on contact. *Hurry, ambulance.*

Time moved like a sea slug while Kenzie splashed water over the turtle and herself.

A siren sounded. Would a turtle ambulance have a siren? Salty whined as the blaring grew louder and higher in pitch. Then *blip.* It stopped.

Moments later, Salty barked an alarm.

"What is it, puppy?"

The pup spun in excited circles as a muscular, bow-legged man and an athletic, lanky woman hustled toward them. Each wore a gray Turtle

31

Hospital T-shirt.

Cool. Sirens for turtles.

Kenzie stepped across the rocks to the sand. "You're here."

"Without a lick of trouble," the man said. "Your friend gave us clear directions."

"Great job bringing in the turtle," the woman said, splashing into the tide pool. She lifted the towels off the turtle. "Ed, this is amazing. It's a hawksbill. A mature female. They're so rare here. We can't lose this one." She stooped beside the turtle and inspected its shell.

The man held out his hand to Kenzie. "I'm Ed Thompkins."

"Ed," the woman called again, "I bet she nested here on Turtle Beach. Wouldn't that be wonderful?"

Ed tipped his head toward the woman. "That bundle of enthusiasm is Melissa. Are you Kenzie?"

"Yes, sir."

Salty barked and butted Ed's leg.

"I'm sorry," Kenzie said. "He's only playing."

The puppy bumped Ed again, then splashed through the tide pools to the turtle.

"I think he's trying to tell me something." Ed saluted Salty. "Right, Turtle Dog, sir. I'm on it." He negotiated the rocks to join Melissa and Salty.

Kenzie swallowed a load of questions and followed.

Salty sniffed Melissa's knees, and she patted his head. "What's your name, puppy?"

"He's Salty."

Melissa lifted his bandaged paw. "Is Salty hurt, too?"

"His dewclaw's cut a little. He's okay though."

"Good. I'm glad we only have one patient here." Melissa ruffled the fur behind Salty's ears, then stroked the turtle. "Not a single sign of disease that I can see, Ed."

"Are you guys veterinarians?"

"No," Melissa said. "We work with several, though."

Ed's knees cracked as he pushed himself up. "I agree, Melissa. No outward signs of disease. At least we can be thankful for that. The old girl's dehydrated. Probably hasn't eaten for days. Don't know how much we can do for her. We'll give it our best shot. I'll get the stretcher."

"Do you really think she nested on Turtle Beach?" Kenzie asked.

"Because you found her so close to shore, I do." Melissa scooted back to sit on a dry rock. "No one has documented a hawksbill nest. Truthfully, the turtle patrol members wouldn't know a loggerhead's nest from a hawksbill's. There's never been much need to know. Before now, that is."

Turtle patrol? Interesting. "What does the turtle patrol do?" *Whatever their job, it didn't keep poachers away.*

"They count and record data. Things like nests, false crawls, disturbed nest sites. After a hatch, they count eggshells. Sometimes they move nests to safer locations."

I could do that. Kenzie opened her mouth to say so just as Ed appeared with something like a giant pizza pan on poles. She could wait.

Kenzie picked up Salty, then backed out of the way.

Ed placed the stretcher on the sand.

"How much of the bag has she swallowed?" Kenzie asked.

"Hard to tell until we x-ray her. Like Ed said, she appears to be starving. She's swallowed enough that it's blocking her digestive tract."

Ed positioned the stretcher next to the patient. "We'll know when we do the endoscopy. We weren't expecting this. We expected to find another turtle with fibropapilloma."

Endoscopy? Fibro what? Kenzie didn't remember reading these terms while researching her sea turtle project.

Melissa and Ed crouched on either side of the hawksbill and grasped her shell.

"Careful," Ed said. "These rocks are slippery."

"Ready?" Melissa asked. "One, two, three."

They heaved the turtle off the rocks, sidestepped, and lowered it onto the stretcher.

Salty whimpered and struggled until Kenzie set him down. He crept forward to nuzzle the turtle's beak-like nose. Kenzie stooped beside him. "What did you say you thought the turtle would have?"

"Fibropapilloma," Ed said. "However, there's no sign of external tumors."

"What is fibro...pap...fibro-whatever anyway?"

"Topic for another time. We need to get this old gal to the hospital."

"On three again." Melissa counted, "One,

two, three."

"Oomph." They lifted the stretcher. Ed gently bounced his end, testing its weight. "I'd say she's close to 150 pounds."

They trudged off the beach into the woods with Kenzie and Salty trailing. By the time Melissa and Ed reached the single-lane county road, sweat beaded their faces and stained their shirts.

They headed for a white ambulance parked across the road. Its sides were splashed with broad orange stripes and the green image of a sea turtle against a red cross. Brilliant orange lettering announced *Turtle Hospital Ambulance. Rescue, Rehab, Release.* The coolest emergency vehicle ever. Its engine roared into life, rousing Kenzie from her wonder. Turtle and crew were already inside.

If only Kenzie could go with them. Two problems: No room. No way. She wasn't even supposed to be on Turtle Beach.

Melissa leaned out the window. "Good job, Kenzie. Come visit the hospital." She gripped the door as the ambulance lurched forward, gravel and dust flying in its wake. Its yellow roof-lights flashed and its siren blared.

The hospital held the answers to so many questions. But how could Kenzie get there? She sort-of-kind-of stole a boat to get *here*.

She collected the towels and hurried back to the house, where Ana waited on the porch. "Is the turtle still alive?"

"She's hanging on."

"That is good news."

Kenzie hung the wet towels over the porch rail. "The hospital team is great."

"*Sí*. They have many successful rescues. Are you ready to see a nesting site?"

"More than ready, but I'm out of time. Mom gets off work early today. She'll go ballistic if she catches me in Angelo's boat by myself. I hate those *You're so thoughtless, impulsive… whatever* lectures of Mom's. She'll ground me for life."

Of course, *if she'd spared time to drive me over here, I wouldn't be in this mess.*

"And Angelo will make chum out of me if he finds out. I've got to get that boat back. Like right now."

"*¡Ay!* You are right. You must hurry. When I parked Doonie, I moved the gas outside the shed door. I hope Angelo's boat uses the same mix as *Papi's*. Leave the can on the beach. *Papi* will get it."

"Ana, I don't want your dad to know—"

36

"Chica, many boaters run out of gas. To help them, we need no name." Ana sparkled with innocence.

Kenzie hugged Ana. A friend. A friend she could trust with secrets.

Ana looked up at Kenzie. "Perhaps next time you go to sea you will carry extra gas and also a cell phone, yes?"

"I promise." Who could she have called though? Not Mom. Ana's number was not stored in her phone, and she sure couldn't call Angelo. "If there is a next time," Kenzie said. "Thanks for everything, Ana. Your number's in the phonebook, right? I *will* call you tonight—if I'm still alive."

She raced Salty down to the beach, thinking about the gasoline mix. Great. Boats could have different fuel requirements. Who knew? She filled the tank. What if this mixture destroyed Angelo's engine? Would their relationship follow? Not that they had much of one—yet. But there had been that hug...

Kenzie dragged the boat into the shallows. Salty leaped in and she climbed aboard.

Please start. Please start.

She pulled the cord.

A BIT OF BLUE SMOKE accompanied the first engine chugs before it rumbled to life. As tense as a tight anchor line, Kenzie waited for a burning odor, a clunking explosion, or at the very least the outboard's refusal to play nice. Fortunately, the motor performed smoothly all the way back to Pine Water Estates. Water and sky cooperated as well. Kenzie offered a prayer of gratitude and hoped the atmosphere between Angelo and her would remain equally calm.

She'd met Angelo when he fished her saltwater-blinded self out of a steeply walled canal. So embarrassing. Ever since, their relationship had been unpredictable. She planned to keep it on an even keel, at least until she could figure out what direction she wanted it to go. She needed to be careful today. Conditions were ripe for a tsunami.

She arrived home at two thirty. No sign of Mom's Jeep. Luck was on her side. Small puddles indicated it had rained here also. That would explain the wet Bimini top as well as any lingering puddles in the boat. With lightning speed, she made Angelo's runabout shipshape— the way he always left it. So far, so good.

To erase any remaining dirt and sand, Kenzie showered herself and bathed Salty. She toweled the pup off, head to tail and spine to paws. *Crud.* His cut oozed again. That was it. Decision made. "No one's getting hurt on that beach again, Salty. Keys Teens Care will clean up that junk for Ana *and* the turtles."

"Hi, sweetie. I'm home."

Salty burst out of the bathroom. Kenzie followed. He scrabbled across the tile floor to greet Mom with ear-piercing yaps and knee-bruising pounces.

"Hello, you little bundle of energy." She snuggled him. "Mmm. Lavender. Salty, you smell wonderful for a change."

Had Salty's cut stained Mom's scrubs? Kenzie examined Mom head to toe. All clear. "Gosh, Mom, you look amazing for someone who spent a day in the ER. It must have been a good day."

"It was. No accidents on land or sea. Hard to believe, but I didn't see one casualty. How about you?"

Casualties? Oh yeah. She'd seen them on both land and sea. Kenzie twisted her ponytail. "I had a good day too, Mom." *More like lucky.* "I learned some things: some geography, a little about weather. Mostly I learned more about sea turtles."

Frowning, Mom eyed the dirty breakfast

dishes that still sat on the counter.

Please, please don't ask.

"You know, sweetie, knowledge is a good thing, but don't spend too much time on that computer." Mom headed toward her bedroom. "Take advantage of your last days of vacation. Spend some time outdoors."

Kenzie nearly choked.

Her mom hesitated, then turned around.

Uh-oh.

"By the way, I haven't forgotten about Turtle Beach. The hospital's shorthanded, so starting tomorrow I'm working longer day shifts. Maybe Mike can take you." Her voice moved down the hall. "Ask him tonight." Then she called from the bedroom. "He's coming to dinner."

Of course he is. Like that's a surprise. In other circumstances, having Mike around would be cool. Interesting things happened in the life of a wildlife officer. He told incredible inside stories about events in the national refuge. He was nice enough. Easy to take in *small* doses. The problem was he practically lived at their house. Sometimes she needed to be alone with Mom—to talk. Like when tears and other weird feelings showed up for no reason. Or when she needed to go shopping for girl stuff.

Salty nudged her ankle. Whimpering, he raised his hurt paw. "Oh, quit it. You're fine. I'm fine. The hawksbill's going to be fine. Everything's fine."

What a bunch of crud. *I'm lying to my dog, now.* She slumped forward on the counter, chin on crossed arms. Things weren't fine. She missed

40

her dad. Yeah, he'd dumped Mom and her. Still, she missed him. She missed her lifelong New York friends at St. Joe's. *Sorry, Sister Martha. I mean St. Joseph's Academy for Girls.*

Add school to the *not fine* list. She'd have to attend a co-ed school with boys. Boys—one more thing she wanted to talk with Mom about. She didn't get boys; all that punching, poking, and wrestling. How would she deal with a school full of boy noise? She opened the cabinet and grabbed a snack bar. She'd find out soon. Too soon.

Crazy, but some girls at St. Joe's begged to transfer to co-ed high schools. Of course, not all boys were obnoxious. Not all the time. Angelo could be amazing. *Sometimes.* When he wasn't fuming. Or brooding. Or arguing.

Mom returned to the living room, brushing her cropped blonde hair and shouldering the phone. "Hold on, Mike, another call's coming in."

"Ana, hello, dear.... Fine, thank you. And your family? I've been working so much; I haven't made it to church to see you.... Wonderful. Hold on. She's right here."

Mom punched a button. "Mike, Ana's calling Kenzie. Dinner should be ready at seven thirty. See you then." She switched the line and held out the phone.

"Hey, Ana." Kenzie went to her room and sprawled across the bed. She lowered her voice. "I was so-oo lucky." "Everything's cool. I even had time to bathe Salty. Mom would have grilled me about his sandy coat."

"Your news is good," Ana said. "But I have bad news. *Papi* found baby loggerheads crushed in the marina parking lot. They are so small, a driver cannot see them. He found only one alive, searching for the sea."

"Oh, Ana, no. The pole lights must have confused them. The poacher didn't get them, but they died anyway." *So unfair.* "What'd your dad do with the one that survived?"

"He brought it home for me to release. Tonight will be dark and stormy. But tomorrow evening will be good. I will release it near some nests. You will come, yes?"

Kenzie sat up. "Awesome."

"Sunset will be around eight o'clock. Can you come before that time?"

"I hope so."

"I know you will tell Angelo. Invite him to come also."

Tell Angelo?

"See you tomorrow, chica."

Salty leaped onto Kenzie's lap. "Guess what, puppy? Tomorrow we start our investigation. We're going to the scene of the crimes. Should we ask Angelo?"

Salty licked her cheek.

"You think so, huh?" How could she ask? What would she say? She wasn't ready to *face* him. Never mind ask him to go somewhere with her. One big problem. She'd *have* to see him. He was coming for his boat—any minute now.

Wait, it didn't have to be a problem. She'd simply play not-at-home. If he figured out she used his boat, though—not-at-home wouldn't be far enough away.

Angelo examined his boat so carefully, you'd think he had to pass inspection before he could return to sea. She'd stowed everything on board in its place. She'd wiped everything down, including all footprints. He shouldn't have a clue she'd taken it. What else could she do? Nothing except wait.

"Kenzie," Mom called from the hallway, "I need a few more things for dinner. I should be back before six. And please, get those breakfast dishes cleaned up."

"I will, Mom. Take your time." *Phew*. She'd dodged another bullet. Plus, she could count on the Jeep being gone at least an hour. If Angelo came soon, she could get away with not being home. He'd probably go straight to the dock anyway. She wouldn't have to show her face.

She stared at the TV drama, not caring if the screen displayed an image or not. Could she really hide from Angelo? It would be like trying to ignore a gallon of rocky road ice cream. She couldn't stop thinking about him or dreaming of his warm, dark eyes searching for her in a crowd.

Right. Like that would ever happen. Shoot, she might as well wish to *be* ice cream.

Woof. Salty jolted her out of her stupor. Footsteps clomped up the stairs. Kenzie chewed her knuckles.

Angelo?

Salty scampered out on the screen porch, barking a happy welcome.

"Salty. Dude."

Definitely Angelo.

The screen door creaked open.

He's on the porch.

Kenzie inhaled. Why hadn't she closed the front door?

Angelo stooped to pet the leaping puppy. "Hey, Spiceman. You sure liven up things around here."

"Come on in, Angelo." She clicked off the remote.

Angelo, deeply tanned from hours on the water, ambled into the house.

Don't look in his eyes. Kenzie's heart flopped like a freshly hooked snapper. She stared at his beat-up sneakers—every bloody stain on them. The coolest shoes ever.

"You're growing by the minute, Spiceman. What's he weigh? About twenty pounds now?"

A faint odor of sea, fish, sweat, and chlorine swirled in the air. Angelo's signature fish-house cologne. *Heaven.* The living area—never spacious—shrank. *Steady, girl.*

"Kenzie, you all right?"

"Uh—Yeah."

Move, girl—kitchen. "Actually he weighs

44

twenty-two, to be exact." *Delay the boat inspection. How?*

"Whoa, Salty. You're gonna hang with the big dogs soon."

Food. "Angelo, are you hungry?"

"Nah. I rode over to get my boat. Tide's high enough to get her home today. Word is snapper are thick out there."

"There's leftover pizza." She opened the refrigerator door. "You never turn that down."

"With pepperoni?"

"The works."

Angelo wrapped his long legs around the barstool and turned his ball cap backwards, exposing his thick, dark hair.

"Want me to heat it?"

"Nope."

Kenzie moved papers and dishes out of the way before sliding the pizza box in front of him. "Here you go, Sharkman."

His brown eyes narrowed. "You still callin' me that?"

"You're the one who says Keys people need a nickname. I'm *Red*. Not that I'm happy about it. You even nicknamed Salty."

"True." Pizza garbled his words. "But I don't need a lame nickname. Got a good one already."

"Right, Angelo, the Italian pizza nut. It fits." She opened a cabinet. "I like your real name, *Ángel*." She held a napkin out to him. "But it's a tough name to live up to."

"Yeah." He stared at the napkin as if it were a window to a tragic memory. "It is."

What's that about? Kenzie waved the napkin

in front of his face.

He blinked and took it.

"Okay, no more *Sharkman*. I'll stick to *Angelo*, the angler. Anyway, I'm glad you can fish this evening since you worked this morning."

"Lousy morning to fish anyway. The lobster guys said storms oceanside were brutal."

"I didn't think they were that...bad." Kenzie's heart sank the second her words escaped. Her mind raced for an explanation.

"Like you would know."

"Well, from what I heard on the radio, I mean."

"What'd they say?"

"The usual stuff about waves, tides, and wind."

What now? Where had she stashed her brain? On ice? Speaking of... She opened the refrigerator. She had to get him out of here.

"Want a soda for the ride?" She set a can on the counter and dug a sandwich bag out of a drawer. "Here, I'll pack the last slice for you. I know you want to fish before the tide turns."

Angelo wiped his sauce-stained mouth. "Right, thanks." He grabbed the drink and pizza. "I'm out of here."

"Good luck." Kenzie's stomach knotted as he went out the door. How soon before relief would arrive? She wanted him gone from the dock, distracted with the business of fish. Gone before he figured out she'd taken his boat. She'd already exceeded today's trauma limit.

Her right leg trembled as she leaned on the

sink and peered through the kitchen window. Angelo walked his bike to the dock, balancing his collection of rods across its basket. He unloaded his gear, stepped into the boat, and unhooked two straps on the Bimini top. After folding it down like a convertible car top, he positioned his fishing rods in their holders.

So far, so good.

He lifted his bike off the dock, turned, then froze, holding the bike in midair.

What's wrong? Kenzie chewed her lower lip. *What's he doing?*

Angelo scanned the boat from bow to stern, then back again. He returned his bike to the dock, then stood in the boat and shook his head back and forth like a pendulum keeping time. Left. Right. Left. Right. He whipped off his ball cap—*Whoosh*—flung it to the floorboards. *Whap.*

Kenzie flinched.

Angelo glared up at the house.

He knew.

Angelo sprang to the dock.

Kenzie ducked from the window. Made it to the barstool a split second before the back door slammed into the wall. She cringed.

Salty fled.

"*Ship*, Red, tell me you didn't."

Naughty nautical talk. Never a good sign.

"You couldn't. Not you."

I couldn't?

"Fisher's motor died. I told him to take my boat if he needed it. It was Fisher, right?" He narrowed his eyes. "No. Fisher wouldn't leave the anchor line tangled." He poked Kenzie's arm. "Tell me."

It would be so easy to say *yes*—the eccentric sponge fisherman, her friend,—had borrowed the boat. But it would be so wrong. She met Angelo's black-ice eyes.

"I didn't damage anything. Honest."

"You better hope that's true." He paced, arms flailing. "You're nuts. I knew it the day you moved here and fell in the canal. Definitely crazy."

"As if you've never done anything crazy with that boat." Kenzie stacked dishes and stomped to the sink.

"I'm talkin' about you." Angelo clenched his fists. "You don't know my boat. You don't know the water. You don't know anything."

Kenzie jammed the dishes into the sink. "Like being a grade ahead of me makes you so smart?" She blasted the plates with soap and water. "I'm not stupid. I've been in your boat lots of times."

"Not alone." Angelo jerked a stool from under the counter, then straddled it. "Where'd you take it?"

Kenzie stared out the window, rubbing a sponge round and round the surface of a plate.

"I repeat. Where—did—you—take—it?" Each word intensified like a gathering storm.

She squeezed the sponge. Suds poured over Kenzie's knuckles. She had to come clean.

"Hey, Red, a little help here." He cupped his hands around his mouth. "MAYDAY, MAYDAY, MAYDAY. Coastguard Cutter Angelo, attempting contact with disabled vessel, Kenzie. Anyone there? Over."

She should be calling MAYDAY. She was about to capsize.

She exhaled—long and hard. Gripping the sink to steady herself, she turned slightly toward him, gulped, and dived in. "You know how I always ask everybody to take me to see the turtle nests?"

49

As if he could block the truth, Angelo closed his eyes.

"But no one ever has time..."

He winced. "No way." He pounded the counter, faced facts, and fired. "You took my boat to Turtle Beach, didn't you?"

"Well..." Not ready to face him, Kenzie returned to her task. "I—"

"Turtle Beach is on the other side of the island. Even you can't be that nuts."

Kenzie stared out the window and rinsed a plate. *Get it over with, girl. Admit it*. Water splashed the counter. Splash? A sly grin tickled. Would it work? Could she flip his quick-to-come, quick-to-go temper?

"So, I'm not that nuts... " She aimed the sprayer at him. "Want to bet?"

"You wouldn't."

Splat. She squirted and held her breath.

Angelo stilled. Eyes closed. Water dripped down his face. He lifted the hem of his T-shirt to his hairline.

Tight, tanned. *Oh...* She stared. Gulped.

He wiped his forehead and eyes, then raised his shirt higher in search of dry fabric. She gulped again. He *had* to lift weights. Maybe this co-ed school thing wasn't going to be so bad after all.

Angelo dabbed his nose. His cheeks. His chin. Finally, he lowered his shirt and grinned. A crooked *aha!* grin. As if, though he'd lost a juvenile marlin, he'd figured out how to hook the big one.

What was he—?

Angelo snatched her soda.

Uh-oh.

He shook the can, aimed, and blasted.

His eyes sparkled. Hers dripped.

"So..." He smirked, staring at...?

The wet blotches spreading across her tank top. She crossed her arms over her chest and wanted to die.

His focus snapped to her face. "I'm cool now."

She wasn't. Heat crawled up her neck. *Forget it.* Her fingers curled into fists. *You got what you asked for.* She eyed the sprayer in her hand. *Let... it... go, Kenzie.* Slowly, she replaced it in its slot. "Yeah. Me too."

"Truce?"

"Yep." She patted her face with paper towels. "We're even."

"Sure you didn't hit my prop on a sandbar?"

"Didn't come close."

"Crack or stress anything?"

Stress anything? Not on the boat. She mopped up the floor at his feet. "You're the one who taught me to read the water."

"So..." Angelo rubbed his temples. "You and little Spiceman were out in those squalls."

"One caught us. No big deal."

"Yeah, right."

"The storm *wasn't* the big deal," Kenzie said. "Wait 'til you hear what—"

"You have any trouble gassing up?"

Crap. Just when she thought she was home free. *Think fast.* Skirt the issue. The truth—her stupidity—would set him off again. She perched on the stool across from him as if it were the hot seat in an interrogation room. She'd no clue what would come out of her mouth.

"Guess not," Angelo said. "You've been with me enough times when I filled up at the marina."

He'd answered his own question. Unbelievable. "Exactly." This word, at least, was true.

After piloting through dangerous Angelo territory, she could finally share her morning adventure. Like air released from a swollen balloon, her words gushed from beginning to end.

"And the amazing thing is I even had time to bathe Salty." Kenzie completed the minute-by-minute account of *almost* all of her adventures. "Mom didn't have a clue."

"You're unbelievably lucky, Red."

"It all seemed unbelievable, Angelo. Poor Salty. I think that crazy lady really would shoot him if she got a chance. And you can't imagine the size of that turtle or the condition of her shell. All covered with slimy algae and barnacles and her skinny neck and that bag hanging out of her mouth." Kenzie gulped a breath. "But the good news is, Ana's dad found a baby loggerhead. At least one hatchling escaped the turtle egg thief. We have to stop him, you know. She'll release it tomorrow night."

Angelo signaled time out. "Stop who? Who's releasing what?"

"Stop the thief. Ana's releasing the hatchling tomorrow night. Want to come?" she asked, not waiting for an answer. "I can't wait to watch it take off, even though I don't know how a tiny turtle can crawl over all that trash.

It's disgusting. Ana can't go anywhere except right in front of her house. That beach is a real dunkyard."

"Dunkyard?"

"Oh, you know what I mean—junk, dump—whatever."

Angelo ripped off a side of the pizza box. "Junked up beach. Stolen eggs." He tore the cardboard into pieces. "Wrecked nests... Keys Teens Care—"

"A.K.A. the KTC," Kenzie interrupted, in her best mystery narrator's voice.

"Right, Detective Ryan. The *KTC* needs to be all over this."

"We'll clean up the entire shoreline on that side of the island. Our parents won't suspect we're after the poacher. But we can't wait three more days for the meeting at church. We need to get started now." Kenzie glanced at the wall clock. "It's only five. We have a little time before Mom gets home."

She handed Angelo another Coke.

He chugged it. "If we get lucky, another jerk will go down."

"Prep work for the beach sweep would be the perfect cover for the initial investigation. Only the Keys' Teens will know what's really going on." Kenzie rummaged through a drawer until she found paper and a pencil. "Let's list what we need to do."

Angelo crushed his empty can. "Easy. Shouldn't be any different than what we did for the refuge cleanup. The kids can handle the same jobs they did before." He cocked his head.

"Did you hear that?"

"Yep. Thunder."

"It's coming from the north. Guess fishing's out." He pitched the can in the recycling bucket. "Want me to call Ted and get him going?"

"Yes. I'll call Kish. They can contact the others." Kenzie chewed the end of her pencil. "Anything else?"

"You know nesting season's almost over, right?"

"That's why we can't wait." Kenzie drummed her pencil on the counter like a woodpecker attacking a tree. "We have to be at Turtle Beach as often as possible—the poacher will be working overtime. You and I can start monitoring the beach right away. Let's say we're scouting for places to put the food tables and spots to stash trash bags and gloves for the workers. Safe places where no one will trample nests by accident. We have to be sure the nest markers are all in place."

Angelo reviewed the list. "We've got it covered."

Over the Gulf of Mexico, rumbling rolled. Louder and closer. Angelo stepped out to the front porch. "Ugly out there."

"I'm sorry I held you up."

"Don't be. Good thing I didn't go out. Lots to do at the fish house anyway." An aura of sorrow lingered after his words.

His mother's work. He never talked about his mother's death. She'd died six months ago, and since then he'd taken on her role in the Sánchez fishing business.

"I'll make my calls later," he said, passing

through the living room. "I want to beat that storm."

"Angelo..."

"Yeah?"

Kenzie twisted her ponytail. "I won't take your boat again."

"I figured that, Red."

She followed him out the back door to check the towels on the railing. *Dry.* She gathered them up.

"Hey," he called from the bottom step. "How you gettin' to Ana's tomorrow night?"

"I'm not sure." Kenzie bit her lip. "Maybe I'll ask Mike."

"He'll do it. Don't leave without me. It'd be cool to see that little guy take off."

"Can you get here by seven?"

"*No problema.*" Angelo retrieved his rods, bungeed them on his bike's basket, and pedaled for home.

Kenzie completed her KTC calls in record time. Because every member of the group loved Ana, they eagerly agreed to work on the cleanup. The bonus of protecting the long-besieged sea turtles, in Ted's words, "iced the cake." He threatened to stake out the nests on Turtle Beach—baseball bat in hand—and bash anyone who approached. Lakisha responded with fury: "Raiding a nest is the same as killing a hundred babies all at once."

Later, during dinner, Kenzie avoided any comment that would hint at the group's scheme to catch the turtle egg thief. She did, however, talk about the hatchlings Ana's father found.

Mike scraped the last bits of icing off his plate. "No matter how many times stories like that get reported to the refuge, I never get used to the tragedy of it. Most of our residents are happy to comply with the lights-out rule during nesting season. Sadly, a few refuse to cooperate."

"At least one hatchling survived. Ana and her dad are going to release it tomorrow." *Ask him now, Kenzie.* She twisted her ponytail so tight it shrank to half its length. *He's well-fed and relaxed.*

Mom gently loosened the hair from Kenzie's fist. She winked at Kenzie, piled a second piece of cake on Mike's plate, and asked, "Mike, is there any chance you could drive Kenzie to Ana's tomorrow evening?"

"You need a ride tomorrow evening, huh?" Mike eyed Kenzie over the rim of his coffee mug before turning his attention to Mom. "I've always maintained that the way to a man's help is through his stomach." He sipped. Asked for a refill. Sipped again.

Was he waiting to digest his entire meal?

At last he set his mug down and answered in what Mom called his velvet voice. "Unfortunately, I'm on night patrol tomorrow."

There goes that idea.

Mike placed his hand over his wildlife refuge badge. Tucking his chin in mock sincerity, he declared, "However, it is my responsibility to ensure the welfare of all threatened species. It would be a dereliction of duty if I didn't support the release of a hatchling."

Yes.

His voice returned to normal. "I'll see if I can rearrange the schedule."

Sometimes having Mike around wasn't so bad after all.

The next evening, to fill the time before Mike was to pick her up, Kenzie logged on to the Turtle Hospital website. She couldn't wait to visit it for real. Until then, she could enjoy the virtual tour. Her hawksbill wasn't featured on the site yet, so she followed the surgery and recovery of other turtles. Their icky fibropapilloma tumors reminded her of lumpy cauliflower—a vegetable that would never touch her lips again.

Woof. Woof. Salty's guard-dog bark accompanied the *click, click* of an approaching engine—unmistakably, Mom's Cherokee. Popping gravel announced the arrival of another vehicle before Mom's Jeep door banged shut. What was going on?

"It's me." Mom called from the kitchen. "Another nurse wanted to work this evening."

Cool. Kenzie stood. Ready to go. Her mom could take her to Turtle Beach after all.

Mom paused by Kenzie's room on the way down the hall. "What a nightmare of a day. We were short-staffed. The ER rivaled terror at the zoo. Imagine scores of uncaged animals and dozens of hysterical kindergartners." She leaned on the doorframe. "Two overdoses, two diving accidents, couple of stabbings—after three car wrecks I quit counting. I don't think I sat all day. And to top it off, Mike and I have to attend an emergency meeting for everyone who lives or works in the refuge."

What? This isn't happening. Seething, Kenzie sank in her chair. *After one day they've forgotten about Turtle Beach?* Her stomach boiled.

"Since I won't be fixing dinner, I picked up

fried chicken for you. The meeting's catered. I assume in honor of the regional chief. He flew down from the mainland. Some important refuge issue."

Hello... threatened turtle rescue and release. Like that's not an important refuge issue. She clenched her jaws and swallowed a bomb of destructive words. "Mom, did you forget anything?" She studied Mom's reflection in the wall mirror for a response. *Nada.* No clue.

"I don't think so. I remembered gravy, and I got all-white meat."

Unbelievable. Mom totally missed it. IT'S NOT ABOUT FOOD!

"Great." Kenzie snapped. "Just great." She attacked the arrow key like it might reverse time.

Her mom came in and kissed the top of her head. "Do you want me to warm the chicken in the oven?"

I want you to forget Mike and remember me. "Don't bother."

"Well, I better get changed." Mom's uniform shoes squeaked as she hurried to her room.

Kenzie's eyes clouded. The computer screen blurred. She clamped her lips shut, dead-bolting them with her teeth. If the hint of a syllable leaked, her verbal logjam would break, and it would be *she*, not Mom, who drowned in the torrent. Kenzie gripped the mouse and banged it on the pad as if it were a hammer.

"Maggie?" Mike called from the porch. "Are you about ready?"

"On my way." Mom rushed down the hall,

sandals flapping.

Nothing had changed. It's all about Mike. All the time. Neither of them remembered. She wasn't going to remind them. *They'll figure it out when they come back, and I'm gone.*

After the truck door slammed, Kenzie hit speed dial. "Angelo, can you get the truck tonight? You are not going to believe what happened."

Although Mr. Sánchez needed the truck for a business meeting, it was on Big Pine Key, so he offered to drive Kenzie and Angelo to Turtle Beach. Salty's excitement built as the pickup rattled along the last mile of Turtle Beach Road, and he stumbled from lap to lap. When Mr. Sánchez pulled up to Ana's house, the sun was slipping into the sea, tinting it shades of pink and orange. The clear sky promised an infinite canopy of star shine and moonlight.

Ana waved from the deck. "I will be right down."

Kenzie fastened Salty's leash to the railing as Ana rolled off the elevator. "Angelo, you came with Kenzie. I hoped you would."

"Yeah, well... " He flashed Kenzie a crooked grin.

As Ana patted Salty, she grasped Kenzie's hand and whispered. "Does Angelo know you took—"

"Yeah. He knows. It's all good."

"*¿Verdad?* I knew it. You and Angelo—*muy buenos amigos.*" Her words twinkled as if she knew a huge secret. Like who would win the lottery, when, and how much. Then she headed toward Doonie. "There is news." She spoke over her shoulder. "Something unexpected."

Unexpected? Kenzie didn't want any other surprises tonight. She caught up with Ana. "What do you mean—unexpected?"

"One of the nests is caving in."

"Caving in? What's wrong? What happened? What can we do?"

"Chill, Red." Angelo poked her with his elbow. "The turtles are hatching."

"Oh, right. Sinkholes. I knew that." Kenzie nudged him back. "Ana, this is great. Your little turtle can race with the others. With competition, its muscles might strengthen more than if it crawled alone."

"*Sí, chica.* Also, if it is a female, she may have friends to come home with when it is time to lay her own eggs."

"There are bigger *ifs* than that," Angelo said. "Like *if* she survives."

"True and *if* we're still living here in fifteen to twenty years when she is old enough." Ana switched chairs and rolled toward the steps.

"Hey guys," Kenzie said, "that's enough depressing talk for now. We're on a mission of hope here."

"You are right. We must be...optimistic, yes?" Ana retrieved a red sand bucket, then rested it on her lap.

Angelo and Kenzie peered in the bucket of wet sand. The miniature loggerhead's shell appeared no bigger than a soupspoon. Its front flippers were longer than the width of its shell. Could this tiny creature really grow to three hundred pounds?

"Hey, little dude." Angelo touched its thumbnail-size head. "You're not gonna take off alone after all."

Ana indicated a shelf in the shed. "Please bring the flashlights. Soon it will be dark, but *Papi* will not turn on the floodlights. He does not want to confuse *these* turtles."

Ana switched Doonie into gear, then led the way down a wooded trail unfamiliar to Kenzie.

Where the trail met the beach, a tangle of net, broken traps, and old boards blocked Ana's progress. "*Papi* told me to go another way. Instead I came this shorter path. I should have listened."

Kenzie caught up to Ana. "It'll be easier soon. KTC is planning a beach cleanup."

"¡*Qué maravilloso!* When will this be?"

Angelo's eyes flashed. "Not soon enough." He stomped ahead to kick and heave junk out of the path. Chickens roosting in a nearby tree flapped and muttered at his outburst. Returning, he grasped the handles on Ana's chair so tightly it looked as if he'd chuck it next.

"Angelo, I will be okay now." Ana touched Doonie's controls. "Follow me. It is not far." She wedged the bucket between her legs, then motored Doonie up the bumpy dune.

Angelo shadowed Ana. Twice Doonie struggled. Each time, with a move that tugged at Kenzie's heart, Angelo discreetly nudged the chair until it rolled free. This was the *amazing* Angelo at work.

A few yards past the dune Ana stopped. "There, in front of us."

Where? This place looked like any other spot on the beach, except for the stakes and caution tape.

"*Pero, ¿por qué es...* The warning tape. It is down."

"Oh no." Kenzie covered her face. "We're too late."

"Maybe not." Angelo inspected the area around the five-foot square perimeter of the staked-off area. "Relax. Hoof prints. A deer ran through the tape." He secured the trampled barrier.

Kenzie lowered her hands. "Thank goodness."

"Looks like more good news." Angelo kneeled to examine the area inside the barricade. "Yup. Sand's sinking in two places."

"Today." Kenzie squeezed Ana's hand. "They're hatching today."

"Good news, *sí. Pero no sólo hoy.* Not only today. For many days they have been hatching. The turtle watchers explained to me. The first hatchlings wait in the nest. Each time an egg hatches there is more space for babies to wiggle. One moves, it bumps another. That turtle bumps another, until—"

"Look." Kenzie stooped and pointed. "More sinkholes."

"*Esto no es normal.* They do not usually emerge before it is completely dark."

Angelo talked to the nest. "You guys in a hurry? Go. Dig on, dudes."

Ana wheeled Doonie foward. "They do not really dig, you know." When her knees hit the caution tape, she set Doonie's brakes. "They wiggle to make the nest cave in. Sand falls and fills the bottom of the nest little by little." Ana slowly lifted her hands as she spoke. "That pushes the hatchlings to the top."

"They ride up." Kenzie giggled. "Like we do on your elevator."

"Okay. Wiggle on, dudes." Angelo moved to the far side of the nest. "Hey, here comes one. No, two."

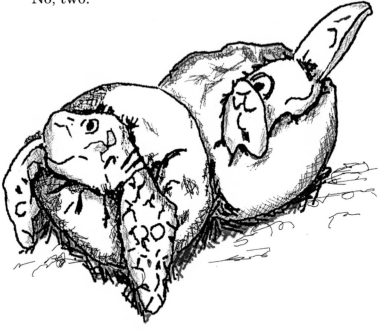

"Three, four," Ana cried.

Kenzie cheered. "Five, six, seven."

Handing the bucket to Kenzie, Ana said, "Please put this baby near the others."

Kenzie placed the bucket on its side. The nest erupted, and dozens of tiny turtles clambered out, scurrying and scampering on top of each other like ants fleeing an anthill. In seconds, Ana's turtle joined the swarm.

Some crawled over debris only to flip upside down on the other side. After struggling to right themselves with their flippers, they returned to the race. One or two seemed confused and headed the wrong way. When oncoming turtle traffic blocked them, they soon got it right.

"How can they move so fast after being crammed inside those shells for over a month? Hey—" Kenzie cocked her head. "What's that laughing?"

The distant *ha ha ha ha—haah haah* intensified. Hordes of screeching black-and-white birds zoomed overhead like fighter planes. *Ha ha ha ha.* Swoop. *Haah haah.* The creatures circled in the darkening sky. Lower and lower. Shriek after shriek.

"They're obnoxious." Kenzie yelled. "What are they?"

"Laughing gulls. I've never seen them feed this late in the day. Run, little guys." Angelo yelled at the hatchlings. "Faster."

"They're diving at the turtles." Kenzie leaped and batted at the birds with her flashlight. "Stop it. Leave them alone."

One after another, the birds attacked the helpless babies.

Shifting Doonie into gear, Anna rolled beside the trail of turtles. "*Shoo. Vete de aquí.* Get out of here. *Lárguense.*" Her free arm sliced the sky like a saber.

Angelo swore. He swatted black-feathered heads and flapping wings with his hat. He picked

up pebbles and shell fragments. "Eat these." One by one, he lobbed the bits high into the air. A few gulls chased them, but soon returned to their tasty prey.

Woof. Woof. Woof. Salty, sounding three times his size, hurtled out of the woods onto the beach.

"How did he get loose?" Kenzie yelled.

"Who cares?" Angelo said. "Get 'em, Spiceman."

The puppy seemed determined to keep the seagulls away. They screeched and dive-bombed his head. *Haah haah.* He nipped and barked. *Woof. Woof.* He checked the babies. Leaped at the gulls. Over and over. A shepherd defending his flock.

Out of a hundred or more, only a few tiny turtles were snatched before they reached the water. There, protected only by their camouflage, they'd face an ocean of predators.

The gulls retreated as the sea gobbled the sun. In the moonlight the last hatchling crossed the glowing sand, then splashed into the surf. Salty stood, sides heaving and tongue hanging.

Kenzie stooped and called him to her. "What a good dog you are." She blinked back tears and waited for doggie kisses. Instead, he growled—a big-dog rumble. He spun toward shore and tore across the moonlit sand, barking ferociously.

"No, Salty, no." Kenzie started after him, then stopped. She couldn't leave Ana.

"Go. Both of you." Ana waved them off with her flashlight. "I will be fine. I will take the other path."

Kenzie and Angelo raced after the puppy. He turned sharply and disappeared into the trees.

Kenzie tripped, switched on her flashlight, then stumbled ahead. "Angelo, he's headed toward Angry Edna's house."

"Keep calling him. She'll hear us coming. She won't do anything."

"But I don't hear him."

"He'll be fine. We'll catch him. He can't be that far ahead."

Finally. Angelo's light beam caught Salty a few yards ahead. Nose to the ground.

"Salty. What are you—?"

The puppy scooped up something and gobbled it. He sniffed and scooped again.

"Salty, drop it." Kenzie rushed forward. Pried open his jaws. Wiped her fingers over his tongue. No use. He'd already swallowed. "Oh, Salty, what did you eat?"

"Probably something dead and gross," Angelo mumbled.

"You were just being a dog, I guess." Kenzie ruffled Salty's furry neck. "Hey, where's your collar? Is that how you broke loose? Angelo, did you notice if he wore it on the beach?"

"Uh—I was pretty busy back there."

"Maybe we can find it." Kenzie slid the flashlight into her pocket and picked up Salty. "I'll follow you."

"Look at this." Angelo aimed the light. "Dog tracks. Shoe prints too. He was chasin' somebody."

Purple Shirt. "Bet it's the same person he chased yesterday—the thief. Shine the light back on the footprints. Crud. The sand's too dry. The pattern of the sole's unclear. Wait. This one's sharper. Look at that logo. It's a Surf Sandal tread." She placed her foot beside the print. "It's about two inches bigger than my sneaker. Try yours."

"Close," he said.

"So, we're looking for someone with Surf Sandals and a foot about the size of yours. That's something at least. Can you see well enough to follow these tracks back to the beach? He probably lost his collar in the chase."

"Maybe. You okay carrying the Spiceman?"

"Yeah. He's too tired to give me much trouble."

They snaked, bumped, and stumbled through the trees for much longer than it should have taken to return to the beach.

"Angelo, are we still following the trail?"

Without warning, he stopped.

Kenzie rammed him.

Salty yipped.

"Hey. What happened? Did you find the collar?"

He lowered his flashlight, and it went dark.

"Angelo. Why'd you stop? Did you find it?"

"Aw, Red... You don't want to know what I found."

"Angelo. What is it?" She poked him in the back. "Why can't you show me?" Her eyes adjusted. Through the trees ahead, moonlight sparkled on the beach. "Never mind. I'll see for myself." She barged ahead of him.

"Watch it." He grabbed her shoulder and aimed his light at a disturbed place a few feet in front of them.

Kenzie yelled, "No way."

Salty flinched.

"Not another raid."

Salty struggled free. He raced to the spot marked by Angelo's light. The pup sniffed every inch of the shallow hole, emitting a symphony of whimpers, growls, and whines.

Flashing his light in a wide radius around the nest, Angelo joined Salty's inspection. "Looks like the eggs are okay."

"Please, please be right." Kenzie stepped forward. "Maybe it was a raccoon or a dog."

"No animal tracks anywhere except Salty's.

Shoe prints though. Looks like the same pattern. It's the poacher all right." Angelo bent down and scratched Salty's ears. "Must have thought he'd be safe with all the chaos. Salty surprised him. Before he reached any eggs, luckily."

"Angelo, Salty knows who it is. He's the only one who does."

"Too bad he can't talk."

"Not with words, anyway. Come here, puppy." She picked him up. "Let's go before Ana gets worried."

They turned to go back, and Angelo's phone sounded, startling them. He pulled it out of his pocket. "Hi, Dad... Yup... Okay."

"He's on his way?" Kenzie asked.

"Yeah. We have to go, but..." In the ambient beam from the flashlight, his face glowed with an expression that...what? "I need to tell you something. The reason I couldn't have the truck tonight—or any time soon—I can't drive. Well, I can. Just not legally. I don't have my license."

That explained the glow. Embarrassment.

"Geesh, you could have just said so."

"Yeah, I should have. So now you know. You can't rely on me to drive you anywhere."

Wrong. "What's the big deal? I like traveling by boat."

"For real?"

"You said it before. Around here there's more water than road. More freedom in a boat."

"I said this before too." He shot her a hesitant grin. "You catch on quick for a city girl." Then he leaned forward—*Is he going to?*—and ruffled Salty's fur.

71

Mr. Sánchez's headlights swept the driveway, illuminating Ana where she sat by the bottom step. Salty's leash remained tied to the railing. His open collar dangled from its end.

"Thanks to God. You are back. I was so worried. *Mira.* Salty's buckle must have been loose."

"I don't see how." Kenzie reattached Salty's collar, hooking it one hole tighter than normal. "But it won't come off now."

"My parents did not know Salty disappeared until I told them you were looking for him." Ana lowered her voice. "Why did he run? What happened?"

"Scumbag poacher." Angelo placed his flashlight on the step.

"It was the creep for sure," Kenzie said. "But the good news is this time he—"

"Came when she called." Angelo kicked Kenzie's foot and shot a look behind her. "Hi, Dad."

Kenzie mouthed, "Thanks."

"*Niños, Señor Sánchez,*" Mrs. Muñoz called from the porch above. "Come, please, we have ice cream."

"*Gracias, Señora Muñoz.*"

"Do we have time, Dad?"

Mr. Sánchez patted Angelo's shoulder. "We cannot refuse such an invitation, *Ángel.* We must be polite."

Angelo scaled the steps two at a time. Riding up on the elevator, Kenzie quickly detailed the story of Salty and the poacher for Ana.

Pleased with the successful release, Ana's parents asked many questions about the new hatchlings' race to the sea and Salty's escapades.

Careful, guys. A look pinballed from Kenzie to Ana to Angelo. Worried parents would mean much less freedom. The ultimate plan would fall apart. As they described the excitement on the beach, not a word slipped out concerning the close encounter with the poacher.

The clock on the truck's dash displayed ten fifteen as Mr. Sánchez drove through the maze of roads and canals in Kenzie's neighborhood. Her apprehension increased as home neared. She'd taken off without permission. Did Mom believe Kenzie had gone to Ana's? Not to some unknown or risky place? Was Mom awake and waiting? Her verbal arsenal primed?

They passed the vacant lot across the canal from her house. Pale reflections, like beams from a fading flashlight, lit the quiet canal water. She glanced at the house. *No way.* Her stomach lurched. Mike's truck sat under the streetlight by her house. *Crud.* Outnumbered two to one. How would she deal with this storm? She needed time to think.

"Thank you, Mr. Sánchez. Please let me out at the stop sign. I need to walk Salty."

"*No, niña.* It is late."

Kenzie gave Angelo her best help-me-out-here look.

"Don't worry, Mr. Sánchez. I walk Salty this time every night. Right before I go to bed."

"It's cool, Dad." Angelo opened the door and

hopped out.

"Thank you, Mr. Sánchez." She scooted out and lowered Salty to the ground.

"Night, Kenzie. Maybe I'll see you at the flea market tomorrow," Angelo said. Making small talk while his eyes signaled, *What was that about?*

The walk down the block didn't boost Kenzie's courage. Mom and Mike were there, sitting under the dim porch light. Waiting. She reached the bottom of the steps and still didn't know how to greet Mom. Take an offensive approach? Too dangerous. Kenzie's anger boiled. Nonchalant? No way she could act like nothing happened. Apologize? That would totally throw Mom off. Not a chance. Not when they'd let her down, dropping her as if she were an anchor too heavy for their two-person boat.

Mom and Mike sat in deafening silence. *One of you say something. Anything. Give me a clue.* They must have seen her coming. The streetlight lit half the block. She could play this game too. She delayed the taking-off-without-permission lecture by unreeling the hose and rinsing a sandy, exhausted Salty. He'd never been so wiped out.

Kenzie pulled a towel from the clothesline and rubbed him down. "Run interference for me, puppy." When she released him, instead of his usual rush to the porch, he shook, then lay down at her feet. "Guess you're done playing hero for the night." Kenzie wanted to collapse beside him.

The walls of their little stilt house echoed with the voice of Kenzie's grandmother who'd spent so many winters here. Kenzie sighed. *I hear you Nana. Time to face the music.* Chewing her lip, she lifted Salty, then trudged up the steps.

Mike nodded at her before focusing again on his newspaper. Deep in concentration. Storm-shuttered against a gale.

"Mom, I know you're—"

"Not now, young lady." Mom raised one hand in traffic-cop pose. "We'll discuss this later."

"But Mom, I want—"

Her mother pointed a finger. "Not now." Her eyes screamed, *Grounded. Grounded. Grounded.*

Kenzie shivered as if she'd been drenched with ice water. She buried her face in Salty's neck and fled to her room. Grounded, she'd be no help to the turtles. She needed to talk to Mom. Make her understand. But Mike was here. *In the way—again.*

She filled Salty's dishes. He nibbled a few bites, then drained his water dish. "Wow, Salty. You're super dehydrated. No wonder you're beat." She replenished his water, coaxed him into his kennel, and curled up on her bed as exhausted as Salty.

Down, down, down. Push. Kick. She struggled for the surface. Another wave smacked her down. The undertow sucked her deeper. She gurgled and coughed. Swallowed more...air. Not salt water. Air. She opened her eyes—dry eyes. More gurgles. More coughs. *Not a dream*—Salty. The gurgles and coughs weren't his regular sleeping snuffles and snores. She switched on the light.

His eyelids fluttered.

"Poor puppy." She stroked his head. "Are you having bad dreams, too?"

His eyes opened, but he didn't budge.

"We'll both sleep better with Nana's warm milk cure." She opened her door. Was the TV on? She paused to listen. No TV. Harsh whispers. Where? She stepped to the middle of the hall. Out on the porch.

"It's not right, Maggie. Don't be that way."

Mike. Still here. Were he and Mom fighting?

"Mike, I have every right."

Ohhh. Intense. They were arguing. *Too bad.* Kenzie shared a smirk with the dancing devil on her shoulder.

"I pretty much promised I'd take her to Turtle Beach," Mike said. "I should have remembered."

You bet you should have. You both should have.

"You said you'd see if you could."

"The problem is, I never told her I couldn't. Give her a break, Maggie. She left a note saying how and where she went."

"And that's supposed to make it all right? A note that I didn't see until after I nearly had a heart attack? She put that note under the cell phone she purposely didn't take. She may as well have written, 'P.S. Don't bother to check on me.'"

I forgot my phone. I didn't mean to leave it.

"You believe Kenzie, don't you? About where she went? You must since you didn't call Mrs. Muñoz."

"And what could I have said? That I... That Kenzie... Was she...?"

76

"Well, there you have it. It's complicated. So don't be so upset with Kenzie. You and I both had horrible days. But the fact remains, we forgot. And all because of a supposed emergency meeting. A meeting that in reality was a self-aggrandizing tribute for a political wannabe."

Yeah, Mom. Listen to him. Wait. What am I thinking? Don't listen to him. If you do, he'll never leave.

"She's so stubborn, Mike. She could have reminded us before we left. Why didn't she? We could have taken her on our way to the refuge meeting."

"Yes, we could have. Fortunately, she was safe riding with Angelo's father. I guess she was too annoyed to remind us. She had reason to be."

You've got that right.

Seconds went by. Mom rested her head on Mike's shoulder and murmured something unintelligible, like the whisper of a smothered flame.

Kenzie's shoulder-devil dissolved. She sighed and tiptoed back to bed. Sleep or no sleep, getting caught in the kitchen now was not a good idea.

"Kenzie, it's almost eight. Are you awake in there?"

Mom? Kenzie rubbed her gritty eyes against the lingering images of monsters that coughed up flocks of winged creatures.

"Honey, are you going with me to the flea

market?"

The flea market? Had she escaped being grounded?

"If you're going, get dressed and take Salty out."

Salty. Why hadn't he awakened her? Every day since he came to live with them three weeks ago, he'd begged her to go out by seven o'clock. This morning, he had yet to move.

"Kenzie, did you hear me?"

"Yes, Mom. I'm up." She moved to Salty's kennel and reached in. "What's wrong, puppy?" He looked up at her, but made no effort to stand.

Kenzie opened her bedroom door. "I'll go, Mom. I don't want to stay long. Okay? Salty's acting weird. He doesn't want to leave his kennel."

Mom shouted over the sound of ice dumping in the cooler. "Did he play a lot on the beach last night?"

"Uh... yeah." She grimaced. *And the day before.*

"He's probably worn out. Shake a leg. We need to get on the road. The shrimp and lobster sell out fast."

Mom was quiet—too quiet—on the long, slow drive through the Key Deer Refuge. The silence was torture, like sitting in class as graded finals are returned. You gauge your teacher's disappointment as he plods toward you holding the last exam—yours—the only one you ever forgot to study for. It wasn't going to be pretty. When would Mom's heavy lecture start? When would the you're-grounded ax fall?

Worrying only makes it worse, girl. Concen-

trate on something else. The cleanup. Would enough people participate? The poacher. How can we stop him? And Salty. Poor puppy. Something was not right with him. It was no use. Anxiety was relentless.

But, Fisher—if he showed up at the flea market—could tell her how Salty's mom handled stress. Dogs inherit personality traits from their parents. Salty might have inherited his moody exhaustion from Jigs. *Maybe it's as simple as that. Maybe he's not sick.*

If only she didn't have to actually see Fisher to talk with him. He didn't have a phone or a computer. He loved his privacy. She got that. But he was an old man living on a boat. He wasn't safe without a phone.

Phone. She touched her pocket. There. Pad and pencil too. All ready for Fisher. Weeks ago she'd retrieved a free-lunch-for-a-month coupon he'd tossed in the flea market trash. When he clearly didn't get its importance, she figured out why: he couldn't read. *I haven't told anyone, Fisher. Not even Angelo.*

Kenzie glanced at Mom, tapping the steering wheel to some golden oldie on the radio. *She would be proud of me. Fisher talks. I write. He's learning to read and write by telling his own stories.* Maybe he had one about turtle egg thieves. He knew the island better than anyone; his insight would be valuable. If only she could illustrate his stories. What pictures they would make: growing up on a remote island with no school; eloquent British father, from a once-wealthy family; beautiful dramatic mother, a former well-known stage actress. Both parents read to him—until his mother died. He'd only been five years old.

Fisher and Angelo... Each were boys when their mother died. She couldn't imagine losing Mom. A dark hollowness crept into her chest.

Was that Mom's voice or the radio? Kenzie glanced over. *Nah, not Mom.* She wasn't doing that one-eye-on-Kenzie, one-on-the-road thing.

So much sadness in Fisher's life. One day when she'd met him at the church for a lesson, he'd said in his usual dramatic style, "My mother's demise terminated my childhood. With all that ensued, lack of the written word seemed inconsequential." Suddenly Kenzie understood his stately manner: Fisher spoke with his parents' grand vocabulary because it was the only way he could use their words.

"Hey, kiddo." Mom patted Kenzie's knee. "Are we talking?"

Uh-oh.

"How about it?"

Mom *had* been talking to her.

"I've apologized for last night several times now. Did you even hear me?"

"Sorry, Mom. What'd you say?"

"Are you still upset that we didn't take you to the beach?"

More like totally forgot me. "I'll get over it." *Careful. Don't set Mom off.* She bit her tongue and stared out the window again.

"You can't imagine how terrified I was when we got home last night. The house was dark, and you weren't in your bed. After the day we had in the ER... Horrible thoughts and images ran through my head. Even after I found your note on the counter, I couldn't stop shaking until Mike calmed me down."

Had Mike talked Mom out of grounding me?
"Guess I should have left the kitchen light on."

"Well..." Her mom zinged a look at Kenzie out of the corner of her eye. "I would have found the note sooner if you had."

"Sorry," Kenzie mumbled. *I almost didn't leave a message at all.*

"Sweetie, before Mike went home last night, he got a call. Someone on Turtle Beach reported a newly raided turtle nest. Luckily it was aborted, but the thief is still out there."

Unbelievable. Mom let it go and changed the subject. If only it hadn't been to this one.

"Did you hear anything about that when you were over there?"

Kenzie gulped. "I... know about it."

"Mike said it's happened a lot lately."

"Yeah. The KTC have been pretty freaked out about it."

"Sweetie, you and your friends aren't going to make me a nervous wreck again, are you?"

"Relax, Mom." Kenzie sat on her crossed fingers. "After seeing all the junk on Turtle Beach, we're more concerned with a beach cleanup campaign."

Mom pulled into the left turn lane and waited for a traffic break. "You thought of that last night?"

"Uh-huh." *We must have thought about it. Sometime during the action.*

"Another cleanup sounds wonderful, sweetie.

81

The KTC signs along US 1 really seem to have decreased highway litter."

"I hope so. Sometimes it doesn't look like it, though."

"Don't sell yourself short. Your success should help recruit lots of support for a beach cleanup. You'll need it too. That's a long strip of shoreline."

"We're working on it."

"Good. I'm proud of you." Her mom hawk-eyed Kenzie. "But if you scare me like that again, you'll be grounded until you're married!"

Kenzie swallowed her giggle.

Traffic finally eased, and Mom turned into the market entrance. She squeezed the Jeep into a shady spot, then reached for the fish cooler behind the seat. "Meet you for breakfast in half an hour. Same table?"

"Sounds good." Kenzie sat for a few seconds, watching Mom prance toward the fish stand, swinging her cooler. *No lecture. Not grounded. Amazing.* The dancing devil appeared on her shoulder for a split second. Was it sprouting wings? *Mike, you old velvet voice, you're smooth.*

Whoa. A positive feeling about Mike? It felt kind of nice. She grimaced. *Get real. It'll pass.*

THE ISLAND READS bookseller tent was jammed with disorganized titles. After extensive digging through random piles, Kenzie found a book on sea turtles. Could some of its photos be local? One in particular looked a lot like Turtle Beach. It was difficult to read its caption in the tent's dark center. She carried it into the sunlight near the public aisle.

"Oops." A woman burdened with shopping bags bumped into the tent pole. Kenzie glanced up and blinked. Had she just seen— *Yes*. It had to be him.

"Fisher!" Kenzie dropped the book onto the nearest table. She raced to catch up with the lean man who flowed in and out of the crowds. How could someone his age move so fast?

She craned her neck to look above the shoppers. She'd lost him. A frightened hen clucked across her path. *Yikes.* Kenzie stumbled backward. *Peep, peep. Cheep, cheep.* Five frantic chicks scooted behind their momma. A delighted child chased them between two vendor tents toward the most wildly painted pickup truck Kenzie'd ever seen. Huge chickens of every imaginable color covered the lavender vehicle. *Unbelievable.* A lavender pickup was weird enough, but when you factored in the chickens? There had to be a story there.

She usually didn't venture beyond the book tent where she often met Fisher. Guess that's why she'd never seen the truck before. It was parked behind the largest tent on the grounds, a shelter shared by many vendors.

In front of the huge tent, two men rummaged through boxes of fishing tackle.

"You know," one of them griped, "it's them dang foreigners stealin' them turtle eggs."

"You got that right," his friend said. "No local would fall for that old wives' tale."

What old wives' tale? Kenzie edged closer, catching one more comment before the men moved on: "They's boat people that swim in. Ain't nobody ever gonna catch 'em."

Oh yeah? The men did have a point. Approaching nesting sites by boat might make the poacher harder to catch. No matter. She'd never quit trying. That old wives' tale, whatever it was, could be an important piece of information, though. Something to track down.

Kenzie wound through the tables toward the dim, rear corner of the tent. *Mom?* Kenzie moved closer. It was Mom all right. Inspecting a department store mannequin dressed in a purple-and-yellow head wrap and enough jewelry to sink a ship. Sure wasn't Mom's style. But who knew what Mom was thinking lately?

Maybe the tropical heat and humidity was—she grinned inwardly—*molding* her mom's brain.

The mannequin posed at a table. Above it hung a hand-painted sign:

SHALIMA'S SECRETS
SOLUTIONS GUARANTEED TO PRODUCE LUXURIOUS HAIR AND RESTORE SKIN TO FLAWLESS RADIANCE

Flawless skin? Between freckles and zits, Kenzie would never have it.

The life-size figure's pale face shimmered with a curious glow-in-the-dark sheen. Its eyes were heavily shadowed, and its lips—*moved*. Kenzie did a double-take. This time it blinked. No mannequin. That was a real, live woman speaking to Mom.

Kenzie arrived at the table as the strange lady, rings sparkling on every finger, handed Mom a small lavender bag. A purple candle flickering on the table below the lady's chin explained her shining face.

"There you are." Mom placed the bag in her purse and checked her watch. "Perfect timing. I saw Lakisha a few minutes ago. She'll join us for breakfast in about fifteen minutes. Sounds like plans are coming together for the beach cleanup. On Tuesday, I think she said."

"Cool." Kenzie studied the odd collection of unlabeled jars and bottles on the table. Something about them bugged her.

Her mom picked up the insulated cooler. "My stomach's growling. Are you ready to eat?"

"Go ahead, Mom. I'll catch up."

Purple. That was it. That color seemed to be popping up a lot lately. The person running away on the beach had worn purple. So did Ancient Angry Edna. This weird woman surrounded herself with it. The color purple and a vague footprint were the only clues she had. And now maybe something about an old wives' tale.

"Hello, my dear." More air than substance, the woman's sticky-sweet, impersonal words leaked from expressionless lips. She swept a hand through the air above the table to the rhythm of clinking bracelets. "Would you care to learn more about Shalima's Secrets?"

Definitely. Kenzie glanced under the table. *Crud and double crud.* The woman's legs and feet were draped in her long skirt. No telling what size they were or if she wore Surf Sandals. She glanced again at the sign. "You're Shalima, right?"

"My name is Shaw-*lee*-ma," the woman said, as if talking to a preschooler.

"Are you like the local Avon lady?"

"Hardly, my dear," she said, her voice pained by the comparison. She placed a hand to her heart and lifted her chin. "I do not deliver. Those who desire the ultimate in beauty come to me."

Kenzie raised a forefinger to her mouth. At the last second, she controlled her urge to mimic the universal puke sign. Spattered rust-tinted spots peppering her arm caught her attention. Those spots were reproducing at an alarming rate since she'd moved to the sun-intense tropics. *Hmmm. You never know...* Might learn something useful if she got the woman talking. She redirected her finger to the bottles. "Are any of those for freckles?"

Shalima inclined her head. "Is someone envious of your dazzle?"

Envious? What planet was this wacko from? Kenzie grimaced at her arms and legs. "Who'd be jealous of these spots?"

Shalima folded her hands on the table. "Surely, you don't wish to fade them."

Maybe she's from Mercury. It's pretty dense. "I sure don't want any more of them."

"My dear, you have been blessed." Shalima leaned toward her. "Your freckles are the spice of God."

Spice... Salty. She'd never talked to Fisher. Hadn't found out if the puppy inherited his weird behavior. What if he was really sick? *Enough of this crazy lady.* Without another word, Kenzie turned and rushed to the food pavilion.

Mom, coffee in hand, waited at a picnic table. She patted the cooler. "Got shrimp. Now, what do you want for breakfast?"

"Can we go home and eat?"

"Don't you want to see Lakisha? She should be here soon."

"I'll call her on the way home." Kenzie twisted her ponytail. "I'm worried about Salty. He's always so lively and active that Angelo calls him 'Spiceman,' but he's been exhausted since last night. We need to check on him."

Mom wrapped an arm around Kenzie. "You're right, sweetie. Let's go."

Kenzie's mother opened the door. "Salty, we're home."

Instead of barking his usual welcome, Salty lay on his side under the shabby captain's chair.

"Hey, you left your kennel." Kenzie knelt by the puppy. "Are you hungry?"

Salty rolled his eyes in her direction and half-lifted his tail in a weary wag.

"Mom, he's no better. What should we do?"

"Let's see if we can entice him to eat a little something for energy. Wash those glasses in the sink, please. While I fix our breakfast, I'll heat some leftover chicken for him. I bet he'll eat that."

"But, Mom? Shouldn't we take him somewhere? Call someone?"

"This will take five minutes. Can you hang on that long? If he eats, that'll be a good sign."

"I'll try." Kenzie filled the sink with soap and water. As she washed the glassware, she forced herself to concentrate on the beach cleanup. With the attention and activity it would bring to Turtle Beach, maybe the remaining nests would be safe. "By the way, you heard Lakisha right, Mom. When I called her, she told me she hopes to organize the cleanup by Tuesday. Do you think it's possible?"

"We'll find out at church. I'm off duty tomorrow, so I can meet with the KTC parents."

Kenzie washed the last glass. "I bet we can do it. The Key Deer Boulevard cleanup came together really fast. Since everyone on this island seems to know everyone else, it's easy to communicate. Is the chicken ready?"

"Yes. I fixed some instant rice for him too."

Kenzie fixed a little plate and took it into the living room. She set it in front of the chair.

One glance and Salty turned his head.

"Salty, come out and eat."

His nose didn't so much as twitch.

"Mom, he won't come out from under the chair. He's not at all interested." Kenzie lay on the floor, then pushed a chunk of chicken toward the puppy. No luck. "And he's making weird noises when he breathes. Like a whistle full of water."

Mom crouched by the chair, stethoscope in hand. "Salty, come out from under there."

Kenzie scooted out of the way.

Gently, Mom slid Salty out into the middle of the floor. "Stand up, boy." Supporting him on his rubbery legs, she listened to his chest. "His lungs sound congested. Watch him a minute, Kenzie. He's fairly steady for now. Let me think." Mom sat on the floor, rubbing her chin in concentration.

Why was he licking his nose so much? *Oh no.* "Mom, he's bleeding. His nose is bleeding."

"Stay calm, sweetie." Mom lifted Salty's upper lip. "Hmm. Looks a bit pale. Okay, let's review the symptoms." Switching into total nurse mode, Mom listed: "Decreased appetite, pale mucous membrane, lethargy, possible pulmonary edema."

Wobbling, Salty circled, stopped and sniffed his tail.

Visually monitoring Salty, she continued, "Now, we add epistaxis to the—" She bolted backward. "Kenzie, move!"

A stream of dark, red mud spewed from the puppy's rear end.

THE STENCH WAS DEADLY. Porta potty times ten. Kenzie gagged. *Do not get sick.* "Mom, that stuff's bloody too. He's bleeding at both ends."

"That's it. We need help." Mom rushed to the cabinet, then yanked out the phone book. With card-shark speed she flipped through the Yellow Pages. "Not many local vets. Here's one. Shoot. Big Pine office is closed Saturday. Emergency veterinarian? No listing. Twenty-four-hour vet clinics ? Nothing."

Kenzie's head throbbed and pounded. *Calm down. Salty's frightened enough.* She stretched out beside the captain's chair where Salty had again retreated. "It's all right, puppy. We'll get help." Salty arched his back and heaved. "Oh no. Mom, he's going to throw up next. What do we do?"

"We clean it up." She slapped the phone book shut. "I can't find anything in this old book. Where's the new one? I've got to find a vet."

Kenzie sat up. "What about Mike? He gets emergency calls about injured deer. He must know a vet."

"Of course. Call him."

Me?

Mom gathered paper towels and disinfectant. As if it were an everyday task, she scrubbed the floor tiles and then swiped them dry. "All right then, we're ready for whatever comes next," she said, kneeling in front of the chair.

Kenzie dialed. After three rings that felt like twenty, Mike answered.

"Mike, help. It's awful. He's breathing all bubbly-like, and his nose is running, and this awful bloody-runny-stinky-stuff's coming out, and we don't know anyone— Excuse me?"

"Yes, *Salty*." Kenzie wiped her eyes. "I'll try." She took a deep breath. "He's having trouble breathing. Nose bleed? Yes. Not yet. He acts like he wants to. Yes, diarrhea. It's dark, reddish-purple. You will? Thank you." She put down the phone. Tears streaked her cheeks.

The minutes dragged. Though the wall clock timed fifteen minutes, it felt like hours before Mike rushed through the door. "Ladies, I've called Lily. She's on her way in her vet mobile." He squatted next to Kenzie by Salty's chair.

"Hey, fella. Come out and say hello to me." He spread his hands, blanket-like, over Salty's back.

With Mike's encouragement, the puppy inched forward on his belly. Mike scratched Salty's ears. "Now, what's going on?" He poked Kenzie's foot. "You first, green eyes."

"He started acting weird late yesterday."

Salty struggled to his feet, then wobbled

forward. His tail hung between his legs. As if trying to wag, he weakly lifted his tail. But he didn't wag, he squirted. Next he threw up, spattering Mike's ankles and drenching his shoes.

Kenzie cringed. *Could it get any worse?*

Mike lifted Salty's chin. "Now, that's no way to treat a guy who came to help you. I could have gone sailing, you know."

"Don't move." Kenzie's mom sopped up the floor around Mike.

"You really are having trouble, aren't you, little guy?" Mike gently massaged Salty's back. "All your plumbing got messed up at the same time."

The puppy wheezed and flopped to the floor.

Kenzie wiped the toes of Mike's shoes. Her heart plunged to her stomach. *This is all my fault.*

Mike touched her hand. "Forget the shoes. They've been through a lot worse." He pushed himself off the floor. "This little guy definitely needs Doc Lily."

My fault he got cold and wet in the storm. It made him sick.

"We've treated deer with similar symptoms."

My fault his paw was cut. It's infected and spreading.

"And you know deer will eat practically anything."

Wait. Eat? What's Mike saying?

"Ladies, could Salty have eaten some kind of poison? Maybe rat poison?"

Poison?

Her mom rose, hands on her hips. "Not in this house. I would never store rat poison where Salty could get into it."

"Easy, Maggie. I wasn't implying *you* would."

Last night. "Mom, he ate something on Turtle Beach. I don't know what it was. He swallowed it too fast."

"Near a house?" Mike asked.

"Yes. Ancient Angry Edna's."

"Who?" Mike and Mom asked in unison.

"Some mean old woman. She poisoned him."

"Now, sweetie, don't jump—"

"Mom, she hates dogs. She's mean, and sneaky, and hiding something. I know it. She's probably stealing turtle eggs too."

"What do you have to support these accusations?" Mom sounded Supreme-Court serious.

Kenzie chewed her lip, mentally searching the universe for a solid clue.

Her mother waited, head cocked and intent. "Well? How much evidence?"

"Uh..."

"That much, huh? Well then, you should not accuse her, whoever she is."

"You're right, Maggie, she shouldn't. However, Salty could have gotten into rat poison there by accident."

Accident? More like he was treated to a poison burger.

"Did someone say poison?" A woman holding a combination duffel bag and small suitcase stood outside the screen door.

"Lily," Mike said, "we didn't hear you arrive.

Too busy worrying and supposing."

Mom jumped up. "Thank goodness you're here. Come in."

"Sweetie—" Mom drew Kenzie backwards. "Let's move out of Dr. Lily's way."

Mike sat at the counter that separated kitchen from living room.

"Okay, let's take a look at this new puppy of yours." Dr. Lily sat cross-legged on the floor and stroked Salty's head. "Why do you think he's ingested rodenticide?"

While Mom explained Salty's mystery meal and symptoms, the vet unsnapped her carry all and withdrew a thermometer. "But, if he swallowed rodenticide just last night, I wouldn't expect him to present symptoms this soon."

Dr. Lily looked up at Kenzie. "Keep him on his feet while I take his temperature." Moments later, Dr. Lily withdrew the thermometer. "Don't let him lie down yet." When she read Salty's temperature, questions flicked across her face. "No fever." She reached into her bag again.

"That's good, isn't it?" Kenzie asked.

But Dr. Lily was busy listening to Salty's lungs. Next she examined his gums, abdomen, and then rummaged through her supplies.

"How you doing?" Mike mussed Kenzie's hair. "Here. Take this." He handed her a soda. "I think you can let Salty relax now."

"Thanks." Kenzie released Salty and sipped, listening to Dr. Lily soothe and stroke the puppy. Suddenly, Salty yelped. *What the?* Kenzie choked. Dr. Lily had inserted a needle in Salty's neck. And she was playing vampire.

"It's okay, sweetie." Mom rubbed Kenzie's shoulders.

Mom's right. Stay calm. Trust the doc. But it wasn't easy watching Dr. Lily squirt puppy blood into a tube and then rock it back and forth, back and forth, like a pendulum on a ticking clock. Kenzie rocked with it, hugging herself tightly. The blood flowed up and down in the vial. Over and over. Whatever Dr. Lily was doing, it was taking forever, and she wasn't pleased about it. Kenzie's fear factor was off the chart.

Dr. Lily shifted Salty's collar to examine his neck, and then focused on Kenzie. "Taking Salty's age, background, and symptoms into account, I was sure he had Parvovirus. However, that's not the case."

Kenzie sat straighter. "That's good news, right?"

"Sweetie, let Dr. Lily finish."

"Well, it's good that he registers no fever, but his blood isn't clotting as it should."

Not good. Really not good.

The vet lifted Salty's head. "See the spot where I withdrew blood? It should not be swelling like this." She rocked the vial again. "His blood is taking too long to clot. And rodenticides definitely interfere with clotting. Assuming he did ingest poison last night—it was likely not the first time."

Impossible. How could that be? When else had he been out of her sight?

Dr. Lily continued. "Salty's blood vessels are hemorrhaging." *Hemorrhaging. A horrid, horrible word.* "Salty's nose bleed and wheezing are signs of that." Dr. Lily pulled another needle from her bag.

Not again. Salty's eyes focused on the needle. *Think of something else. Anything. Like...has Mom unpacked the crucifix and holy water? Ugh. That was so not funny.* Salty began to quiver. Kenzie shook with him.

Dr. Lily prepared the needle. "Vitamin K_1 shots will boost Salty's blood clotting factor."

Not sucking blood. Injecting medicine. Kenzie closed her eyes, waiting for the yip of pain. What was taking so long? She peeked. The needle was nowhere in sight.

Dr. Lily smiled. "See, that wasn't so bad. Neither of you felt a thing. He'll need several of these over the next few days. I suspect something else is going on here." Dr. Lily flipped her waist-length braid over her shoulder. "The diarrhea and vomiting can also be signs of another problem. Did Salty's previous owners de-worm him?"

Kenzie and her mom exchanged frightened looks.

"No worries. I can take care of that. The rodenticide likely exacerbated an intestinal worm problem and vice versa."

Poison *and* worms? Kenzie's gut spasmed. Trembling, she clutched her rebellious stomach, and whispered. "He's going to the hospital, isn't he?"

"Don't worry." Dr. Lily placed her hand on Kenzie's knee. "Your puppy will be well cared for. Yes, he'll have to spend several days at the clinic. He may need a blood transfusion to build up his clotting ability as well as antibiotics and lots of fluids. Plus, we'll give him medicine to prevent vomiting, because if he can't keep the worm medicine down, it's not going to work."

Salty alone in a cold cage, hooked up to frightening machines, poked with sharp needles. Kenzie's tears poured out.

"Oh, sweetie." Mom took Kenzie's hand. "I know this is hard." She tugged Kenzie to her feet and held her close.

"We'll watch Salty carefully for the next hour or so." Dr. Lily finished packing her medical bag, then stood. "I have a crate behind my seat. Kenzie, why don't you ride with me and keep him company?"

"Great idea." Mom dabbed Kenzie's eyes, then filled her pockets with extra tissues. "I'll be right behind you." She tucked tear-dampened curls behind Kenzie's ears. "I won't let you out of my sight."

"Salty's young and strong," Dr. Lily said. "Before you know it, Kenzie, he'll be home, and *you'll* be taking care of him."

"I need to get my purse and keys. Back in a minute." Mom headed for her bedroom.

"Lily, before you go—" Mike glanced at Kenzie. "Thursday the refuge received notification about an injured hawksbill. Were you called in on that?"

Thursday... Hawksbill... Kenzie's heaving stomach knotted. *How much does he know?*

"Yes, the hospital called me in on the case. It was found off Turtle Beach. Apparently, the boater was a young—"

"How's the turtle doing?" Mike asked.

He interrupted Dr. Lily. He doesn't want her to connect the dots. Cool.

"Amazingly well," Dr. Lily said. "No sign of tumors. It had a digestive tract obstruction which we were able to remove."

"Excellent news."

"Most excellent. It will make a full recovery. If only all our patients were so lucky." She reached into her pocket and pulled out a business card. "I better go down and start the van's AC." As she left, she placed her card on the table by the screen door.

"She's a good vet to have on your team, Kenzie." Mike's eyes commanded attention. "No matter the challenge."

He knows it was me. She twisted her ponytail. *Does he know I took Angelo's boat?* How could she have been so dense? The Key Deer Refuge was responsible for all endangered animals on the island, not only deer. Mike would have heard the whole story. But he hadn't told Mom. Yet.

The flapping of Mom's sandals echoed down the hall into the living room. "Okay, I'm ready. Mike, are you coming with us?"

"No need. I'm leaving you girls in good hands. Lily's the best vet in the Keys." Mike placed his hand on Kenzie's head. "You have no reason to worry. Nor does your mother. Salty will be fine."

"I'm not worried, Mike. I'm sure Salty will be good as new," Mom said.

"Good, Maggie. There's no reason for you to worry about the recovery of a single one of Lily's patients. Never will be." He bent forward and whispered to Kenzie. "No matter the species. Because you, young lady, will *never* put yourself in a dangerous position again." His concerned, serious expression pinned her. "Kenzie... Right?" He didn't give her an ounce of wiggle room.

Kenzie managed a feeble, "Okay." She simultaneously telepathed: *I promise. No more going off alone in a boat.* It was the best she could do. Mike had given her strict orders, without telling Mom what he really meant. *Amazing.* Her insides calmed. If only the jackhammer in her head would do the same.

Mike opened the screen door. "I'll come by this evening for an update." He retreated down the steps.

"We'll be here." Mom turned to Kenzie. "Wish I could be as certain about things as he is."

You can be sure about one thing. You just don't know it. No more boat snatching for me. Kenzie lifted Salty and followed Mom out the door. She paused to glance at Dr. Lily's card. Along the bottom edge were the words *Proud to be affiliated with Marathon Turtle Hospital.* She whispered in Salty's ear. "I know you'll be okay now, puppy. Dr. Lily saved our hawksbill, and she's going to make you well too."

As soon as they returned from the hospital, Kenzie called Ana. Even pouring out her fears didn't lighten her mood. No dark eyes begged beside the dinner table that night. No paws crept onto a knee. Even if they'd eaten hand-tossed New York deli pizza, it would have been the least appetizing meal in history.

Dinner long over, dishes washed, Kenzie slumped on the front porch lounge, watching the remaining coral and sapphire drain from the sky. The vision did nothing to improve her mood. Salty's illness seemed like her punishment for taking Angelo's boat to the far side of the island. As it turned out, it had to do with Thursday. Or did it? He had run after that person on the beach. What if he'd found rat poison that day? He could have been licking more than blood off his paw. Dr. Lily could be right.

But it's still all my fault. Salty would not be sick if she'd secured his collar last night. He would have been safely tied to the porch railing through the whole turtle hatch.

Gravel crunched below the little stilt house. Footsteps. Mike and Mom. Since seven thirty, when Mike returned to ask about Salty, they'd been sitting out back on the dock. He must be leaving. They spoke in hushed but clear voices. Should she let them know she was here? *What, and miss something?*

"Lily tells it pretty much as it is," Mike said. "She wouldn't have reassured Kenzie unless she's confident Salty will pull through."

"You're probably right. Kenzie worries me though. She didn't say a word on the way home from the clinic. She's been unusually quiet the last couple of days. There's a great deal she's not telling me. How does she know this Edna person? And if Kenzie thinks the woman is also involved in that turtle egg business, there's no telling what trouble she'll get into."

"I think I know who Kenzie's talking about. If I'm right, she's not connected with the turtle egg thefts. At least not according to Sheriff Clark. The sheriff believes a gang of men from outside the U.S.—"

Kwawk. Kwawk.

"...steal turtle eggs and sell—"

Kwawk, kwawk, kwawk.

Stupid night heron. Mike said something about a gang stealing eggs and selling them. It sounded like "selling them for *af-ri-dee-zee-acks.*"

"You're kidding," Mom said. "In this day and age? People use turtle eggs as—"

Kwawk. Kwawk.

Why won't that bird shut up? Mom had said that same word, *af-ri-dee-zee-acks. Keep talking, you guys.*

"I know it's strange." They were walking toward his truck. "But these men and their customers are from Caribbean islands where many people still practice the old ways."

What old ways?

"If Sheriff Clark knows this, Mike, why haven't they been caught by now?"

"By the time she figured it out, the destruction came to a standstill."

Wrong. That's what you think.

Mike opened his truck door. "They have to harvest the eggs soon after they're deposited, and the nesting season is slowing down."

He climbed behind the wheel. *Crud.* All hope of hearing more information evaporated.

Mike said a gang of *men.* Why couldn't a woman could be a gang member? Ancient Angry Edna to be precise. She could be from some Caribbean island. Most people in the Keys had originally lived somewhere else.

Edna had to be the thief. Kenzie paced in her bedroom, mentally racing through the last three days. First, on Thursday, someone in a purple shirt ran from Salty. Why? Didn't want to get caught robbing nests. Second, that same day, both she and Salty were threatened by Edna, wearing a purple shirt. Third. that woman's hiding something. Else why the high fence in the middle of the woods? Fourth, the very next day, Salty stopped someone from robbing a nest, and where did the thief run? Surprise. Right toward Ancient Angry Edna's house.

Then there's the Salty factor. He swallowed

the poison right by her house. First she kills baby turtles, and now she wants to kill Salty. Why? Because he's making it hard for her to steal more eggs. She had to be the person Salty chased Thursday. She fed him poison first on Thursday. Two days before he got so sick. Two doses. Like Dr. Lily suspected.

Kenzie's chest swelled and her back straightened. Ancient Angry Edna was going to be ancient history.

For now though, she needed to learn what that *afri*-something-or-other word meant. Clearly, it related somehow to turtle eggs. It could be a major piece of the puzzle. *Find the connection.*

Eggs and afri... Afri... African! African eggs.

Kenzie tiptoed to her room and pulled her dictionary off the shelf. She skimmed two and one half pages of *af* and *aff* words. Not one definition clicked with anything Mike said. What did he mean by *old ways*? Maybe it was related to the old wives' tale those fisherman at the flea market were talking about. It could be a tale about old ways of fishing.

So, there's fishing and African eggs. Lots of Cuban fishermen with African heritage live in the Keys. Mike said the poachers came from island countries. *Cuba's an island country*. Kenzie closed the dictionary. *Angelo. He's Cuban, and he knows all the local fishermen*. Maybe he could explain the *afrideezie*-word thing.

She'd ask him at church tomorrow, and then she'd find out Ancient Angry Edna's background. She probably does lots of things in *old ways*.

She's probably an *old wife*.

No wonder Sheriff Clark's investigation failed. She was looking for a gang of men—way off base. Not a gang of men. *One crazy old woman*.

Kenzie opened one eye a crack. She would have slept long past sunup if not for the coffee grinder. Its buzz snapped her out of a healing Salty dream.

Mom's up? It's her day off. Kenzie padded barefoot to the kitchen. Mom sat at the breakfast bar, watching the coffee drip.

"What are you—" They smiled at their duet.

"You first, Mom."

"You're up early. How come?"

"I guess I'm worried about Salty. What about you?"

"Me?" Mom filled her coffee mug, then gave Kenzie one of those heavy-lidded sideways looks. The kind that usually meant one thousand and one questions hung in the air. "Yes, I *am* worried."

Uh-oh. Mom's evasive tone. "Worried about Salty, right?"

"Sure I'm worried about Salty—and you." Her mom sipped, then sighed. "You know you can talk to me about anything." Mom fixed her eyes on Kenzie. "Right?"

"Un-huh..." *I don't like this. Mom's up to something.*

"Good. I'd rather *know* than worry about

what I imagine." She sipped again. "Should I be worried about you?"

"Geesh, Mom. No. Not as long as Salty recovers. What's with you?"

Mom massaged her forehead. "Oh, sweetie— I'm a mother. The only mothers who don't worry are dead."

And if you knew everything, I'd be dead. Kenzie's wince morphed to a teasing grin as she joined her mom at the counter. "That means worry is good thing." She draped an arm over her mom's shoulders. "I mean, if it keeps you alive and all."

"Good thought, sweetie. Remember that the next time I fuss at you." She topped off her coffee. "Sure you're not getting involved in anything troublesome?"

"Oh, *please*, Mom. Stop worrying. It's negative and wastes energy. Salty needs the strongest, most positive vibes we can send his way."

"You're right. How did you get so smart?"

"I have a sharp mom." *Taught me quick thinking under pressure.* Kenzie pecked Mom on the cheek. "Since we're up early, can we visit Salty before church?"

"Absolutely." Mom laid her hand on Kenzie's. "Let's have a full breakfast. Pancakes, eggs, bacon. We'll strengthen our vibes.

At the animal hospital, Mom and the veterinary assistant chatted while Kenzie sat on the back room floor by Salty's cage. The puppy lay with his head on his forepaws, his eyes alert. When Kenzie opened the cage door, his tail flicked from side to side.

"I missed you last night." She stroked Salty's head. "I woke up at the time you always need to go out, even though I wanted to finish my dream. I was close to getting some magical medicine for you called *afrideezie*. If it really existed, you wouldn't be here because it was an instant antidote. We'd be playing chase or tug-of-war at home." She leaned close to his ear. "Or saving turtles."

Salty tilted his head as if he understood every word.

"I needed to pay for the antidote with turtle eggs. And because I love you so-ooo much, I actually stole the eggs."

Salty yipped, then wriggled out of the cage. He rested his head on her lap and whimpered.

"Hey, it was only a dream. Anyway, I didn't rob a nest. I took the eggs from Ancient Angry Edna. No clue how I did that. Shalima, that weird lady from the flea market, was in my dream. She told me about a medicine man who'd trade eggs for the *afrideezie* medication. He lived in an icky, creepy swamp full of snakes and alligators. Old Turtle helped me find him. I can't remember how that happened either. I have a foggy image of me riding his back. Imagine, Old Turtle helping me with a bag of eggs in my hand. Crazy, huh? More crazy—the medicine man looked like Mike, except he had long white hair."

"Kenzie," Mom called from the office. "We better get to church."

"I'm sorry, Salty. You have to go back in the cage now." Kenzie gently lifted and placed him back inside. "You'll be home soon. I promise."

Mom started the engine and turned the AC on high. "The assistant said Salty's doing well, and he sure looked like it to me."

"Positive vibes. Told you."

"Sweetie, some people call that prayer."

They crossed Niles Channel Bridge to Big Pine Key, turned on Key Deer Boulevard, and then onto the bumpy unpaved lane, arriving at St. Francis twenty minutes after leaving the clinic. Kenzie imagined this cozy woodland church through the eyes of her friends back home. *Wait. Accept it. This island's home now.* Her friends in New York wouldn't believe this atmosphere.

St. Francis and St. Joe's operated under totally different dress codes. No fashionistas here. Instead, shorts and sandals—casual comfort. No elaborate, echoing sanctuary lined with frightening renditions of saints. Service was held in a large, peaceful space—a giant screened-in room. Beyond the screened walls, the only distracting sounds were made by whispering pine boughs, clicking palm fronds, and foraging Key deer.

The coolest thing was Father Murphy's dog, Robin. Every Sunday the cheerful dog, who was Salty's father, proudly pranced to the altar carrying the collection basket. Father named his retriever in honor of Robin Hood. "After all," Father had explained, "Robin takes the offering from our rich to provide for our poor."

As usual, after the service, the Keys Teens Care group met under the tiki hut. They shared news and homemade goodies while their families met and socialized on the other side of the building. Before Mass, Father had announced the KTC beach cleanup and explained that a volunteer sheet would circulate. That signup page was making its final round among the KTC members now.

"I haven't been to Turtle Beach since third grade," Lakisha said. "I can't believe it's that messed up."

"Me either." Ted bit into another brownie. "Is it as bad as the shopping center before we cleaned it up?"

"Worse," Kenzie said.

"Trash rides the current. Comes in with the tide there," Angelo said.

"Are you saying most of the trash is from boats?" Kenzie asked. "Not from sunbathers and swimmers?"

"Think about it, Red." Angelo stared at her as if *moron* were etched on her forehead. "How many people did you see on that remote beach?"

True, she hadn't seen any, other than Purple Shirt. But Angelo didn't have to act so snotty about it.

"What about storm trash?" Ted asked. "Debris rides the Gulf Stream all along the coast."

"That, too, dude," Angelo said. "Then there's all that junk along the isolated road. Dumped by lazy sea cukes."

"Sea cukes?" Could he be any more confusing?

Ted laughed. "Seen one yet? Long, brown, like a giant tur—"

"Okay. Okay." Kenzie shushed him with her hand. "I get it. Back to the subject. Ana's house is one of the few on Turtle Beach. And she can't enjoy it because all the trash makes it hard to maneuver her wheelchair." Kenzie leaned forward. "Angelo, tell them how bad it is."

"It's *your* show, Red. You don't need me." Turning his back to her, he straddled the bench. A cowboy riding off into the sunset.

She'd been ditched.

WHAT WAS ANGELO'S PROBLEM? Kenzie fired wicked thoughts and sharp images at Angelo's back.

"Hey!" A shaggy brown dog nudged her elbow. "Jigs, you goofy dog." The big dog plopped her paws on Kenzie's knees. "I didn't know you were here, girl."

"Some detective." Angelo spoke to the air above his head. "You missed a major clue. Robin split from the altar. *Major clue.*"

The Sharkman was out in full force. She couldn't have seen Robin leave. Her line of sight had been blocked by a post. Like it was blocked now by Jigs' big, hairy head. It's no big deal. Why did Angelo keep freezing her out? If she had seen, yes, she would have known Jigs was nearby. Nothing else would pull Robin from Father Murphy's side. The two dogs adored each other. She hid her pain in Jigs' furry neck and ruffled the dog's floppy ears, receiving sloppy kisses in return.

"Gross. Dog breath."

Ted. Always trying to lighten the moment.

"Greetings, young guardians of the island."

Fisher.

Kenzie shifted Jigs' head to the side.

Fisher bowed, sweeping the ground with his floppy hat.

"I knew you couldn't be far away," Kenzie told him. She slipped Jigs a piece of cookie, then tried to pry the big dog's paws from her knees.

"Down, Jigs, my lady. You have made an undignified entrance." The old man's bushy beard framed a contagious grin.

Jigs padded to the leather-skinned man, wearing her best hang-dog-sorry face.

Handing Fisher a cupcake, Lakisha asked, "Why aren't you out sponging?"

He nodded his thanks. "The sea is in a bit of a tempest. Thus, the sponges are granted their day of rest. They've naught to fear from my hook today. This day I labor for the Lord."

"Mom will be glad to see you," Kenzie said. "After you finish your work for Father Murphy, she wants you to fix our roof."

"Ah, a damsel in distress. Come, Jigs." Brushing crumbs from his beard, he curled his fingers around Jigs' collar. "We must not delay." Then he strode off toward the congregational meeting.

Lakisha, serious as a sea captain run aground, asked, "Do you think he's always talked like that?" Her expression cracked, and a mischievous grin appeared.

"Pray tell, fair maiden, what meanest thou?" Ted mimicked.

"Come on, you guys," Kenzie said. "You know he had an actress mom and a British dad. Instead of kid books, they probably read him Shakespeare."

"Shakespeare? That's more disgusting than dog breath." Ted scrunched his nose.

Kenzie rolled her eyes. "Where's the signup list?"

"I'm checking it now." Lakisha studied it a few seconds. "Everything's checked off. We'll be ready."

"Seriously?" Kenzie asked. "By Tuesday?"

Lakisha tapped the list. "If everyone comes through with these promises, yes."

At last Angelo turned around. He batted a fishing weight back and forth on the table, like a cat toying with a mouse. "What about the turtles and the poacher?"

Ted touched his chest with his thumb. "Hey, we're the KTC, right? We've done it before, and we'll do it again. We'll find out who the poacher is."

"Catchin' him would be better," Angelo muttered.

"Here comes Ana," Kenzie said. "Her house is a great stakeout location. She'll be a huge help."

"*Ay, amigas.* I am sorry to be so late. In the offering, there was much change to count today." Ana locked her brakes. "Did I miss anything?"

"We were talking about the turtle nests," Lakisha whispered. "Any idea who the thief is?"

"No. It is so sad. I wish I did."

"Ask the Lone Ranger here." Angelo jerked his head toward Kenzie.

Lone Ranger? What was he talking about *now*? "I do have an idea. What I need is proof." She studied Angelo. He could have been a chunk of granite. "Do you guys have your spy cameras ready?"

Ted saluted. "Locked and loaded."

"I'm using Dad's," Lakisha said. "But after the cleanup, how can we keep it a secret that we're trying to catch the poacher? We'll need another reason to be at Turtle Beach."

"Let's hope it doesn't take that long," Kenzie said.

"If needed"—Ted raised a finger—"Ana could hold endless beach parties."

"*Ay*, my parents would so love that. Not to party, but to start guarding, who can come tomorrow? We will plan where to place tables and supplies. Also, we must be sure the nest marking sticks and warning ribbon are in place. I can tell you where most of the nests are."

"I'll be there," Ted said.

Why was Angelo ignoring Ana's question? When they'd started planning on Thursday, they'd discussed this exact scheme. If only she had telepathic powers. "If I can swing it with Mom, I'll be there." *Say something, Angelo. Say you'll take me.* "But the more Mom knows, the more she worries."

"Like that's not true for all parents," Ted said.

"True. But lately my mom seems to be channeling major suspicions. So it's strictly cleanup talk. Not a word remotely connected to an investigation."

"That'll be easy for you, Red. You're a pro at keeping your mouth shut." Angelo abruptly stood, then leaned against the corner post, and folded his arms.

He sounded more and more ridiculous. How much longer could she ignore his attitude? Even Ted was giving him weird looks. In a fog of Angelo-confusion, Kenzie tuned in and out of the planning finale, hearing an occasional mention of posters, sponsors, and reporters.

"Wake up." Lakisha poked her. "We don't need new T-shirts, do we? The slogan *Please keep our animals alive and our island clean* still works."

"Yeah, sure. We'll wear our old shirts. And don't worry. After people know about our latest project, we'll have an excuse to go to Turtle Beach whenever we can. As far as anyone knows, we'll be there to keep it clean and monitor potential dumpers. Be sure to send me pictures of anything or anyone suspicious, and I'll post them on the KTC site."

In the middle of her fog, she'd made a decision. *Last chance, Sharkman.* Kenzie willed arrows to fly from her eyes, to pin him. "Tell me honestly, Angelo. Do *you* think we can be ready by Tuesday?"

Nothing about his expression changed except his lips. They curled. "Don't ask me. It's your call, Kemo Sabe."

Kee mo what?

"Dude," Ted said, "we can do it." He grabbed the last cookie as Father Murphy joined them.

"How goes the planning?"

"Right on target." Ted licked his fingers.

"Your families are busy organizing a beach cleanup sustenance and support system."

"I saw some parents' names on the signup sheet." Lakisha said. "Did you remind them it's scheduled for Tuesday? Can they be ready?"

"I believe I made that clear." Father Murphy tilted his head skyward as if to check God's memory bank. "But I will check."

"*Oigan, muchachos.*" Mr. Sánchez beamed as he approached them, carrying a tray of sweets.

Father Murphy chuckled. "I see I will not leave you hungry."

"*¿Más dulces?*" Mr. Sánchez set the tray on the table. "*Ángel*, are you soon ready?"

"More than ready."

"*Bueno.* I will get my hat." Mr. Sánchez returned to the church.

As he headed for the truck, Angelo's expression—part angry, part sad—puzzled Kenzie. The sad part wouldn't let her quit. *I am going to get an answer.* She caught up with him. "Angelo, wait. What's wrong with you?"

"Nothing." He leaned against the truck bed, rattling the lead sinkers in his pocket. "Nada."

Okay. Getting nowhere. Try another approach. "Why'd you call me the Lone Ranger? Who's that?"

"Guy on an ancient TV western."

"One you watched?"

"My mother. She watched old shows to learn English."

"Okay... " Kenzie raised her eyebrows and waited for more information.

"My mother said old program plots were simpler and the actors talked slower."Angelo opened the truck door.

"Hey, come on." She plucked the arm of his shirt. "What's an old TV show got to do with me? And what did I do to make you mad this time?"

"Nothin'. Forget it." Like he was conversing with the truck. "*You did nothing.*"

"I did, too, or you wouldn't be jerking me around. Tell me what I did."

"It's what you *didn't* do." He rearranged pebbles with his foot. "You didn't tell me about little Spiceman."

"So? What could you have done?"

"See? That's exactly what I mean." He actually looked her in the eye.

"Excuse me?"

"I was there when Salty ate that poison."

"How did you find—"

"Dr. Lily buys fish from Dad. She told him."

"Angelo, he's fine. Everything's okay."

"Yeah, this time." He kicked a rock under the truck.

"You didn't know it was poison."

"I don't pay attention; bad stuff happens. Every time." He pulled his ball cap out of his back pocket and tugged it low on his forehead. "You and Salty... You're like family."

Wow. How was she supposed to deal with that? *Like family*—intense words—though not exactly what she'd been hoping for in their relationship. "About the Lone Ranger and that other guy *Kee mo* something. I'm still clueless."

"Same dude. Two names. Kemo Sabe's his

Indian name."

"Oh." *This is good. Keep him talking.* "Did that show really teach your mom English?"

Angelo's eyes grew black and shiny, like a bottomless canal. "Not enough to read medicine labels." Several quiet seconds passed. He blinked his eyes brown again and punched her lightly on the arm. "Hey, you don't have to go it alone, you know?"

"What's that supposed to mean?"

"Look, Dad's coming. You'll figure it out."

Figure it out. That weird word Mom and Mike used. She needed his help to figure *that* out.

He had one foot on the running board.

"Angelo, wait. Do Cuban fishermen use something called"—syllable by memorized syllable she repeated—"af-ri-dee-zee-acks?"

Angelo's eyes tripled in size. "Sometimes I wish I'd never pulled you out of that canal." He jumped in the truck and slammed the door, rolled down the window a fraction. "Red, don't even think of asking my dad that."

Rrrriiiinng. Rrrriiiinng.

Monday. The drone of Mom's hairdryer drifted down the hall. *Mom's getting ready for work.*

Rrrriiiinng. Rrrriiiinng.

Kenzie jerked awake, then rushed to the kitchen phone. The vet's cell number displayed. "Hi, Dr. Lily. How's Salty?" She opened the refrigerator door. "He's eating? That's great!" She pulled out the milk carton. "Awesome. I'll tell Mom. Thanks." Kenzie hung up, then lifted the carton to her mouth.

"Kenzie Susannah Ryan, stop that."

Kenzie jumped and nearly dropped the container. "Sorry, Mom. Salty can come home tomorrow. Dr. Lily said his appetite improved, and his vitals are nearly normal."

"Terrific." Her mom opened the cabinet door. "That is cause for celebration." She handed Kenzie a crystal goblet, took one for herself, and filled them both. "Here, have a *glass* of milk." Mom clinked her goblet to Kenzie's. "Cheers."

She downed a few swallows and lowered her glass. "Now, do you remember what to tell Fisher if he comes today?"

"Mom, you've told me a hundred times. The ladder's in the storage room, and the leak's on the canal side of the roof near the vent pipe."

"Perfect. I expect he'll be here. Considering last night's storm and today's wind, I'm sure the water's murky. He won't be able to see the sponges."

"I hope he's not late. Ana's dad is picking me up around ten, remember? Tomorrow's the cleanup, and we have a lot of work to do. I guess I'll be there most of the day." *Keeping a lookout for the turtle-egg thief.*

"That should be no problem. If Fisher's not here by nine, he won't be coming." She snagged her keys. "Mike and I will pick you up at Ana's after work, and we'll all go to dinner together."

Right. Apparently Mom could no longer digest a meal without Mike around. Kenzie still wasn't sure how to deal with the all-the-time-everywhere-ness of it all.

"We'll see you around six, sweetie." Mom kissed Kenzie's cheek. "Have fun." Then she left for the hospital.

Kenzie moved toward the phone. Then hesitated. *Should she contact Angelo?* He'd want to hear the good news about Salty. No She didn't want to deal with his attitude. Not yet. Something about that afri...deezie or dee-zee-ack...whatever-it-was thing had pushed him over the edge. Again. She'd planned to do more research in hopes of figuring it out last night. But the storm forced her to shut down and unplug the computer. While she waited for Fisher, she could try again.

Wait. *Fisher.* She could ask him what that word was. Angelo's warning came back to her: *Don't even think about asking my father.* Maybe asking Fisher wasn't a good idea either.

She went back to her room, hooked up the computer, and continued her search for *anything* about that strange word.

First she typed *African eggs* and found articles about birds and their nesting habits. Tapping out *old fishing methods* led her to articles on Ernest Hemingway's book about an old Cuban fisherman fighting a huge fish, reviews of TV fishing shows, and reports from fishing boat captains. Entering *Cuban eggs* brought up recipes, and no matter how she rearranged letters to spell the puzzling word itself, all she came up with were confusing lyrics to rap songs.

"Ship. Ship. Shiiiiip." *Whoa.* She was using Angelo's no-swear words now. There was not one word about *afrideezie* anything online. Anywhere. Was the stupid computer in on this conspiracy, too?

"All hail within."

Kenzie rushed into the living room. Fisher stood on the top step.

"Come on in. I didn't hear you arrive."

"My noble steed is rather quiet."

"Quiet is good. Plus, you don't have to feed a bike."

"True. Even so, ungrateful mount that she is, upon occasion she lets me down—flat." He raised his ever-twinkling eyes to the roof. "Shall I begin the assault?"

"Would you like a cold glass of tea first?"

"Thank you, kind lady. Unlike my steed, I do take pleasure in a refreshing drink. How fares the young pup?"

"He's coming home tomorrow."

"Splendid."

"Please, sit down." Kenzie reached into the refrigerator, rearranging bottles and cartons to reach the pitcher. Behind a juice carton was a shiny, purple jar labeled: *SHALIMA'S SECRETS FACE BALM*. Why was it in the refrigerator? Mom must've been distracted again. Once, when she was fixing Mike a drink, she'd stashed her keys in the freezer. Kenzie removed both the tea and the jar.

She poured Fisher's tea. While he drank, she inspected the exotic jar. The back label stated, *One hundred percent natural wonders. No artificial preservatives. Refrigerate.*

What natural wonders? Shouldn't they be listed? Kind of weird to refrigerate face cream. Maybe you could smear it on toast as well as your face.

"Tea most admirable, Kenzie." Fisher raised his glass. "Now, why so pensive? Is it something about the vessel in your possession?"

"Well..." Kenzie pictured Fisher traveling the island block by block, collecting discards, sharing his poetic tales, and gathering news. He'd even heard about Salty. The entire island functioned as Fisher's stage, and he knew everyone in the production. She placed the jar in front of him. "Do you know anything about this or the woman who makes it?"

He stared blankly at the label. "Perhaps, my dear, this would be a good time for my next reading lesson."

"Oh, sorry. I wanted to do that at the flea market Saturday. You disappeared before I could catch up with you."

Kenzie sat across the counter from him, then read the label, pointing to one word at a time. "*Shalima's...Secrets...Face...Balm.*"

Fisher took the jar and studied the label intently. Then, he pulled a notepad from his pocket. Spelling each word out loud, he printed them on his pad.

"*B-a-l-m.* That word, balm, I would have pronounced correctly. However, Shalima's name is confusing. It ends with the same letters as the bean—lima. Why does she not pronounce it with a long i sound?"

"People pronounce their names any way they want," Kenzie said.

"So it would appear." Fisher touched the word *face* and stroked his beard. "Here, I remember, the letter c causes the letter a to make a long sound. But, I do not understand why the first e is long in the word *secret.*"

Kenzie shrugged. "Actually, I don't get that either."

"I have come to the conclusion far more rules exist to be broken in the English language than in the English law."

"At least breaking language rules doesn't hurt anyone."

"Only the speaker, perhaps. On to your query regarding Shalima and her vessels. These royal purple gems first appeared in roadside treasure chests this spring. It pains me that I can find no use for them."

Roadside treasure chests? After a second it clicked. He meant recycle bins.

So the bottles started showing up in the spring—the beginning of turtle nesting season. Interesting.

"Fisher, when you go through the neighborhoods collecting recyclables, you see everything that's going on and talk with everybody you meet. You must know something about Shalima."

"Ah, you wish to interrogate Fisher, pirate of the discarded." He removed a bandana from his rear pocket, wrapped it around his head, and knotted it at the back. "Aargh, what has I seen? Eh, matey?" He curled his fingers around an imaginary spyglass, raised his hands high, and peered through it.

Kenzie rolled her eyes and stood to put the purple jar back in the refrigerator.

"Well then, Kenzie, me lass." He took off his bandana and began to talk almost like an ordinary person. "I'll tell you what little I have heard. As you know, Shalima creates unique, enticing concoctions. These she sells from her home, where she also nurtures rescued fowl."

"She rescues birds?"

He nodded. "Chickens, to be precise."

"Rescues them from what?"

"Irate citizens, I presume." Fisher tied the bandana around his wrist. "The foul fowl destroy gardens and eat beneficial insects and lizards. Furthermore, the regal roosters practice their rowdy oration twenty-four hours a day."

"Their crowing is sure annoying during church. Are they a special breed, or endangered like the Key deer?"

"To my knowledge, they are common yard chickens. Though some claim island fowl are descendants of the original colonists' Bahamian chickens."

Why rescue chickens? She's weird enough without this habit. "That truck. The one with the chickens all over it. That's hers?"

"Indeed."

"How long has she been rescuing chickens?"

"She has resided on the island less than a year. No one seems to care much about her origin. I suppose that enhances the veil of mystery she weaves around herself and her products."

Maybe other people appreciated the mystery. But to Kenzie, Shalima's love of purple, the timing of her appearance, and her chicken obsession were challenges. Would someone who saved chickens kill baby turtles? Can't rule out the possibility. What size were her feet and what shoes did she wear? Who was she really—underneath that spotless skin, that exotic head scarf, and yards and yards of clothing?

"Fisher, do you think Shalima's pretty?"

He gulped his tea. The ice slid, smacking him in the nose. He set the glass down, wiped a hand across his face, and mumbled, "Yes... Yes, I do."

He gathered his thick gray hair into a ponytail, stood abruptly, and carried his glass to the sink. "Now, I must fulfill my mission before the sun reaches its zenith."

Mr. Muñoz arrived for Kenzie promptly at ten. As Kenzie rushed down the steps, she shouted goodbye to Fisher who was busy working on the roof.

Ana suggested that they waste no time before exploring the beach. Already 80 degrees, the temperature continued to rise.

They'd just picked a shaded site for the refreshment table when forever-hungry Ted showed up, eyeing the spot as if goodies might appear at any moment. "I approve. Easy to get to. Plenty of shade. So, what's my assignment?"

Kenzie gave him a handful of large garbage bags. "Find about a dozen places along the shore. Spots far away from any nest. Spread one of the bags out at each spot so we'll know where to pile supplies tomorrow."

Ted kicked a half-buried jug, heavy with slimy sea water. "I won't have any trouble finding stuff to weigh them down."

"This week the tides are rising," Ana said. "Put the bags far from the water."

Kenzie cleared a path for Doonie so she and Ana could repair damaged nest markers. On their way back to Ana's house, they came to the final nest. The spot where Angelo had helped Ana cross the sand. Where he'd been so kind.

So, what happened to him yesterday? Kenzie wrapped the marker tape around the stake, then yanked so hard it ripped in two.

"Chica, what is wrong?" Ana tied the pieces together.

"Angelo. He got over the boat issue. Then yesterday he got super ticked off again."

"*Sí*, he *was* in a bad temper."

"He was angry because I didn't tell him about Salty, and when I asked him about some Cuban fishing tradition, he freaked out big time. Do you know anything about Cuban fishing traditions?"

"No. Perhaps we can ask *Papi*."

Probably not a good idea. "No, it's not that big a deal. Besides, I think it's more than that. Something else is going on with him." Kenzie pounded the stake in the sand with a rock. "He won't even talk to me now. Since I went to a girls' school my whole life, I haven't spent much time with boys."

"At school, boys often fight. Why I do not know. But they do not stay angry long."

"I sure hope you're right, Ana."

"This beach is under the protection of Ted the Terrible." The voice of a would-be pirate bellowed across the sand. "Captain of the Keys Teens Care."

"Look at Ted," Ana said. "If he became angry, you could hand him a brownie, and he would be happy again."

Ted continued to march along the shore, whacking invisible enemies with his baseball bat. "I dare anyone to mess with our turtles."

As far as Kenzie could tell, other than Ana

and her, only birds and fish were around to hear him. The attention placed on the beach by community papers, posters, and radio seemed to be scaring the thief—or thieves—off. *Be careful what you hope for,* her brain warned.

How do you catch a thief who's been frightened away?

"THIS EVENING IT IS SO PLEASANT. We should wait on the porch for your mother and Mike." Ana clicked the mosquito lantern button until a trace of insect repellent drifted on the sea breeze. She positioned her chair beside Kenzie. "You look worried, chica. Are you afraid there will not be enough volunteers tomorrow?"

"Angelo's the only one I'm worried about. He's so mad at me, *he* might not show up. I think lots of other people will come, though. Even people who aren't members of our church."

"Our plans are important to Angelo. He will come. He may not speak to you, but he will participate."

"I wish I knew why asking about a Cuban tradition made him so furious. I only wanted to know why someone would buy turtle eggs. It's all about motive. The thief must be making money off them. *How* is the question."

"We will visit the Turtle Hospital, yes? Maybe someone there will know."

"Good thinking. I hope we can go soon. Speaking of going..." Kenzie stood. "Mom should be here soon." She brushed off her shorts and tucked in her T-shirt. When she sat down, her shirttail pulled out again. "I give up. Hope Mike takes us someplace super casual."

Ana touched Kenzie's ragged shirttail. "I remember this design. Is this the shirt you wore Thursday?"

"Yeah. I ripped a strip off the bottom to bandage Salty's paw. When I put it on, I wasn't thinking about going out to eat. At least it's clean."

Ana stretched and smoothed Kenzie's T-shirt. "These are beautiful snow-capped mountains." She read the words beneath the image, "Montana. Big sky. Big dreams," then released the shirt. "Have you been there? Did it make you dream big?"

"No." *Stupid shirt.* Something Dad and the new wife got on vacation. She should have tossed it months ago. "*Dad* had the big dreams."

Ana stared out to sea as if she were searching for a missing ship. "Do you have any dreams, Kenzie?"

Dreams? Well, there was Angelo. Actually, that was more like a wish. And she'd given up on Dad. Then, like the sudden haze on the inside of a windshield, a foggy veil curtained Kenzie's eyes, and Old Turtle's haunting image wavered before her. "For me, saving the turtles is dream enough." Kenzie blinked until Ana reappeared. "What about you?"

"Once I had a big dream."

"Tell me."

Ana whispered into the breeze. "I dreamed that one day I would walk."

Oh no. Kenzie winced. *And I was whining.*

"Then I learned the truth." Ana's gaze shifted from the sea to Kenzie. "I never will."

Kenzie wanted to die. Right there. Right then. She swallowed. "What happened, Ana? Were you in a—"

"I was born this way. I have spina bifada."

"Oh." What was spina bifada? Kenzie was afraid to open her mouth. Afraid she'd burst into tears. Somehow she'd always thought Ana's wheelchair was temporary. No. She *wanted* to believe that. *Another fantasy. Like the one about Dad coming home.*

Ana touched Kenzie's arm.

Geesh. Ana's comforting me. I'm such a jerk.

"It happens, chica. Not often, but it happens. My spine didn't develop the right way."

Kenzie willed her eyes to dry and her words to come. She choked out a froggy, "I'm so sorry, Ana. Really sorry." *For being a self-centered whiner.*

"*Gracias, chica.* I am actually very lucky. I could be much worse."

Lucky, right. Kenzie refused to think about what Ana meant by *much worse.*

During the lazy drive to the restaurant with Mom and Mike, Kenzie stared out the passenger window. Her two best friends were dealing with serious issues. Ana would never walk. Angelo's mother was dead. While she'd been feeling sorry for herself. *Pathetic.*

She wanted to ask Mom about Ana's illness. About Mrs. Sánchez's death. About the mystery word. She'd probably never have a chance to ask any of those questions. Not with Mike around all the time.

"Look at that." Mom's voice startled Kenzie into the moment. "I love seeing all the painted cars down here."

Kenzie looked to the left. An old van covered with tropical fish designs—similar to Shalima's chicken-decorated lavender pickup—passed by. You didn't drive vehicles like those unless you wanted to be noticed.

"So Maggie, want me to paint deer all over my refuge truck?"

"Only if you want to get fired."

"Darn, it seemed like such a good idea." Mike tapped his horn as he approached a bicycle outfitted with two heavy-duty contractor buckets hanging like saddlebags over the rear tire. Mike slowed and rolled down the window. "Hey, Fisher. How's it going?"

Fisher flashed the thumbs-up sign. Displaying the treasures in his basket, he swept his hand above a lamp and some pots he'd collected from people's refuse cans. An umbrella and odd pieces of metal and wood were heaped in the buckets behind.

After they'd moved on, Kenzie asked, "Does he make much money saving what people throw out?"

"A little," Mike answered. "I think he simply hates things to be wasted. Of course, sponge fishing doesn't pay well, so he does need extra money. That's why he works odd jobs. How'd he do on your roof today, Maggie?"

"Fine, I suppose. He's not finished though. He told Kenzie he'd be back Wednesday."

As they pulled into the restaurant's lot, a skateboarder in baggy shorts zoomed in front of the truck. Like lightning, Mike stomped the brakes, jerking them forward.

"Sorry, dude," the boy shouted.

Mike parked, switched off the ignition, and shut his eyes.

"Too close," Mom said. "He's one lucky young man."

The skateboarder glided to the abandoned lot next door, joining other boarders deftly leaping and twisting around a homemade obstacle course. In the shadow of a tree, a lone figure stood watching, board in hand. *Angelo*.

Mike and Mom claimed a picnic table under a striped awning.

"I'll be right back." Kenzie walked along the edge of the parking lot until she got Angelo's attention. "I didn't know you skated."

His face a stone-cold mask, he plunked down the board and skated to his bike. He jumped off, flipped and caught the board, then plopped it into his basket. Without a backward glance, he pedaled off.

133

Kenzie sat on the bench across the table from Mike and Mom, absently twirling spaghetti on her fork while eyeing the skateboarders next door. She sighed and shifted her focus. "Do you think I'd understand boys any better if I'd gone to school with them, or maybe had a brother?"

Mom and Mike exchanged raised-eyebrow looks.

"Well,"—Mom scratched the back of her neck—"I attended co-ed schools, and it didn't help me any. Your uncle Jack was no help either. In fact, living with him made me think I'd never learn to get along with the opposite sex."

Kenzie wrestled with a mouthful of pasta. *If Mom and I had understood Dad, would he have stayed?*

"Mike, what do you think?" Mom asked.

"Oh no, leave me out of this one. This is a mother-daughter, no-males-allowed discussion. You two tackle this one later." He concentrated on his hamburger.

Mom poked him in the ribs. "What a chicken."

Ick. They're actually flirting.

A sudden breeze threatened to carry their napkins away. Mike and Mom rearranged tableware to anchor them. Kenzie slapped her hand on an abandoned newspaper that flapped open on the empty bench next to her. "Hey, you guys, speaking of chicken, look." Kenzie grabbed the paper. "Here's a letter to the editor from Shalima."

That got Mom's attention. "What's the chicken connection?"

"She rescues chickens. At least that's what

Fisher told me today."

"Oh, that's a nice thing to do," Mom said. "I guess."

"I know who you're talking about," Mike said. "Sometimes we call her when we find nuisance chickens on refuge land. She's a colorful bird herself."

Kenzie skimmed the letter. "She says she's appalled by the turtle egg poachers."

"As she should be, sweetie."

"Listen to this." Kenzie read, "As one who protects and defends the much-maligned chicken, I am appalled that anyone could hurt such treasured, helpless, harmless, and threatened creatures. We must do all we can to protect these turtles as I protect the noble hen and rooster."

Kenzie lowered the paper. Should she take Shalima off the suspect list?

"I'm sure glad I decided not to have the grilled chicken," Mike said. "I might have had to arrest myself."

Mom gazed at Mike as if he were Prince Charming, heir to the Kingdom of Wit, come to rescue her from dungeon drudgery.

More ick.

"Officer Kaczynski," Mom teased, "did I detect a note of irony in that statement? Somehow you seemed less than sincere."

"Certainly not."

Kenzie stared. This was more than icky flirting. Something else was happening. Mom was really relaxed. Having fun. It was seriously time to rethink this Mike and Maggie thing.

"Shalima may be a little over the top," Mom said, "but I do enjoy her skin care products." Mom's wicked smile promised something good. "You'll never guess the reason Shalima gives for keeping her head covered in those scarves."

"What?" Kenzie asked.

Mom sat straight up and sucked in her stomach. "Allow me to quote." She stroked her cheeks as if they were a rare treasure. Then she lifted her hands and pretended to adjust a head wrap. Raising her chin skyward, she spoke, sounding so much like Shalima it was spooky. "'The beauty and allure of my long, silken hair would simply drive foolish men crazy. Why, I wouldn't get a moment's peace.'"

"Foolish men, huh?" Mike shook his head.

Mom hadn't been this loose or funny in years. She made a good point. Shalima was over the top. A dramatic character actress. If only Kenzie could read the script.

To Kenzie's surprise, Mike went straight home after escorting his "two favorite ladies" to the door.

"I'm going to shower and change," Mom said. "Why don't you get comfy too?" Mom's code for, "We have serious business to discuss."

No wonder Mike didn't stick around. Maybe those two were finally catching on. A girl needs *some* exclusive Mom time.

A few minutes after the shower stopped, Mom, dressed in cut-off scrubs and carrying two mugs of tea, tapped on Kenzie's door. "We're overdue for a little girl time. Don't you think?"

"O...kay?" Grinning to herself, Kenzie crawled onto her bed.

Mom handed a mug to Kenzie and sat on the edge of the bed. "So, I take it you're having boy trouble?"

Finally, her chance. Kenzie took several long sips. How to begin?

"You do know, sweetie, there's not a girl alive who hasn't had boy trouble. What's the problem?"

"I don't get them."

"Get them in what way? A little context, please."

"Like with Angelo. I can't figure out what goes on in his head. And if I ask, he won't tell me."

"I see." Mom placed her mug on the nightstand. "Scoot over." She positioned herself beside Kenzie, her back against the headboard. "That's one mystery you may never solve. Let me share my observations about the opposite sex. Male pride is fragile. Boys are often as insecure around girls as you are around them. Angelo may open up more if you compliment him."

Right. Angelo was bigheaded enough. Besides, she'd tried that, and it didn't work.

"And practice the art of listening to him."

He doesn't say enough to practice. "It's hard to listen, Mom. Especially when he's angry."

"I know. Sometimes men allow their temper to flare when women would silently lock it in, then hold onto it for a long time. Most men let go of their anger quickly though. Give Angelo some time."

Ana had said something like this. But Angelo wasn't letting go, and it hurt.

Mom rested her head against Kenzie's. "What do you think?"

I think it's hopeless.

"Am I making any sense?"

"Maybe." Kenzie sipped her tea.

"You don't sound convinced, sweetie." Mom retrieved her mug, then tipped it high to drain the last drop. "And no wonder." She placed it on the nightstand again. "I'm not the best person to be giving advice on the subject."

Kenzie touched Mom's arm. "Look, I know what you're thinking. But Dad's only one guy. You're doing all right with Mike."

"So far." Mom ran her fingers through Kenzie's untamed hair, trying to loosen its snarls. "In my experience though"—she held up a tangled lock—"men do seem to respond better to us when we look our best." She tugged on a strand.

"Ouch, Mom." Kenzie freed her hair. "My hair's harder to control than Salty. Nothing works on it."

"We can work on other areas." Mom switched her Understanding-the-Male-of-the-Species lecture for Intro-to-Beauty-Products, concentrating on the benefits of skin creams, one brand in particular: Shalima's Secrets.

Mom droned on. Kenzie practiced the illusion of listening while mentally drifting. If only Shalima had a solution for Kenzie's major problem—the poaching mystery. The woman was all about mysterious secrets.

Maybe she'd been too quick to take Shalima off the suspect list. Something seemed off with that letter to the editor. A bit over the top. Could it have been a cover-up? Of course everything about Shalima was over the top. There was no connection between Shalima and the destroyed nests, but what about those mysterious products? Could their ingredients provide a clue?

Mom waved a hand in front of Kenzie's face.

"Not real interested in this topic, are you? So, what else do we need to talk about?"

Not the time to obsess on Shalima. She had Mom's full attention. *Ask those other questions.* "About Angelo's mom...I've been wondering... "

"Yes?" Mom shifted her position to face Kenzie. "Go on."

"Do you know how she died?"

"Oh, honey." Mom took a few moments before answering. "It happened eight or nine weeks before we moved. When I first started at the hospital, I heard talk. Mrs. Sánchez was under treatment for cancer and depression. Apparently, she confused her dosages, with fatal results."

"You mean she mixed up her pills?"

Mom nodded. "Cancer patients often need several medications. Keeping track of them all can be confusing."

"So she took the wrong ones together, or the wrong amount?"

"I'm afraid so."

"I get what Angelo meant now." Kenzie's chest ached. "He said she couldn't read medicine bottles."

"That might explain things. It was ruled accidental, in spite of suicide rumors."

Kenzie bit her fingers. "Mom, Angelo thinks it's his fault."

Mom took Kenzie's mug and set it down. "Sweetie, that's often the case when someone dies suddenly. A loved one believes if he or she had done something differently, the death could have been prevented. Of course, that's rarely the case." She pulled Kenzie close and rubbed her back. "Angelo must really be hurting. I'm sure that's one reason it's difficult to know what he's thinking. And why he's full of anger."

Kenzie rested her chin on Mom's shoulder. *It's now or never.* "Mom..." Her words drifted into the fabric of her mother's shirt. "Do af-ri-dee-zee-acks have anything to do with men?"

"What?" Her mother pulled sharply back.

"Or with fishing?"

"Do *what* have something to do with men and fishing?"

Kenzie repeated, syllable by syllable, "af-ri-dee-zee-acks."

Mom closed her eyes for a second, then inhaled deeply and said, "Well...certain things attract men to women—"

"Mom, we already covered that. Compliments, listening, looking good..."

"I guess we did." Mom hesitated, mangled a few false starts, and began a drawn-out medical explanation. Halfway through it Kenzie's eyes widened.

"Sex," she shrieked. "That stupid *afrideezie* word has something to do with sex?" Kenzie buried her face in her pillow.

Mom sighed. "In a manner of speaking. Superstitious people consider such things love potions."

Oh ship. Angelo knew that word. *Ship, ship, ship.* Unbelievable. She'd asked him about a love potion. At that moment, Kenzie would have welcomed a poison potion.

Mom's nurse engine revved as she switched

141

into diagnostic gear. "Let's talk about this scientifically, sweetie."

Let's not. Kenzie lifted her head. "You're starting that whole reproduction lecture you gave me years ago. Aren't you? Gross." She hid her face again.

"Sweetie, this is because of the turtles, isn't it? You saw what Sheriff Clark said about the gang of thieves in the paper."

There was something in the newspaper? Kenzie rubbed her face up and down on the pillow, scratching a mosquito bite. It wasn't her fault if Mom took that for a *yes*.

"Actually, I'm surprised you didn't find an answer on the Internet."

"It's not like I didn't try."

"How did you spell it?"

Kenzie rolled over and sat. "I tried every way I could think of, starting with *a-f-r-i*—"

"It's *p-h*," her mom said. "Not *f*."

I'm a total idiot. Kenzie covered her face with both hands.

"And *ro*, not *ri*."

"I'm so embarrassed."

"Because you didn't know how to spell it?"

The answer struggled past the wall of Kenzie's hands. "No."

Mom wrapped an arm around Kenzie and squeezed. "So, what is it then?"

"I asked Angelo if Cuban fishermen used... that word."

"Oh, dear. Why'd you do that?"

"I thought it had something to do with fishing."

"What made you...? Never mind. It doesn't matter." Mom gently pried Kenzie's hands away from her face. "What did Angelo say?"

Hiding behind a curtain of hair, Kenzie stared at her lap. "It was awful. You should have seen his face. He said he wished he'd left me in the canal where he found me. Why was he that angry?"

"I'm sure it was a question he'd never expect, especially from you. My guess is he was confused, embarrassed, and a little insulted. Sometimes anger is the only credible response to such a mix of emotions."

"So, all this boy-talk was about Angelo." Mom smiled. "Have we covered everything?"

Except for how to explain I don't really think it's a magic potion that makes Angelo so brilliant and adorable. Kenzie nodded.

"Do you want some more tea?"

"No. I want to die."

"Sweetie, we talked about how boys get angry fast and then quickly get over it. Angelo won't be annoyed long."

"I don't think Angelo knows about the anger timeline." A tiny grin tweaked Kenzie's lips.

"That's the spirit." Mom kissed her forehead. "Now, I'm going to bring you some warm milk to help you sleep."

Two hours later, Kenzie lay in bed staring at the ceiling. So much for warm milk. Even if Angelo tried to speak to her again, she wouldn't be able to face him. *Wait a minute.* She sat up. She didn't have to face him. She hopped out of bed. There was always e-mail. She smacked her forehead. E-mail had spell-check. Why hadn't she tried spell-check when she couldn't find the mystery word?

Kenzie tapped a message to Angelo. She explained what she'd learned from Mom and ended with:

> *I'm really, really sorry. Try to understand. I overheard Mike and Mom talking and misunderstood what he said. I thought aphrodisiacs had something to do with Cuban traditions and fishing techniques. I know it's crazy, but that's why I asked you that question.*
>
> *Sheriff Clark thinks it's a gang of men stealing the eggs and selling them for aphrodisiacs. What do you think of that theory?*
>
> *Still friends?*
>
> *Kenzie (AKA Red)*

Before she could chicken out, she clicked *Send*.

Kenzie checked her inbox and found several messages from KTC night owls. Cleanup assignments were going well, but no one had pictures to post on the webpage yet, and no one had noticed anything suspicious on the beach. *Relax*, she told herself. It had only been one day since they'd really geared up.

Kenzie worried herself back to sleep, wondering if Angelo would bother to answer her message. Nightmares rattled her. Shalima's Secrets Face Balm turned out to be a poisonous potion. Its application placed Mom under the evil spell of cruel creatures covered with red and yellow feathers.

KTC photos kept arriving in her dream mailbox. Each one showed the thief poking a stick in the sand to find turtle nests. One after the other, the photos appeared with increased focus and detail, until the poacher, wearing a purple shirt and shorts, began to look familiar. Just as she was about to identify the poacher, the image evaporated.

Kenzie opened her eyes in the depths of the sea, wrapped in a web and sandwiched between two monstrous shells—a helpless sea turtle caught in a shrimp net. Beside her, Old Turtle floated upside down. From a boat overhead, Angelo ducked his head below the surface and stared at her. He waved through the ripples. The boat motored away.

Wriggling and twisting, Kenzie opened her eyes to the morning sun. High and dry. Wrapped in sheets. Safe and sound.

It's Tuesday, beach cleanup day. Salty's coming home!

She'd just pulled on her cargo shorts and KTC shirt when the bedroom door creaked open. Salty scrambled through, leaping and yipping.

"Puppy, you're home." Kenzie sat on the floor and hugged the wiggling dog until he washed every pore on her face. "Mom, I wanted to go with you to pick him up."

"Dr. Lily brought him. She was making a house call down the street. She left his medicine. Two pills a day."

"Cool. I'm your nurse now." Kenzie lifted the puppy to eye level. "I prescribe fun. We're going to the beach today."

"Now, Kenzie—"

"I'll keep him on the leash. Don't worry. I'm sorry you have to work today."

"Me, too. I'd love to help."

"You did help. You baked your yummy brownies, didn't you? I smell them."

"Sweetie, you know what I mean. I'm dropping you off on my way to the hospital. So hurry and get dressed.

"I will." *Soon as I check messages.*

Her mailbox was empty. Not a word. She sighed. Angelo hadn't checked messages yet. That was all. Give him time.

Ana sat in her parents' driveway, perched in Doonie and ready to work. "On the beach already people are busy. But I did not see Angelo. Did you hear from him?"

"No. He showed up in a dream last night, and he wasn't talking then either. It's creeping me out."

Salty propped his front paws on Ana's lap. "*Perrito,* I am happy you are home to cheer Kenzie." She ruffled his furry ears. "Get down now. We must go help the others."

They followed the path to the beach until they reached a long table cluttered with food, fuel for the volunteers. Drink coolers crowded the ground under it. Kenzie added Mom's brownies to the snack collection on the table.

Fisher and Father Murphy piled black garbage bags and green recycling bags in the designated locations. Kenzie counted six kids and four adults spread out along the beach. Most were wearing work gloves and dragging bags.

Wearing turquoise KTC shirts, the volunteers inspected the beach intently, as if searching for treasured shells instead of discarded rubble.

Ana withdrew what looked like a sawed-off broom handle from Doonie's backpack. "See what *Papi* made for me." She touched the tip of a nail projecting from the stick's end.

"Nice." Kenzie scanned the beach. Ana aimed and jabbed trash. Kenzie scanned the beach again.

After Ana's nail bounced off a plastic bottle three times, she stabbed a candy wrapper. "This is not easy."

"No, it isn't." *Where is he?* Kenzie felt like stabbing something herself.

"Kenzita, he will come." Ana touched Kenzie's hand. "Be patient."

"I'm trying."

Ana scowled at her stick. "This works with small papers only. Doonie and I can carry trash bags to the road. That will be helpful, yes?"

"Very. Especially since you know where the garbage pickup spots are. I'll go tell everybody to bring their bags to you." Kenzie pushed the loop of Salty's leash up on her wrist and pulled on work gloves. "Come on, Salty. Let's get to work."

She headed toward the distant marina, picking up trash to deposit in various bags along the beach and passing Ana's message to the workers.

Ted signaled to Kenzie. "Look at this loot." Excited as Santa on Christmas Eve, he opened his bag. "You won't believe what I found—shoes, plates, an old dog dish—"

"I know. It's crazy. When the bag's full, take it to Ana. She'll haul it to the road for you."

He came.

"Hey, what's up?" Ted looked behind him to see what Kenzie was staring at. "It's about time that dude got here."

Angelo glanced toward Kenzie, then picked up an empty black garbage bag. He trudged toward Lakisha and her mom, who were struggling with something in the tide pool.

"I need to tell Lakisha what to do with her bags. See you, Ted." Kenzie lowered her hat against the sun and followed Angelo. He couldn't ignore her forever. Salty trotted beside her.

She stood several yards behind the little group as Angelo freed monofilament from the rocks. He handed it to Lakisha and her mom, then they jammed the hazardous fishing line into their bag.

"Hi, guys. Need more help?" Kenzie asked, watching Angelo.

"We're fine," Lakisha said.

Kenzie might as well have been a ghost. Salty stretched his leash and whined. Angelo even ignored him.

She'd fix that. She unhooked his leash. Salty leaped once, then halted, hackles raised. His eyes seemed locked on a cordoned-off turtle nest. Kenzie spotted the raccoon the moment Salty bolted, barking his big dog barks.

Kenzie's mind raced as fast as her legs. *Raccoons eat eggs. Raccoons carry rabies. Raccoons are vicious.* Salty didn't stand a chance. "Salty, no. Stop!"

He stopped—nose to nose with the monster raccoon. Instantly, Salty transformed. In his place—possessed Devil Dog. Devil Dog, hackles raised, stood guard over the damaged turtle nest.

I have to do something. Adrenalin roared through Kenzie. *What?* What could she do?

Devil Dog curled his lips. Bared crimson gums. Sprouted barracuda teeth. A canine vampire with a rumbling, savage growl.

The enormous raccoon arched its back. Exposed needle-sharp teeth. Hissing and snarling, it doubled in size.

It's going to kill Salty.

Salty crouched. Slowly, one paw crept forward.

Now. Do something now, Kenzie.

She waved her arms at the raccoon, kicked sand and screamed. "Get. Go. Go."

The masked creature reared, its rage exploding into ear-piercing squalls.

Kenzie frantically searched for a weapon. *There, in the sand.* The glint of sunlight on a bottle neck. She yanked it free. Hurled. *Thunk.* The raccoon dropped to all fours. Its shrieks ended. It hissed and scuttled into the scrub. That bottle—what a beautiful hunk of junk.

Ted, panting and brandishing a worm-eaten board, arrived in time to see the possessed Salty morph into a puppy again. "Awesome. What a dog. No way that coon would get those eggs."

Salty plopped beside the turtle nest.

Angelo was nowhere to be seen. He'd disappeared without even waiting to see if Salty was okay.

Panting, Salty rested his head on her knee while Kenzie scratched his back. "I pity anything that messes with you when you're full-grown. Let's get you some water, puppy." After brushing the dislodged sand over the nest, she secured the fallen nest markers. "I could use some liquid, too."

Kenzie worked her way back to Ana's house. What a difference. Yesterday bottles, cans, knots of fishing line, and piles of other junk littered the beach. Turtle Beach could now pass for a postcard scene.

Without the distraction of visual junk, Kenzie searched the sand for what Nana called a mermaid's purse. They were leathery egg cases of skates, creatures related to stingrays. The size of a match pack with string-like growths on all four corners, they did look a bit like a tiny, brown, pouch purse. They were difficult to spot, but finding a mermaid's purse might bring her good luck.

"You kids are sure doing a bang-up job."

Oops. She'd nearly stepped on a pair of bare feet. They anchored a hairy-legged man she'd never seen.

"I didn't mean to scare you," he said. "Wanted to compliment you. I've never seen so much interest in this beach." He gestured up and down the sand. A straggly gray ponytail hung halfway down his broad back, the only hair on the man's head.

What is it with old guys in the Keys and ponytails? Even Fisher wore a short one.

"What's your dog's name?" He stooped and

held out his hand to Salty.

Salty backed away, growling.

"Whoa, what's the problem, doggie?"

"I'm sorry." Kenzie picked up the puppy. "His name is Salty, and he's usually friendly."

"Hey, Salty. My name's Jake. Glad to meet you." Salty quietly sniffed Jake's hand, and this time accepted his touch.

"Did you come to help the Keys' Teens?" Kenzie asked.

"Actually, I'm monitoring turtle nests. I'm with Protect-a-Turtle." He patted the emblem on the green T-shirt stretched across his barrel chest.

"We protect turtles too. Don't we boy?" Kenzie nuzzled Salty. "He just fought a raccoon that was digging up eggs. Maybe that's why he's grumpy."

"Smart dog," Jake said. "Which nest?"

"The one over—"

"Hey, Kenzie," Ted yelled. "Come on. Ana needs more help."

"On my way. Nice to meet you, Jake. You're helping the Keys' Teens, even if you didn't know it."

Salty jumped out of her arms. They dashed down the beach to the pile of garbage bags where Ted and Lakisha waited.

"Hold on, guys. Let me get Salty some water. I'll tie him up and be right back."

Doonie rolled up the path. Ana's face was hidden by a pile of garbage bags. Was Doonie operating on autopilot and a GPS?

Kenzie placed a water dish in the shade of

a buttonwood tree, then fastened Salty's leash securely to the tree's trunk.

She'd completed her tenth trip lugging bags to the road, when Ana's worried voice sounded through the trees. "Kenzie, where is Salty?"

"Tied to that big buttonwood tree by your house."

"His leash is there. Salty is gone."

Not again. He couldn't have slipped his collar this time. She raced to the tree. Inspected the snap on the leash. It worked perfectly. Someone had unhooked it.

"Kenzita, could he have been kidnapped?" Ana asked.

Liquid fire screamed through Kenzie's veins. "Don't even think that." *Calm down. Concentrate.* "Some little kid probably wanted to play with him. Stay here in case he comes back. He can't be far." Kenzie turned in circles. Which way should she go?

Ana held a hand to her ear. "Do you have your cell?"

"In my pocket." Kenzie stuffed the leash in another pocket and took off in the direction Salty knew best.

Please, don't eat anything, Salty. She searched the hammock area along the beach. Called and whistled. *Don't mess with the raccoons either.* She stopped to listen for his jingling tags, then entered the woods. *And stay off the road.* She paused again. *Clink. Clink. Dog tags.*

The clinking came from the direction of Ancient Angry Edna's house. *No.* That crazy lady took him.

Salty's barks overpowered the sound of his tags. What had he gotten into this time?

Ancient Angry Edna's fence came in sight, and Salty's barks changed to snorts and snuffles. Scratching and splattering sounds muffled the clink of his tags. Digging. Edna had locked Salty in her yard. He was trying to break out.

Kenzie raced round the corner. He *was* digging. But not trapped. Salty wanted *in*. He tunneled furiously. Only his back legs and tail remained outside the fence.

"Salty, get out of there." She grabbed for the vanishing puppy. Too late. Gone. Under the fence. Into the yard.

The branches of a large buttonwood tree hung over the fence into the yard. Kenzie gripped a limb that rested on the fence. She pulled herself up, crawled over its rough bark until it forked, and then flattened—an arm on each branch—surveying the yard.

In the shadows under the little stilt house, something moved. Beside the house at that clump of thatch palm—more movement. *No way.* Four miniature, endangered Key deer. This was illegal captivity.

Salty's tags jingled wildly beneath her. She separated branches to look below. He was vigorously shaking dirt and sand from his coat, showing no pain. Suddenly, he froze within stalking stance. His attention shifted briefly as if something had distracted him. What?

There. Coming this way along the wall of the shed. Another deer? No. Too tall. A person. Someone with a long reach. Reaching for what?

155

The figure moved into the light. Ancient Angry Edna. Not reaching. Pointing—a gun!

"No-oooo." Kenzie's hand flew to her mouth. She lost her balance and fell. *Thud*. Smack into Ancient Angry Edna's yard.

I'M DEAD. Kenzie closed her eyes and waited for the shot.

"You poor thing. Is anything broken?"

Ancient Angry Edna. Who else had that gravelly voice? Something about it was different though. An accent? Maybe the tone—calm, cautious. Not angry, simply ancient. Still, Kenzie kept her eyes shut. She didn't want to face the woman who probably wanted both her and Salty out of the picture. So far though, Edna hadn't hurt Salty. He proved that by vigorously licking Kenzie's face.

"That's right, little dog. Kisses usually help. Come on, child. Sit up. Let's check the damage."

A solid arm reached under Kenzie. A firm hand gripped her elbow. Edna might be ancient, but she was strong. She prodded and pulled until Kenzie sat up. Kenzie opened her eyes. A rugged face, shadowed by a floppy hat, stared down at her. *Purple.* Wrapped around the hat's brim was a purple bandana. Below the hat, dressed in heavily pocketed khaki, Ancient Angry Edna seemed prepared for a safari.

"Tell me what hurts."

Hands. Knees. Her pride. Was that a gun on the ground next to her? Soon there could be other body parts in pain. Trembling, Kenzie stared at the weapon.

"Oh, don't worry about that thing." Edna picked up the pistol. "I keep it mostly for effect. When I heard this dog carrying on, I figured he was tangling with a rabid raccoon. There've been a passel of sick coons this season. Found more than one dead. Had to shoot a couple others."

Whimpering, Salty nosed Kenzie until she petted him. "I'm okay, Salty."

"Salty, hunh? Good name." When Edna reached to pet him, he yapped and charged the deer, scattering them like frightened rabbits.

"Don't do that." Tank-like, Edna marched toward the fracas. "Stop it, now! Stop it." Gun held high and arms spread wide, she herded the deer toward a fenced-in pen under her stilt house.

I need to get up. Move. Not easy. Kenzie's head was spinning. She'd fallen into a nightmare.

"Yo, Red."

Yo, Red? Above her. In the tree. *No way.*

Thud.

She flinched. Looked behind her.

Angelo. For real.

"Come on, Spiceman. Leave the deer. Come here, bud."

Yipping, Salty raced to Angelo.

Angelo snared the wriggling puppy. Moving in front of Kenzie, he asked, "You okay?"

Kenzie rolled her shoulders and neck. "I think so."

The last deer trotted into the pen. Edna, still holding the gun, fastened the chain-link gate.

"Hey, lady, what's with the gun?"

Edna glared at Angelo, then up at the tree. "If I don't cut that branch, somebody's going to catch m—" She scratched her nose. "Somebody's going to get hurt."

Kenzie whispered. "I don't think we need to worry about the gun."

"No?"

"I'm pretty sure."

Angelo released Salty, then pulled Kenzie to her feet.

"Lady," he said, facing Edna. "The gun?"

"Oh." She stuck the pistol in a pocket. "Well, since you both dropped in... " Her lips twitched into a crooked grin. "You might as well visit a while." Edna directed them to two white plastic chairs. "Sit yourselves down." She patted the gun. "I'll tell you about this thing."

Glancing sideways at each other, Kenzie and Angelo did as they were told.

"You skinned your knee, child. Let me see those hands." Edna walked over and turned up Kenzie's palms. "Uh-huh. Be right back."

When Edna was halfway up the stairs, Kenzie whispered, "What are you doing here?"

"Me? What about you?"

"I came to get Salty. Did you see that hole he crawled through?"

"Yeah. I'm guessing you crawled too. Just a little higher." He looked up at the tree, then down at her knees. "Ever heard of ringing a bell?"

"Cute. You've seen that sign by her bell. It sure doesn't say 'welcome.' She hates dogs, and she poisoned Salty. Do you think I wanted her to know we were here?"

"Salty wasn't quietly sneaking around. I think she'd have figured it out."

"Your turn. Why are you here? I thought you were mad at me."

"Got your message." As he spoke, he focused on Edna's slow descent—step down, feet together; step down, feet together—a cardboard box clutched against her body. Angelo lowered his volume. "And I don't think much of Sheriff Clark's gang theory either."

Edna handed Angelo and Kenzie each a can of soda, flipped the box upside down, and placed a plate of cookies on it. She moved an empty chair and sat, forming a tight little circle. Crazy lady, Angelo, and Kenzie.

"Usually, a person knows the names of her guests, especially those she's doctoring. I'm Edna Jenkins, though I expect you call me Ancient Angry Edna."

Kenzie's fingers froze on her soda tab. "Oh, no ma'am, we wouldn't—"

"Of course you would." Edna held out a cloth and a tube of antiseptic cream. "I do everything I can to live up to that name. Here, wash yourself off, and put this on those skid marks. Good thing there's plenty of mulch under that branch. It's a whole lot softer than pea rock."

She prodded Angelo. "You first. What's your name?"

"I go by Angelo. She's Kenzie."

"You lived here long, children?"

"Angelo grew up here," Kenzie said, as Salty inspected the yard square foot by square foot. "I moved down a few months ago." She capped the tube and returned it to Edna.

Edna applied bandages to Kenzie's hands and knees, then leaned back in her chair and rubbed her cheek. "Kenzie, hunh? Memorable name. Are you the youngster that had something to do with catching that Key deer killer?"

"Yes, ma'am."

"Well then, you've got to be wondering about those deer." She nodded at the pen. "I know good and well it's illegal for me to be keeping these Key deer, seeing as how they're endangered. There's something wrong with every one of them though. If they tried to fend for themselves until they're healed, they'd get run over or killed by dogs, sure as shootin'. Aren't you going to have some cookies with those sodas?"

Behind his hand, Angelo mouthed, *No way*.

Rat poison on her mind, Kenzie nodded her agreement. Who knew what Edna put in those cookies? "No, thank you. Ms. Jenkins, don't the refuge officers take care of sick deer?"

"*Hunh*. They're supposed to. Must be short-handed seeing as how they need to recruit community volunteers. Call me a secret volunteer. Since Mr. Jenkins died five years ago, rest his soul, I've been a tad lonely. We never had children—she shifted her focus to the deer pen—"and these babies are all I have."

Intent on his scent survey, Salty approached

161

the pen.

Edna's leg twitched.

Ignoring the deer, Salty appeared excessively interested in the covered buckets between two long, low freezers.

Edna's leg twitched faster.

"Ms. Jenkins, is that why you scare people away? So they won't see your deer?"

Edna's shoulder jerked as if she were shooing a fly. "People and dogs." Her leg twitched. "Dogs attract attention. All that sniffing and barking." Her eyes narrowed. "You better put yours on the leash. We don't want him scooting out that crater he dug."

Salty was nowhere near that hole. What was really worrying Edna? Her jitters were contagious. "Angelo, we should go. We need to finish the cleanup."

"I'd have helped you youngsters, but I've been feeling poorly. Had a doctor's appointment this morning. I was just getting home when that dog of yours started fussin' up a storm."

"That's okay. Lots of people came. Let's go, Salty." Kenzie fastened the leash to his collar and stood. "I'm sorry for the trouble we caused, Ms. Jenkins."

"I've had worse."

Angelo and Kenzie headed for the gate in the high wooden fence, quickening their steps as Edna closed in behind.

"Wait, children." Edna barreled past them. She reached for a hammer hanging by the gate.

Angelo sprang toward her. "What the—?"

"I need to loosen the latch." Edna banged

the sliding bar over and over. It didn't budge. "Blasted thing's corroded."

Kenzie's leg was twitching now. *Please, please open.*

Sweat beaded on Edna's brow. She removed the bandana from her hat and used it to wipe her forehead.

A purple bandana. Forget it. Even if Kenzie could connect it to a purple plaid shirt and Surf Sandals, it would be weak evidence.

Angelo held out his hand. "Let me." He moved to Edna's side. She stood spine-straight at his approach. Angelo was tall, but Edna had two or three inches on him. He glanced at Kenzie and casually positioned his foot close to Edna's. His toe in line with her heel.

Nice move, Angelo. Their sneakers were close in size. But it still wasn't much to go on.

Edna hesitated, then handed Angelo the hammer.

Whack. He banged the latch open. They escaped without another word as if Ancient Angry Edna might decide to shoot them after all.

Salty took the lead, dragging Kenzie behind him. They were halfway to the beach when a chain saw buzzed into action. A loud *crack* sounded.

Swish, clatter, thump.

Angelo stopped and snorted. "Guess no one's gonna climb into that lady's yard again."

"What'd you think of her?" Kenzie asked.

"She shoots," he said, picking up a stick. He used it to demonstrate his words. "She hammers. She saws." He flung the branch into the woods

163

and started walking again. "She's not sick. Doctor's appointment? No way."

"Yeah, that was suspicious." Kenzie caught up to him. "With all the beach activity, she could have been busy hiding something. Did you see anything purple there? Besides her hatband. A rag, a shirt, a plastic bag? Anything?"

"Why? What's with purple?"

"Whenever anything suspicious or weird happens, it seems like purple's involved. But it's probably nothing."

Angelo pulled a slip of paper from his pocket. "Here's something."

"What's that?"

"A receipt for two bicycle tires." He handed it to Kenzie. "I found it when I was following you."

"Jerry's Bike Shop. So?"

"It was by the nest we found Friday."

"Angelo, this is awesome." Bouncing, she waved the receipt in the air. "This is a serious clue. It must have fallen out of the creep's pocket."

"I'll check it out with Jerry." Angelo retrieved the receipt. "She never got around to the gun story, you know."

"She said she needs it to shoot rabid raccoons. She thought Salty was fighting with one."

"*Ship*, Red. You fell for that?" He reached into his pocket. Replacing the receipt, he withdrew his metal fishing weights. A sure sign of frustration.

Kenzie swatted the bill of his ball cap. "Actually, I fell before that."

"No joke, Red." He straightened his hat.

"She knows you'd never let Salty dig under her fence. That raccoon story was quick thinking. She figured he was alone."

Kenzie stopped and grabbed Angelo's elbow. "You think she planned to shoot Salty?"

"You're the one who said she hates dogs. Think it through." Angelo paused as if he were waiting for her to make notes. "Dogs dig when they smell something." The sinkers rolled and clinked in his hand.

"He smelled the deer."

Angelo tweaked Salty's leash. "Spiceman, have you ever chased deer?"

Salty cocked his head without so much as a whimper.

"See? Not once. The times he's taken off... most had something in common. Right?"

Kenzie mentally replayed chases, escapes, and battles. "Turtles and eggs." She stooped. "Salty, turtles don't nest in Edna's yard. What were you doing?" Salty wagged his tail. "Guess he's not talking. Let's go."

"Keep thinking, Red." With each step, Angelo tossed a fishing weight in the air, then snatched it in his fist. Higher and higher. Faster and faster. He stopped dead and faced Kenzie. "Salty zoned right in on those buckets."

"He's always sniffing. Look at him now."

"*Mmm.* Coon poop."

"*E-ew.*" Kenzie shook the leash. "Salty, quit it."

"What do you think's in those freezers, Red?"

"How would I know?"

"Down here, outdoor freezer chests like those

mean big time hunting and fishing. I didn't see tackle anywhere. Believe me. I looked. Even through the storage room window. *Nada.*"

"So, what are you saying?"

"You believe her about the deer? You think she's really takin' care of them?"

"I..." Kenzie shifted her feet. "I...want to."

"We got one bad dude jailed, Red. Doesn't mean no other creeps shoot Key deer."

"But they're protected."

"So are sea turtles. You ever see Key deer that fat? Know why farmers overfeed livestock and lock them in pens?"

"Angelo, she could have deer in those freezers."

"Yup, and eggs in the buckets." He tossed a sinker. Snatched it. "There wasn't fishing tackle in the storage room, but I saw something interesting."

Kenzie poked him. "What?"

Toss. *Whap.* A two-handed catch.

"An old bike with two brand-new tires."

When they reached the beach, Father Murphy, blue cooler in hand, greeted them. "There you are. Our volunteers were beginning to go home, so Ana and I had to start the celebration without you. I was concerned."

"Sorry, Father." Angelo rushed his words. "We ran into some problems back in the thicket. Got kind of scraped up getting out of the mess. It's all good now."

Kenzie bit the inside of her cheek, praying she wouldn't giggle.

"You don't seem too worse for wear. I applaud your diligence." He lifted the cooler lid. "Congratulations are in order. You've pulled off another successful KTC project." Father scanned them head to toe. "I see a few battle scars though. You both look like you need a refresher." He held up an ice cream bar. I have only one. Who gets it?"

Kenzie nudged Angelo. "You deserve it." *Yikes*. She'd almost winked at him.

"Thank you, Father." Angelo took the ice

cream, ripped the wrapper open with his teeth, and placed the wrapper in the overflowing trash barrel. "You first." He offered it to Kenzie. "Take a couple bites."

A breeze fluttered along with Kenzie's heart. "Thanks."

The wrapper blew out of the barrel. "I better take care of this trash." Angelo caught the ice cream paper, stuck it in the trash again, then tightly tied the bag.

Kenzie swallowed. "Better eat this before it melts."

Clutching the bar in his mouth, Angelo lifted the bag, then trudged toward the road.

"I'm going to find Ana. See you in a few," Kenzie said. Within minutes, Kenzie heard Ana's delighted cry. "Kenzita, you found Salty. He is okay, yes?"

"*He* is."

Ana waved an ice cream bar as she rolled toward Kenzie. "This may be the last one. Eat it before Ted sees it."

"We'll share it." She took a bite and gave it back to Ana. "It's all yours. Did Ted say whether he can get back here tomorrow? Until we catch the creep, people still need to hang around the beach."

"No. Only Lakisha. Friday she will come for a beach party." Ana looked up. "Last bite?" Kenzie shook her head. Ana's eyes widened. "Chica, your hands. Your knees...You are hurt. How?"

"It's a long story." Kenzie jiggled Salty's leash. "He's going to get one of us seriously hurt if he doesn't quit taking off."

"*Tu perro sólo tiene...* Your dog is only six months old. He will learn to obey."

"Spiceman—obey? Yeah, right."

Angelo. Kenzie turned around. "How'd you get back so fast?"

"I didn't have far to go. Someone started a new pile of trash bags just through those trees." He nodded at the road.

"Ana and I were talking about patrols this week. Any ideas?"

Shifting his ballcap, Angelo squinted as if he were envisioning something. "Can't be more than a few cars a day." He turned toward Turtle Beach Road, slowly moving his head to the far right and back to the left. "Make a good skateboarding course. I'll call around. See if I can get some guys to practice over here."

Ana clapped. "*Perfecto.*"

"Sorry, girls. But we gotta go. Mike's parked up there waiting to take us home."

Ana tugged Kenzie's shirttail and motioned for her to lean down. "Whatever happened, it must be good. Angelo is talking to you." Her eyes sparkled with questions and mischief. "Call me."

"I will. You are definitely not going to believe it."

After dropping Angelo at his house, Mike and Kenzie rode in relaxed silence until she remembered Edna's captive deer. *Goodbye, relaxation.* She should tell Mike. After all, his

major responsibility was protecting the deer.
But Edna would know who ratted on her. *Hello,
tension*. Who knew what a truly angry Edna
might do with that gun? She could harm KTC
beach patrollers. Kenzie *couldn't* tell him. Not
yet.

"Ken...zie?" Mike drew out the two syllables
of her name. His tone was loaded with unspoken
questions. "I bet you want to visit your hawksbill
at the hospital, don't you?"

My hawksbill? Uh-oh. She should have
known. He'd finally told Mom. He couldn't ignore
her rule-breaking boat-taking forever. Even if
it resulted in a turtle rescue. *Mike—Mom's hit
man*. Hands on her ears, she was ready to muffle
the coming words: impulsive, irresponsible,
thoughtless—

"So, what do you think? Want to go?"

What?

"Maybe tomorrow?" More of Mike's words
broke through. "She'll be there after four."

She who? Be where?

Kenzie eased her hands backward to the
scrunchy on her ponytail and rewrapped her
hair. "Tomorrow?" The least dumb response she
could think of.

"Yes, tomorrow." Mike smiled. A smile that
seemed amused and aware. "Dr. Lily examined
a late-season fawn at the refuge this morning."
He stopped his truck in front of Kenzie's house.
"She told me tomorrow would be a good day for
you and Ana to visit the Turtle Hospital. She'll
be there to answer your questions."

"Awesome. I'll call Ana right away." As

she opened the truck door, Salty leaped out. Kenzie stepped down, then turned around, one hand clutching the door. "Mike..." What could she say? He was running interference for her. Granting her immunity from prosecution. How do you thank someone for that?

Eyebrows raised, Mike lowered his sunglasses and peered down at her. "Yes?"

"Thanks... You know, for everything." She closed the door, then chased Salty up the stairs.

The next day at three thirty, Salty yapped his someone's-at-the-door-hurry-hurry bark. Kenzie replaced the cap on her sunscreen bottle, then peeked out to the screen porch. Ana's father stood at the top of the front steps.

"I'll be right there, Mr. Muñoz." Kenzie placed Salty in his kennel. "You're staying home and out of trouble today." She handed him a biscuit and rushed out.

Ana waved through the open rear window. "This is going to be so much fun."

"Please climb in," Mr. Muñoz said, opening the front passenger door.

Ana leaned forward. "Of course it will not be as exciting for you as yesterday."

The driver's door opened.

"Mr. Muñoz, it's nice of you to take us to the Turtle Hospital. Especially since you just got off work."

"*No hay problema.* It is my pleasure. Today I go to Marathon to buy tools. The hospital is very near."

As they drove over the Seven Mile Bridge, the road climbed up and up with no view of the downward slope on the other side. They traveled eye-to-eye with high-gliding pelicans. Far below, tiny waves glistened, toy boats sailed, and miniature seagulls soared. Sapphire sky and turquoise sea stretched forever in all directions.

Kenzie had first crossed the Seven Mile Bridge only a few months ago—from the opposite direction. Her eyes had been closed to the unwelcome world and the dramatic architecture. It was all a glaring symbol of passage. The end of life as she knew it. That day the crossing had been torture. Today it seemed magical.

Minutes after arriving in Marathon, Kenzie sighted the parked turtle ambulance even before she saw the hospital sign.

"Please, park by the ambulance, Mr. Muñoz. When I called this morning, they said to knock at the door of the medical building. It's that square, concrete-block building behind the ambulance."

After Ana's father turned off the ignition, he made no move to get out.

Was he waiting for Kenzie to help? "Ana, wait." Kenzie unlatched her door.

"Kenzita." Mr. Muñoz raised a halting hand and shook his head.

Kenzie turned around to see Ana maneuvering a wheelchair toward the open rear door beside her. It was folded side-to-side accordion-style—a chair Kenzie hadn't seen before.

Ana opened her chair with a single movement, then deftly lowered it to the ground. To the left of the van's sliding door was a vertical handrail. Ana grabbed it and inched down the step onto the chair's seat.

I should have known. An internal beam of sunshine spread throughout Kenzie's chest. She'd never imagined having a friend like Ana. Could anything stop that girl?

Mr. Muñoz patted Kenzie's hand. "We must allow my Ana her dignity." His face radiated with cheerful pride. "Go now and enjoy your visit." Then he pushed a button to close the back door.

Kenzie hopped out. Mr. Muñoz started the engine. "I will return at five thirty, *niñas*."

Ana's folding wheelchair wasn't motorized, but in spite of the bumpy, gravel parking lot, she kept up with Kenzie.

Kenzie tapped the chair's back. "How many of these things do you have?"

"Three. At home there is the big chair, *Cushy*, for comfort. *Doonie* for the beach. And this new one to travel with ease."

"It doesn't have a name?"

"I did not name it yet." Ana stopped in mid-roll. She grinned and clasped her hands. "This I must do."

"Not now. Come on. Let's find out how the hawksbill's doing."

The medical building appeared closed to visitors. Kenzie knocked and waited. A latch clicked. The door opened, and Melissa peered out, blinking against the sunshine.

"Hi, girls." She aimed a wide smile at Ana. "You're Kenzie's friend who called for the ambulance. Ana, right?"

"*Si. Yo soy Ana y este es...*" Flicking a gotcha look at Kenzie, she lovingly tapped the arms of her chair. "This is *Viajero.*"

Kenzie peered sideways at Ana. "Excuse me?"

"Traveler. His name is Traveler."

Kenzie knuckle-bumped Ana's shoulder. "Good one." Then she spread her arms, palms up. "But geesh. What took you so long?"

Melissa waved them through the open door. "Well, travel on in," she said, locking it behind them.

They entered a large, open space resembling an old classroom. A dry-erase board hung on the wall, just like the ones at St. Joe's Academy.

"Did this used to be a school?" Kenzie asked.

"No. A motel." Melissa gestured to the rows of folding chairs. "But we do hold classes and seminars, and it serves as home base for PAT, Monroe County's Protect-A-Turtle group."

Kenzie scanned the PAT wall chart next to the whiteboard. Turtle watch duties were listed by members' initials. Two names began with the letter *J.* "Melissa, yesterday, I met a man named Jake patrolling Turtle Beach. Do you know him?"

"I bet you met Jake Rogers. Long gray pony tail?"

"Yep."

"I hear he's one of the most active members. Bet he never misses a meeting."

"Those shapes." Ana steered Traveler to the whiteboard and stared up at it. "What do they mean?"

"That's a chart of our patients." Melissa moved to the board. "This large rectangle refers to our recovery pool, originally the motel swimming pool. The circles around it represent isolating tanks. The color of each turtle's name tells you whether they're here for life, rehabilitation, or research."

Ana touched two letters near the circles. "In this tank the turtle is named Snuffy Face. Why are his initials *Cm?*"

"The initials are scientific names. Genus and species. *Cm* is *Chelonia mydas*, the green turtle. The other initials represent *Eretmochelys imbricate* for hawksbill. *Lepidochelys kempii* for Kemp's ridley, and these initials belong to the majority of our patients—"

"*Caretta caretta*," Kenzie blurted. Her fingers flew to her mouth. Had she been rude?

"You got it." Melissa patted her on the back. "The loggerhead."

"It's the only name I can pronounce," Kenzie said. "I always thought it sounded like a dance or a pasta dish."

"No food references, please." Melissa smiled. "Wouldn't want it to get back to the turtles." She touched the rectangle. "Short Tail and his friends are recovering well from fibropapilloma surgery. To gain strength, they exercise six months in the saltwater pool before release."

"That disease," Kenzie said, "fibro... "

"Fibropapilloma. It's the main focus of our research."

"When Ana called you, that's what you figured our turtle had, right?"

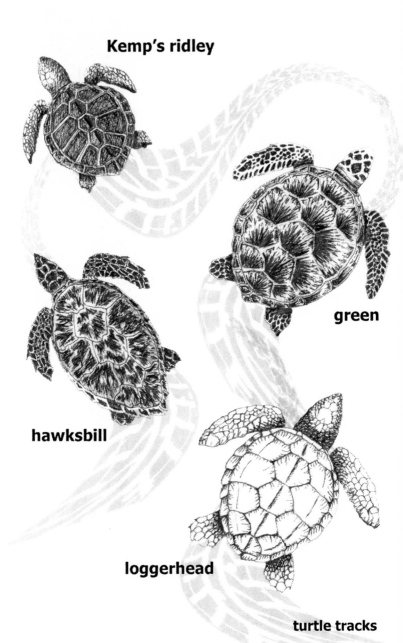

Kemp's ridley

green

hawksbill

loggerhead

turtle tracks

"Until we examined it, yes." Melissa raised her head to the sound of a door closing. "And we were very happy to be wrong, weren't we Dr. Lily?"

"We certainly were. Nice to see you again, Kenzie." Dr. Lily gently shook Ana's hand. "Ana, I'm pleased to meet you. Ready for a tour?" Dr. Lily gestured at the door through which she'd entered. "I know you two want to see your rescued hawksbill. We'll take a quick walk through the hospital on our way to the pool."

"I'll catch up with you outside," Melissa said. "You can help feed the patients."

The surgery room sparkled with stainless steel equipment and fascinating machines. Large lights hung above an operating table. Mounted on the wall was a light box with an unbelievable image clipped to it.

"Does that x-ray show the inside of a turtle's stomach?" Kenzie asked.

"It does. A very sad case. Over time it had swallowed an enormous quantity of trash." Dr. Lily opened a drawer. "Here's what we extracted from its stomach." She took out a large clear box crammed with a tangle of green nylon rope, shredded bits of plastic bag, and other unidentifiable junk. She emptied it onto the counter.

"Oh, no." Kenzie envisioned Old Turtle's sad eyes. "One turtle swallowed that whole pile?"

Ana's hands cupped her cheeks. "*¡Dios mío! Que*— What is all that?"

"The obvious bit is green mooring line." Dr. Lily took a pen from her lab coat pocket and picked at the snarled rope, freeing the leather sole of a shoe, a rice bag label, ballpoint pens, and a plastic wine cork. "I could keep going, but you get the idea."

"*Pobrecito.*" Ana grasped Traveler's arm rests, her knuckles shining smooth and white with tension. "Turtle Beach suffered much trash also. After our cleanup the beach is like new." Ana backed away from the counter. "Cleanup I think is not so easy for a turtle."

Studying endangered sea turtles hadn't prepared Kenzie for the graphic reality of living in the Keys. Experiencing—up close and personal—the horrible turtle accidents and diseases. Her stomach rolled as if she were on rough seas, and her intestines twisted like lines in the waves. *I didn't know things were so bad, Old Turtle. I'll do everything I can to save your babies, but I can't cure disease or stop injuries.*

Still, she had to know. "Dr. Lily, did that turtle survive?"

THE IMAGE OF OLD TURTLE tormented Kenzie as if *he'd* swallowed that agonizing load of garbage. Could he have experienced such a tragedy? He wouldn't have begged for help unless he knew the dangers to his species. How was that knowledge possible? Only one way— Old Turtle had once lived free.

Kenzie's spirits sank lower and lower while she waited for Dr. Lily's answer. *Did that turtle survive?*

Finally, as if Dr. Lily could find no way to avoid it, she released a defeated sigh. "No, we couldn't save it." She jammed the fatal debris back in the container. "The poor thing didn't stand a—"

"Dr. Lily," Ana called from an adjoining room. "What do you do in here?"

When had Ana left them? Blinking out of her heartbreaking trance, Kenzie followed Dr. Lily into what had once been a kitchen.

"This is where we clean the turtles," Dr. Lily explained. "We remove barnacles and algae from their shells."

With a rusty screwdriver in hand and a puzzled expression on her face, Ana was parked next to a large stainless steel sink.

"Now, Ana..." Dr. Lily held up a warning finger. "You be careful with that." Her words danced with the release of humor. "It's one of our crucial surgical instruments." She took the tool from Ana and tapped its flat end. "We use this to scrape off barnacles. Turtles are difficult to handle until their shells are free of sharp and slippery growth."

"I noticed."

"Actually, Kenzie, in light of what we usually see, your hawksbill didn't have many barnacles. The loggerheads are the ones most plastered with organisms." Dr. Lily glanced at her watch. "It's feeding time." She placed the screwdriver back on the counter. "Melissa and Ed are waiting for you."

Once outside, they headed toward the saltwater pool. Housed under a roof and enclosed by a chain-link fence, it sat mere yards from shore. "Our location," Dr. Lily explained as she opened a gate, "is ideal. It provides the rescue and release teams easy access to both the Gulf of Mexico and Atlantic Ocean."

Kenzie sniffed. "Why does it smell like bleach and fish stew?"

"I think you smell this." Dr. Lily lifted a bottle marked *Sodium Hypochlorite* 0.5% from an equipment bin. "The equipment was recently sterilized. You probably smell the turtles' dinner, as well. It's all prepared." She gestured toward Ed, who sat a few yards away on a stool surrounded by buckets. "But I know you want to see your hawksbill first."

"Hey, girls," Melissa called from the far end of the enclosure. "Over here." She was leaning against one of many tanks larger in diameter than a kiddy pool and at least three times as high.

Ana sped ahead, nearly rolling into Melissa before engaging Traveler's hand brakes. She jerked forward, then back again in her seat.

Kenzie hollered, "Ana, you all right?"

"*Sí, sí. Estoy bien.*" Ana touched a small plaque on the tank with her other hand. "*Chica, vamos, rápido.* Hurry. This name. You will love it."

"You need an airbag on this thing, girl," Kenzie said, grasping Traveler's handles. "So what's the big deal?" She leaned over Ana and read the sign, "*Salty's Hawk.* Cool."

"Ed named him," Melissa said. "Your dog's concern for this turtle really impressed him."

Kenzie peered over the tank wall. A huge beak-like nose bobbed to the surface. Jets of water squirted her face. "Yikes." Kenzie jumped back, wiping her eyes and laughing. "She hosed me. She looks so good. I can't believe this is the same turtle I rescued."

Melissa patted its tapered head. "She's the only hawksbill in residence."

Equipment cleats were spaced at ladder-like intervals on the tank. Ana grasped the lowest with one hand and lifted herself out of her chair. Then she reached for the next cleat and pulled, rising little by little until she stood clutching the shoulder-level rim. "*¡Que bonita!* Now she is beautiful. She is lucky you came to Turtle Beach, Kenzie."

From behind, the sound of squishing footsteps approached, accompanied by a potent fish odor. "And she's lucky you called us, Ana," Ed said as he sat a small bucket on the concrete. "Dr. Lily fixed her up good. Tell them, Doc."

"Well, when we performed an endoscopy..."

Casting each other clueless looks, Kenzie and Ana shrugged.

"We put a little camera down her throat," Dr. Lily said. "The bag was jammed tightly in the curve of the turtle's esophagus right before it connects with the stomach. It was challenging to extract the bag without leaving bits of plastic in the esophagus. I'm pleased to say we removed it all."

"I bet you have a sore throat." Kenzie shook her finger at the turtle. "No more plastic meals for you." The hawksbill's eyes locked on her, drawing her into a churning sea. A shiver flowed through Kenzie. Waves of dizziness blurred her vision. She reached for the tank wall, steadied herself, and returned to solid ground.

What was that about? It must be hotter than she'd realized. She needed water. That had to be it, she thought as the turtle's narrow head began to morph, enlarging in size and paling in color. What was happening? Its sharp beak smoothed into thick, blunt jaws—loggerhead features. Swaying, Kenzie clung tighter to the tank rim. Salty's Hawk was channeling Old Turtle.

What, Old Turtle? What more can I do? I'm doing my best to catch the poacher. What else—

Whoa. Kenzie straightened. It had been smack in front of her all along. So obvious. *Plastic.* True, she couldn't prevent *all* injuries. But if... If she could reduce the number of plastic bags in the water—

Dr. Lily's voice drifted into Kenzie's awareness. "As for tumors—"

Tumors? Kenzie jolted into the moment. *Please, no tumors.*

"—the endoscopy uncovered good news. There were no internal tumors." Dr. Lily continued. "Nothing else in her system, except a mass of gravel and shells, and we're cleaning that out with enemas."

"Oooow." Kenzie grabbed her bottom. "Poor turtle."

"It's not what you're thinking." Ed hid half a grin behind his fist. "We don't do it from that end. It's down the hatch for turtles." He tapped the bucket. "So, ready to feed Salty's Hawk?"

"Absolutely," Kenzie said.

Ed reached into the pail. "Hold out your hand, then."

Ana made no move, but Kenzie eagerly followed Ed's direction.

He dropped a pale, rubbery, slime-covered, could-have-once-been-alive thing on her palm. *Blech.* It slipped. Instinctively she squeezed the vase-like form. *Yuck.* It slid out of her fist. She captured it in both hands. *Eek.* Popping out of her clasped hands were floppy, suction cup-covered tentacles and—eyes. Big round eyes. *Ewww.*

Ana gasped.

Kenzie squealed, and for a moment her own eyes mimicked the wide-open expression on what could only be a dead squid.

Steady, Kenzie. Her science teacher's voice—*It's only a dead mollusk*—shamed her into control. One breath. Two breaths. Three. Shifting her weight to one leg, Kenzie stared Ed down as if he'd told *her* to eat the squid. She held the oily thing an arms' length away. "Okay. Now what?"

With eyes radiating mischief, Ed rocked on his heels. "You're going to feed Salty's Hawk *and* give her an enema."

Bee boogers. The man was nuts. "I'll give her this squid, but an enema? Not a chance."

"Ed, give her a break." Melissa's tone was serious. Her lips, however, twitched as if corralling a giggle. "That squid is the enema, Kenzie. It's filled with vegetable oil. You squeezed some out. Mixing squid with laxatives cleans her system gradually. Go ahead. Drop it into the tank."

Kenzie couldn't dump it fast enough. *Plop.* The turtle gracefully turned, dove, and snapped up her snack. Kenzie stared at her hands.

"That wasn't so bad, was it?" Ed asked, handing Kenzie a wipe.

"Not for the turtle." Kenzie tossed the used cloth at him. "Bet you're sorry you missed that chance, Ana."

"Your fun was also mine." Ana giggled before lowering herself onto Traveler. She moved to the next tank which was labeled *P*. "This is the tank for diseased turtles, yes?"

Kenzie followed her. "Ana, maybe you shouldn't get so close."

"Not to worry," Dr. Lily said. "Their papilloma tumors have all been removed by lasers. In any case, the virus can't be passed to humans, only

185

to other turtles."

"Virus?" Ana asked. "This is like a cold?"

"More like chicken pox. Turtles get tumors instead of spotty rashes."

Kenzie examined the spots on her arms. As much as she despised her freckles, they were way better than tumors. "Where does the virus come from?"

"Pollutants? Other environmental changes? Parasites? So much is unknown. One thing scientists believe is that infected turtles pass on weakened immune systems to their hatchlings. Those babies are likely to succumb to the disease."

Diseased turtles with tumors. Who'd want sick turtles covered with bumps? People who raise sea turtles for food or exhibit wouldn't buy the poacher's eggs. Not with this disease being so common. So who did buy them and why? What was the real motive for stealing eggs?

"Dr. Lily, why would—"

A ringtone sounded, and Dr. Lily patted her lab coat pocket. "Excuse me, Kenzie." The vet retrieved her phone, then read its display. "I need to go, girls. I'm on emergency call. Melissa and Ed can answer any other questions you have."

Crud. Kenzie had planned to ask her how people could make money from sea turtle eggs.

A few steps outside the chain link fence, Dr. Lily turned. "Kenzie, I'd like to come by tomorrow around noon and check on Salty. Will you be home?"

Tomorrow. She'd ask then. "Yes, ma'am."

"Enough of the depressing stuff." Ed rubbed his hands together. "Let's have some fun. Follow me to the buckets, ladies." He had lifted the first bucket no more than two feet in the air when the turtles grew restless, gliding in rapid crazy eights near the surface. Several paddled to the concrete wall and floated, holding their heads above water. Sea turtle beggars.

Ed sprinkled chow into the pool. *Plop. Spatter. Splat.* "Here. Take a handful." He held the bucket out, first to Ana, then to Kenzie. "Have at it."

With each toss they made, the water erupted in whirlpools, and an army of shiny-scaled torpedoes zoomed among the gliding sea turtles.

"What kind of fish are those?" Thrusting her head forward, Kenzie stuck out her lower jaw. "They look mean."

"That's not a bad imitation." Ed laughed. "They're tarpon."

The turtles gobbled, splashed, and dived, but the huge, grumpy-faced fish gulped most of the sinking chunks.

Kenzie crossed her arms, pouting. "That's not fair. Those tarpon are too fast."

"Maybe that's why they've been around over a hundred million years," Melissa shouted above the flapping turtle flippers and thrashing fish tails. "Don't worry. Competing for food forces the turtles to exercise. It's good for them."

Ed pulled several stinky squid out of another bucket and threw them one at a time into the pool. "Here, your turn." He offered a squid to Ana.

She backed away, wrinkling her nose. "Kenzie, we should go. *Papi* will be here soon."

"You don't know what you're missing." Ed flipped the squid into the pool.

Melissa glanced at her watch. "I need to go in anyway. There's a PAT meeting in a few minutes. I have to open the classroom for them. Come on, girls. Carry on, Ed."

Closing the pool gate behind them, Melissa said, "Kenzie, I remember you asked about Protect-A-Turtle the day we picked up the hawksbill. If your friend, Jake, comes for the meeting, you can ask him about his experiences."

Whoa. Brain wave. Kenzie stopped, forefinger twirling a loose strand of hair. She needed to do more than talk to Jake, she needed to join PAT. *Perfect work for a spy.* "Melissa, do you think I could volunteer with PAT sometime?" *Perfect way to find evidence.* "I could work with Jake." *Perfect alibi to get out of the house.* "In case I don't see him before we leave, do you know how I can contact him?"

"Call me here Friday or Saturday."

This could really work. "Thanks."

They wound back through the hospital to the front classroom. In passing, Kenzie checked the PAT duty chart. JR was scribbled on two dates. Then she leafed through the PAT logbook on the table below the chart, finding Jake's signature on lots of nest reports. He was definitely dedicated to the task. "Melissa, someone with the initials JR is monitoring nests today and Friday. Is that Jake?"

"Sorry, can't answer that one." She smiled at

Ana and then at Kenzie. "But did we answer all your other questions?"

Ana poked Kenzie's thigh and mouthed, *The poacher?*

Right. Why not get Melissa's thoughts? "Well, we *have* been wondering about the poaching problem. Do you know why a person would steal turtle eggs?"

"And do you have an idea who is this poacher?" Ana asked.

"I have no clue who—or why—at least not why here. People in other parts of the world believe— Well, no. *I* don't."

There it was again. The aphrodisiac theory. Kenzie still wasn't buying it. Where was the market? Too much trouble for too little reward.

"Ed suspects the poacher's someone who lives on Turtle Beach. As he said, who else would benefit so easily from familiarity and access?"

Kenzie twisted her ponytail. One more reason to keep Ancient Angry Edna at the top of her suspect list.

Melissa inserted her key in the front door. "Of course, anyone could get to Turtle Beach by boat. To discourage that approach, a friend of mine plans to fish the sponge beds off Turtle Beach. Even plans to move his houseboat there."

"*The Bard?*" Kenzie asked.

"Yes." Melissa turned the key. "How—?"

"Fisher!" Ana and Kenzie said together.

"You two know Fisher?"

Kenzie and Ana exchanged smiles.

"At our church, Fisher does much work," Ana said.

189

"And his dog, Jigs, is Salty's mother," Kenzie said.

Nodding, Melissa relaxed against the doorframe. "That's why Salty's such a good puppy."

"He is good"—Ana winced—"at getting into trouble."

"Great. As if I don't hear enough of that from Angelo."

"Let's see if Jake's outside," Melissa said, opening the door.

Several cars were parked in the lot, along with five or six bicycles jumbled in the bike stand. More than a dozen people wearing Protect-A-Turtle shirts waited at the entrance. No Jake.

"Already *Papi* is here. His van is under the big tree. *Todo fue maravilloso.* Everything was wonderful. *Muchísimas gracias*, Melissa."

"Yes, thanks a gazillion."

The girls headed for the van, excusing themselves as they moved through the PAT members.

"Wait, girls." Melissa cut through the oncoming rush of green shirts. "Kenzie, I just thought of something. Fisher fills in sometimes when one of the PAT members can't work. He's doing a count on Turtle Beach tomorrow. If you can find him, you could go along."

"Perfect. I'll ask him today. He's finishing a job at my house this afternoon."

Kenzie and Ana saluted each other with hopeful crossed fingers as the back door of the van slid open. Ana pulled herself up onto the seat. Before Kenzie could be chastised, she handed Traveler to Ana, amazed that the chair weighed little more than Salty.

While Mr. Muñoz waited for traffic to clear, Kenzie caught a glimpse in the side mirror of someone exiting the hospital door. Jake? Yes, and he was walking in their direction. He must have checked the chart, learned he had patrol duty today, and couldn't stay for the meeting. Why hadn't they seen him? Kenzie rolled down her window to speak to him. The van lurched forward, tossing her against the seatback. *Oomph.* Mr. Muñoz gunned his motor, zipped onto U.S. #1, and Jake crossed the highway.

Crud. She'd missed her chance to patrol with a full-time PAT member. Kenzie slumped in her seat. A rush of humid air blasted her face, but couldn't drive away her disappointment.

Caught in a passing car's draft, a discarded plastic bag lifted into the air, meandering toward the ocean. Something definitely had to be done about those deadly shopping bags.

Later that evening, Mom skipped down the front steps. "Sweetie, wait for me. I could use some exercise."

Salty turned, tail wagging. Kenzie waited, mind boggling. Her eyes narrowed in suspicion. After a long day, Mom usually collapsed feet up, teacup in hand.

"So, how was your tour today?" Mom asked. "Was this Ana's first visit to the Turtle Hospital too?"

"Yep, and we both loved it. You wouldn't believe what awesome things they do."

"Like what?"

Mom never felt like talking when she first came home. Where was she going with this? "Uh, they remove disgusting tumors, treat wounds caused by propellers and sharks—sometimes they even have to amputate flippers. They remove garbage from turtles' digestive systems too—lots of plastic grocery bags."

"I see those bags along the highway. I never

thought about them blowing into the water. Hold on a second." Mom stooped to untangle a sandspur from Salty's tail. She eased the sharp bur loose and continued. "The organic grocery store in Key West has the right idea. They're no longer offering plastic bags. I read it in this week's *Island Times.*"

"That's great. If *they* banned the bags, maybe we can get the stores up here to do the same. The KTC will jump all over this."

"It's certainly worth a shot. You kids have pulled off great feats before." Mom took a pack of gum from her shorts' pocket. "Want a stick?"

"Yes, please." A major compliment followed by a sweet treat. Mom had to be building up to something. Kenzie tried to focus on a ban-the-bags plan, chewing intently, as if the effort might deflect whatever distraction Mom had in the works. The taste of spearmint mingled pleasantly with the sultry evening air and tangy sea breezes. But it did nothing to relax Kenzie's guard.

"Sweetie..."

Uh-oh. Mom's syrupy tone.

Mom gently touched Kenzie's hand.

Here it comes.

"I know about your hawksbill rescue."

Gulp. Kenzie nearly choked on her gum.

"And I know you borrowed Angelo's boat." She placed particular emphasis on *borrowed.*

Mike couldn't have. "How—"

"Dr. Lily's office manager. I stopped by to make a payment. You forget how small this island is."

Bee boogers. Kenzie led Salty a few steps ahead. *This was seriously bad news*. At least she didn't know the *really* dangerous part. Did she? Chewing her ponytail, Kenzie waited for the tirade.

The *flip flop* of Mom's sandals closed in on Kenzie. "You're going to get gum in your hair." With a light shoulder squeeze, Mom turned her around. "Sweetie..."—*not syrupy, hesitant*— "Relax."

Relax? I've broken just about every rule in the house.

Mom freed the ponytail from Kenzie's mouth. "At first I was furious. However, I'm practicing reflection before action. Having sole parental responsibility is new to me."

Kenzie fixed her gaze groundward. An ant boldly approached her sandal.

"I'm guessing you and Angelo already had a... *discussion* about this. Right?"

"Kind of." Kenzie managed to whisper. The ant marched closer.

"And something good—saving a turtle—did come out of your reckless behavior."

Kenzie groaned. *Reckless*. A common start for the Mom Lecture. That ant was going to die.

"Oh, come on." Mom brushed a forefinger over Kenzie's nose. "I had to get in one dig. It's my maternal right. I'm hoping you've already learned a lesson."

Kenzie chanced an upward, raised-eyebrow look at Mom. "So, I'm not grounded?"

"Oh, you are grounded. Solid-as-a-rock, feet-on-terra-firma grounded. You are never to go anywhere in Angelo's boat again. Unless he's in it. Deal?"

Unbelievable. Not only was Mom not furious, she was teasing in an out-of-practice kind of way. It was a miracle. "Deal." Kenzie hugged her tightly, and the ant crawled on.

Salty pounced first on Kenzie, then her mother. Mom lifted the puppy to her face. "That goes for you too, Salty." She set him down. "Now, let's go home. I need a cup of tea and a good book."

In easy peace, they moved on to the tune of rustling palm fronds and the occasional *plop-splash* of fish in the nearby canals. Mom put her arm around Kenzie and matched her stride. "If you had visited the Turtle Hospital before your science project last year, you might have won the New York state prize. Maybe you can in Florida."

"I have other projects now."

"Oh?" Mom cocked her head. "More than the beach cleanup and banning plastic bags?"

"Way more." *As in catching the poacher.* "I want to work with an environmental group called PAT. Protect-A-Turtle."

"Sounds interesting. Right up your alley."

"At the hospital, Melissa—she came in the ambulance to get the turtle—told me that Fisher's filling in for a PAT volunteer tomorrow morning."

"And that means what?"

"He's going to Turtle Beach to check nests and count hatched eggs. When I got home today, he was still at the house. He said I could go with him. So"—she squeezed Mom's arm— "since I'm not exactly grounded, can I?"

"Cheeky child." Mom squeezed back. "Do you need me to take you?"

"No. Fisher's building a fence for Mrs. Grable tomorrow and—"

"She's the church choir director, right?"

"Right. She's going to drop Fisher off at Turtle Beach when she goes shopping and pick him up afterward. I could bike to her house and ride along."

"Sounds good to me."

"Great. By the way, Fisher's coming Saturday afternoon for his pay."

"That's fine. I'll have it then." Chuckling, Mom nodded across the canal to three Key deer surrounding a child on a tricycle. The little boy pedaled in circles, stopping to pat the German-shepherd-sized deer each time he passed them.

Hands on her face in wonder, Mom said, "Now that's a vision. I don't think I'll ever get used to such sights."

Kenzie contained her smile. *You should see the visions I have.*

Mom closed her eyes, her face a picture of bliss. "Mmm. Smells like plumeria." She opened her eyes, then scanned the area. "Ah, there. That tree covered with pink blossoms." She sniffed again. "Isn't it sweet?"

No tirade. No third degree. No grounded-for-life. It was sweet all right. Real sweet.

Kenzie placed the fragrant blossoms by her

computer before opening her mail. Angelo's came up first.

> *Turtle Beach patrol covered. Skate-boarding course a big hit.*
>
> *No sign of poacher today.*
>
> *Talked to Jerry. He wasn't working the day the tires were sold. Said those tires aren't common.*
>
> *I sketched the tread design. Might be useful.New thought. Exploding ping-pong balls. We fill them with dye. Camouflage them in a nest. Set a timer.*
>
> *Surprise. The thief is permanently marked. Haven't found a formula for dye yet. Timer might be a problem too.*

The boarders would skate up and down the entire road. That had been a great idea. Exploding ping-pong balls. Not so much.

She opened Ted's next. He'd attached a photo of a car with a Florida plate. It was illegally parked in the trees along Turtle Beach Road. So? Cars did that all the time. The bike was the important thing. But she posted Ted's photo on the KTC site anyway.

Lakisha reported:

> *No news. Couldn't get to beach. Not giving up.*

Kenzie messaged all the KTC members:

> *Watch for suspicious bike riders wearing purple.*
>
> *PAT duty with Fisher tomorrow on Turtle Beach.*
>
> *Will look for clues. Fisher moving The*

Bard to Turtle Beach. Will watch all boat traffic.

Also, organic market in Key West banned plastic bags. How can we get stores on BPK to do that? Ideas?

In minutes, Ted responded:

People trust Fisher. Me? Not so sure.

Working with PAT? Y?

Anchoring houseboat at Turtle Beach? Convenient, ya think?

Bikes everywhere picking up junk. Easy to dig up a nest anytime. Steal turtle eggs.

KEEP YOUR EYES OPEN.

PS That bag thing sounds tough to pull off.

How could Ted suspect Fisher? That was absolutely nuts.

Another message from Lakisha popped up:

I'll see if my aunt will mention banning plastic bags to her boss at the grocery store.

Mom knocked on the doorframe. "I'm going to shower. Do you need to use the bathroom first?"

"No. Go ahead." Kenzie stared at the purple jar in Mom's hand.

Smiling, Mom raised the jar in champagne-toast style. "To Shalima's Secrets. A girl needs all the magic she can get." Then she retreated to the bathroom.

Exactly what secrets did Shalima have? Even though all signs indicated that Ancient

Angry Edna was the one with dangerous—likely criminal—secrets, it was difficult to ignore Shalima. Kenzie Googled *Shalima*, hoping to find a website for her merchandise. No luck. She did find some interesting information about the name *Shalima*. Inspired by the Arabic *Salimah* or *Saleema* it had multiple meanings: 1) *flawless*, 2) *safe*, 3) *healthy*, 4) *peaceful*, 5) *faultless*. But there was nothing to be found about the mysterious local lady.

Her search for Shalima's skin care products led to beauty sites that detailed recipes using raw chicken eggs for skin and hair care. One source said that egg yolks contain a kind of Vitamin B for healthy hair and clear skin. Simply eating eggs didn't improve skin or hair; to be useful, eggs needed to be processed and blended into a topical cream.

There were documented recipes as far back as the 1600s. A French queen, Maria de Medici, used honey and raw chicken egg on her face. In the 1700s, Marie Antoinette shampooed with raw chicken eggs, rum, and vinegar. But she'd been beheaded. Kenzie grimaced. That hadn't worked out so well. Shalima closely guarded the product she used on her own hair. Something made it so "alluring" that she kept it hidden. Ha. Maybe she hid it because she knew about Marie Antoinette's fate.

Eggs and cream. Shalima could be using turtle eggs in her *Shalima's Secrets* formulas. Major secret. Wait, that didn't make sense. Nests were still being destroyed. This late in the season, turtle eggs were too developed for processing. Unless turtle eggs really did contain a unique, magical ingredient—something yet to be proven—why go to the trouble and risk of locating and robbing turtle eggs when you had an unlimited supply of chicken eggs?

Shalima's secret was simply her formula. Kenzie had discovered the basic ingredient, raw egg, which explained why the face cream must be refrigerated. If it wasn't...yuck. Kenzie wrinkled her nose.

Who knew why Shalima used purple packaging? Though it seemed crazy, her name, along with extraordinary creams, miraculous shampoos, and chicken rescues were starting to make strange sense.

Shalima—mysterious? Absolutely. Shalima—brilliant? For sure. So much so that she'd even found herself a nearly perfect name. Consider her name's Arabic meanings: she had *flawless* skin; she provided a *safe* home for chickens; she seemed *healthy* and *peaceful*, in a weird kind of way. But was she *faultless*? Good question.

THE PINK SUNRISE SKY promised to turn blue in minutes and remain that way all day. It would be a scorcher on the beach. Good thing Fisher planned to complete his PAT patrol early.

Kenzie wheeled her bike out from under the stilt-house. After two miles of pedaling, she approached an old light pole taller than the surrounding scrub woods. The post—as if it were a giant's straw-hat rack—was topped with a ragged osprey nest. The masked raptors had made it impossible to miss the turn onto Mango Lane. Kenzie coasted around the corner and met a breeze, welcoming her to Mrs. Grable's street.

Houses on Mango Lane backed up to a canal like the one behind Kenzie's house. All were painted pastel colors—sky blue, buttery yellow, or mint green, as if this neighborhood had a dress code for homes. She approached a tangle of tall trees, rolled past them, and then braked with a screech. Open-mouthed, she stood staring at a rebellious house painted in Crayola blue-purple, laser-lemon, and pink-flamingo.

Shalima's Secrets

Kenzie squinted. There—straight from the flea market, squeezed deep in the jungle that threatened to swallow the colorful house—was the chicken-painted pickup. A rooster crowed from the roof. Two hens flapped in a tree. Another perched on a shiny, purple sign: *Shalima's Secrets*. This was Headquarters Shalima. But she sure wasn't keeping it a secret, upping her score in the innocent column.

Three houses down, Fisher's bike rested against the mailbox. Kenzie found him drilling postholes in the solid, coral rock. Fisher was one hard-working, good-hearted man. Ted was definitely crazy to suspect him. Still, with a touch of guilt, she checked his tires as she chained her bike next to it. The back was bald. The front one was new. *Crud. It can't match Angelo's sketch. It just can't.*

The telltale chirp of a remote car key sounded. Mrs. Grable appeared, waving to Kenzie and calling to Fisher.

Fisher passed Kenzie, greeted her with his usual flourish, and retrieved a loose-leaf binder from his bike's basket. Eyes twinkling, he handed it to her and said, "Follow this guide as we complete our task. Wisely, and slow. They stumble that run fast."

Twenty minutes later, Fisher and Kenzie shed their shoes on Turtle Beach. His were two inches longer than hers. Though suspicious in size, they were nothing like the robber's Surf Sandals. Fisher wore boat shoes. She'd never seen him in anything else.

Kenzie smiled. Barefoot. Toes curling deep

into soft, warm sand. Something she wouldn't have considered doing here two days ago for fear of injury.

Fisher scanned the beach and bowed slightly. "Fair lady, you are to be congratulated. This slice of paradise has been restored to its former splendor."

Tucking Fisher's notebook under her arm, Kenzie folded her hands prayerfully. "Let's hope it stays that way." A pencil dropped from the binder. She picked it up and asked, "I know we're looking for hatched eggs. What else? Will we find turtle crawl tracks?"

"I think not. The time has passed for the gentle ladies to come ashore. Thus, the emergence of hatchlings is near an end."

"Are there many nests that haven't hatched?" She swallowed. *Or been raided.*

"To my knowledge, we await five. We draw near the first."

Five? How did Fisher know the exact number? She shook off Ted's suspicion. All PAT volunteers would know the statistics.

"There." Kenzie rushed toward a fence of yellow warning tape attached to yardstick-sized posts. It surrounded a large indentation in the sand.

"Allow me to alter my prediction. These have departed one and all. We await only four. Shall we?"

Fisher knelt and dug his calloused hands into the sand. He pulled out one after another of what appeared to be squashed, slashed, and otherwise mangled ping-pong balls. So different from what she'd expected. How could a baby turtle hatch without breaking its shell into pieces? She gently squeezed one. Flexible, it didn't shatter like a chicken eggshell would. Cool.

Fisher piled the empty eggshells to one side. Then he dug elbow-deep and found six round eggs, their shells dimpled and sunken.

Preparing to record Fisher's counts, Kenzie flipped through pages of illustrated PAT forms. The book included directions, several blank forms, and many sheets that had been completed. She found no initials J.R., however, on any signature line. Was this the only record book? Maybe Jake used a different one. Had he even carried one that day he was on patrol? She searched her memory. Nothing. Jake had not used a notebook. "Fisher, do all volunteers use a binder like this?"

"Final counts must always be filed in such notebooks." He studied the sand sifting through his fingers. "However, few volunteers need visual guidance."

That made sense. Though Fisher had no problem with numbers—he'd kept records for his sponge and fish catches forever—reading directions challenged him. He needed the forms to show how other PAT volunteers completed them. Jake didn't need a reference; he could carry blank forms in his pocket. It'd sounded like Fisher meant there were several notebooks. Jake's forms could easily be in another binder.

Fisher grew silent. Kenzie grew uncomfortable, like the uneasiness she experienced in hospital rooms. Had her question embarrassed him? "Fisher, the reason I asked about the notebook... I... Well, the day we cleaned the beach, I met a PAT volunteer who didn't use one—Jake. Do you know him?"

"Ah, a frequent defender, Jake. Now, if you please, count every three-quarters of a shell. You may skip the smaller pieces."

Clearly, it was time to return to their task.

Kenzie counted sixty-three sections. "Do I record the whole eggs, too?"

"In a moment."

Fisher picked up one of the whole eggs. "Now we open these."

"What if—"

"Have no fear. If living, these would be smooth and unblemished."

He opened the six eggs with a pocketknife. After peering inside each egg, he buried them in the bottom of the hole. "Now. We record five unfertilized. There was one hapless baby. Most unfortunate. Therefore, we must also record one fertilized, though unhatched."

"Is that normal?" Kenzie asked as she recorded the information

"I believe it to be natural. However, Protect-A-Turtle will compare these results with others to monitor trends." He began to scoop up the empty shells. "Now, we bury these shells and move on. I do not wish to delay Mrs. Grable."

Ancient Angry Edna's roof soon appeared above the treetops. "Fisher, we're not far from Ana's house."

"We near a nest, as well, if my memory serves." Surprisingly, he moved further from the water as he continued. "Both shrewd and reticent, this determined lady concealed her nest amongst the trees." Fisher examined the tree line. "This way."

They left the beach, spooking five Key deer that bounded farther into the woods. Following the deer's worn path, Kenzie turned her back to a wall of low branches and pushed through. A spot of yellow flashed on the beach. *Ana.* Wearing a yellow tank top. Doonie was rolling freely over the spotless beach. Kenzie beamed with satisfaction.

"Kenzita," Ana called. "I saw you a minute ago. Where are you?"

"Back here in the trees. Fisher and I are patrolling for PAT. There's supposed to be a nest back here. Do you know where it is?"

"Please, come out."

"I'm over here." Kenzie waved her hands. "Which way is the nest?"

"Please, Kenzie. I need to speak with you."

Kenzie followed the path to where Fisher stood. "I'm going to go see what Ana wants."

He nodded, concentrating on the ground and stroking his beard.

Kenzie wound back through the trees until she emerged on the beach. "Ana, I don't get it," she said, brushing leaves out of her hair. "The PAT people told Fisher to check a nest somewhere back there. We can't find it."

"The warning tape is no longer there. The nest is now covered with leaves." Ana spoke more to her lap than to Kenzie.

"That's crazy. I need to tell Fisher. We could

have been walking all over it. We need to put up new marker tape. Are we even close?"

"Kenzita." Ana said Kenzie's name as if she spoke to a small child. "*Escucha*. Listen." Ana touched her ear. "Last night, *Papi* and I went shrimping. We came home very late. Near our house, *Papi's* headlights made something shine: a bicycle."

Kenzie chewed her lip. "The nest...Was the nest—?" She couldn't finish.

"*Sí*, Kenzie. I asked *Papi* to check all the nests this morning. That nest has no more eggs."

Her stomach knotting, Kenzie stared toward the area where Fisher still searched—not far from Ancient Angry Edna's house. *Poacher. Bicycle. Poacher's receipt. Edna's new tires. Edna did it. She's the poacher all right.* But— Kenzie looked at the peak of Edna's roof showing above the treetops. Why would Edna use a bicycle to raid a nest so near her house?

As SHE'D PROMISED at the hospital yesterday, Dr. Lily arrived around lunchtime, soon after Kenzie returned from Turtle Beach. Kenzie asked her the same question she'd asked Melissa. "Why would anyone steal turtle eggs?"

"Food is the only reason I can think of," Dr. Lily said. "Where food is scarce, people eat turtle eggs. Who needs to do that here? One can catch fish from shore with a simple hook and line."

The vet quieted Salty, ran her hands over his stomach, and examined his gums. She paused, stethoscope in midair. "And for goodness sake, egg protein can be had by simply following our wild chickens to a nest." She listened to Salty's heart, patted him, and packed her bag. She rose, then touched Kenzie's shoulder. "You've been a good nurse."

Dr. Lily's words were meant to comfort, but a good nurse wouldn't have let Salty dig into Ancient Angry Edna's yard.

"Don't worry, Kenzie. Salty doesn't need me

anymore. Continue to administer his K_1 pills until they're gone, and don't forget his worm medicine. He's in great shape now. If you keep up with his meds, he'll stay that way."

Right. If she could keep him out of trouble.

Dr. Lily's diagnosis didn't ease Kenzie's mind. She continued to obsess over the morning's disaster and mysterious motives until Angelo arrived and convinced her a snorkeling trip would clear her head. A short twenty minutes after they left the dock, her thoughts were back on shore. So much for distraction.

Kenzie twisted and braided her ponytail. "Angelo, it's great your dad gave you time off. But we shouldn't be playing around on the water." Then she loosened and finger-combed it. "Ana saw a bike near another destroyed nest. We need to track it down. Every second counts. We need a plan. We need to think."

"Red, lighten up. You're wound tighter than a winch cable." Angelo dropped anchor between two small mangrove islands. "I *am* thinking. Out here's where I think best. If you don't calm down, you'll never figure anything out."

"Maybe you're right." Kenzie sighed. "Ana took pictures of the bike. I hope they turn out."

"It'd be a good break."

"Speaking of bikes..." Kenzie hung her head. "I'm embarrassed to even bring this up. I noticed Fisher has a new tire and—"

"I saw Ted's message. Don't worry about it." Angelo set the hook, then tied off the anchor line.

"The thing is... Fisher acted super weird this morning when he learned about that nest."

Angelo pulled his snorkel gear from under the seat. "What'd he do?"

"Not much. That's the thing. I expected him to get furious. Instead, he stared out to sea and quoted Shakespeare."

"What'd he say?"

"Something like, 'I wasted time, and now doth time waste me.'"

Angelo sat on the transom, dangling his feet in the water. "Red, was *The Bard* at Turtle Beach this morning?"

She shook her head.

"Didn't think so."

"Oh geesh. Fisher planned to move his houseboat to protect the beach. Because he hasn't, he blames himself."

"Yup. You know him. When everything's cool, the man uses his own words. Lots of them. Not cool? He borrows someone else's words." Angelo pulled on his fins.

"About Fisher's new tire. Shouldn't you still—?"

"Chill. He'll be at Dad's fish house later today or tomorrow. I'll check it out." He picked up his mask. "Someone could have given it to him. Take a break. Grab your gear."

He's right. Forget that something about the case kept nagging her. Another suspicion that she couldn't quite grasp. She might as well stop worrying about the murdering robber, at least for the moment. There were enough things out here to worry about. One: she'd never been snorkeling. She wasn't about to tell Angelo that. And two: she'd never been with him when she'd been wearing only a swimsuit. And not even a cool one—a boring, competition suit. Maybe that was a good thing. She didn't have much to show off anyway.

Kenzie retrieved a bottle of sunscreen from the snorkel gear bag she'd found in Nana's closet. She opened it and dabbed it on her face and neck.

"Hey, you know that stuff kills coral, don't you?"

"You're kidding, right?"

"I wish." He fished in his gear bag, then tossed her a tube marked *eco-friendly- biodegradable*. "Not much coral in the backcountry, but use this anyway."

She wiped her face with a towel and applied Angelo's cream—slowly—still reluctant to bare her skin in front of him.

"Hey, what's the hold up? Let's go."

It was now or never. Kenzie stripped off her T-shirt and shimmied out of her shorts. Angelo hadn't even looked her way. He was too busy spitting inside his mask. Spitting? "Eew."

He spat again, smeared it over the lenses, and smirked at her. "Keeps it from fogging. You don't have to do it. Unless you want to see." Leaning overboard, he rinsed the mask, then stretched it over his head and positioned it on his face. The snorkel dangled at his ear.

Kenzie copied the procedure. She was no wimp.

Angelo pulled gloves out of his bag. "Put these on. You may have to grab rocks and pull yourself along."

Pull? She was expecting to swim.

Snorkel in place, Angelo jumped overboard.

Kenzie followed his directions. Mask first, fins, then gloves. She grasped her mouthpiece between her teeth and slipped into the water. Floating face down, she practiced breathing through her mouth. In and out of the snorkel. No sweat.

"Stay with me." Angelo mumbled through his snorkel. "It's shallow, but the current's strong."

Though it was easy to stay on the surface in the buoyant salt water, swimming through the narrow channel between the islands was exhausting. At times, it did help to grab rocks and pull. The visibility was awesome. Only three feet below the surface, small conch snails like the ones on the Key West flag nestled among the forest of greenish-brown sea grass—grass that bent toward her in the rushing current.

As if daring Kenzie to enter their space, small black-and-yellow fish darted around donut-shaped sponges the size of car tires. Spiny lobsters, clawless (unlike their northern cousins), ventured from their holes, waving their antennae at her.

Halfway through the channel, a disgusting, familiar material fluttered in the current. Fighting rushing water, Kenzie dislodged the plastic bag from the mangroves, then tucked it inside her elastic glove. At least no turtle would mistake this one for a jellyfish.

Gesturing for her to stay put, Angelo swam to meet her mask to mask. He placed her hand over a root and held it there, then lifted his face out of the water long enough to say, "Going back will be easier. Take a break for a minute." Eyes closed, Kenzie floated beside him and wondered what it would be like to be free of the thick glove, tangled roots, and strong current between them.

With no warning, Angelo shouted a muffled alarm. He pointed at several large rocks on the bottom. His fins splashed, and he dove.

Shark!

Kenzie yanked her legs upward. Knees to chest. Bumped her mask on the root. Water seeped in. She struggled to clear and reposition the mask. Lost her grip. *No.* The powerful current dragged her.

In her panic, her head went under. Salt water poured into her snorkel. Gagging, eyes burning, she lifted her head. *Puh.* She blew water out of the tube. Disoriented, she stroked and kicked, fighting the current.

Stop. That's back toward the shark. She spun and surrendered to the current. *Swish.* She was carried away—a raft in the rapids. There. Straight ahead. Anchor line. *Yes.* She was back at the boat. In one piece.

Angelo swam toward her. His shoulders

215

shook with garbled laughter that escaped his snorkel. Gripping the gunwale, he hauled himself on board.

Kenzie pursed her lips and folded her arms. "It was a harmless nurse shark. Right?"

He responded by dropping his gear on the floorboards. His sheepish grin said it all.

"Okay, Sharkman. You got me." Not in the mood for games, she held up the dripping bag. "Do you have any idea how to get rid of these things? Can we get at least get fishermen to stop taking them on boats?"

"I don't see how. Tackle shops always sell chum boxes in plastic bags. So does Dad. Nobody wants stinky bait to thaw and leak."

"There must be another way."

He toweled off and plopped on the rear seat, rocking the boat.

Splash. Behind them. What? *Splash. Splash.* She froze in place. That had been a harmless nurse shark, hadn't it?

"Speaking of bait, turn around. There's a pelican party." *Splash.* "Look at 'em dive. Must be a huge school of mullet." *Splash. Splash, splash.* "They're gonna have to share with us. Dad needs bait."

Quickly, he lowered the Bimini, then fired the engine. "Pull anchor." Kenzie hauled it on board. Angelo guided his runabout toward the hungry pelicans. As soon as he found a spot free of turtle grass, he cut the motor, and Kenzie dropped the anchor again. The surrounding water boiled with fish.

Angelo planted his feet on the floorboards.

Picking up the main line of his circular cast net, he coiled it around his left wrist. He slid the net's center ring up the line, then lifted and gathered the net in his left hand. Its skirt dangled, weighed down with a hem of lead weights. He clamped a few peanut-sized weights between his teeth, then grabbed another section in his right hand. He stretched his right arm, spun left, twisted right, and tossed. *Whoosh*. Like a giant Frisbee, the net flew and plopped into the water.

After the net settled to the bottom, Angelo pulled the hand line to form a pouch and trap the fish, then hauled the net to the boat. He dumped a pile of flopping, silver fish into his live well—a tank-like device he'd fashioned out of a large cooler and an aerator. One more toss and Angelo's bait tank was filled with round-bodied mullet eight to ten inches long.

"That's so cool," Kenzie said. "Can I try?"

Angelo turned to look at her. One corner of his mouth curled up. "Sure. You can *try*."

"Okay, so I do this." She wrapped the line around her left wrist. "Now what?"

He walked her through the steps. When she'd firmly grasped a section of the weighted hem between her teeth, he straightened her right arm. "Now," he said, "grab it an arm's length away with this hand."

"Got it," Kenzie said through clenched teeth. "Now, I do this." She twisted, rocked the boat to the left, shifted her weight right, then hurled the net.

"Whoa," Angelo yelled.

The boat tipped sideways. *Splat*. The net

dropped into the water beside it. *Splash.* Kenzie followed.

She surfaced sputtering. "At least I didn't get tangled in the net."

"Good thing," Angelo said. "Would have torn it up. It's not made for whales."

Kenzie stuck out her tongue and draped the net over the transom.

Grinning, Angelo hauled her back on board. "Ready to try again? You were doing okay until the toss."

"What'd I do wrong?"

"Leaned into it too much. Go for a smooth toss." He demonstrated a graceful release. "Your timing was a little off. Be sure to let go of everything at once."

"Okay, here goes." She repeated the steps. Coming out of the twist, halfway into the pitch, Angelo shouted, "Don't forget—*Fump* —to let go with your teeth." Kenzie grabbed the gunwale for balance. The net flopped half in, half out of the boat.

"Owie, owie, owie." Kenzie bounced in time with her cries. "Am I bleeding? Did I break a tooth?"

"Easy. Quit rocking the boat. Open up." Angelo played dentist, turning her head side to side, up and down. "You're okay. Hey, it's harder than it looks."

"No kidding. I *am* going to learn, though."

"Take the net home. Practice under your house. At least that way you can't drown."

All the way home, Kenzie sulked and hid behind her flapping hair. Why was she always so klutzy around Angelo? As if falling into canals and out of trees weren't bad enough, now she was falling out of boats.

Angelo slowed his skiff at the entrance to the canal. The engine *glug-glugged* quietly.

"You haven't told me what you think of my exploding ping-pong ball idea," he said.

"Well, it's kind of..." *Impossible*, she thought. "Well, it... You'd need... Did you find a way to make the dye?"

"No. Haven't figured out the timer thing either. Looked on every spy site I could find." He cut the engine and drifted until they bumped into Kenzie's dock.

She was tired of feeling useless. There had to be an easier way to catch the thief. "What if we could rig up some kind of night spy camera? Like stores and banks use."

"That'd be cool. It'd take some bucks. Those things aren't cheap. Listen, I've got to get these fish home. Let's do some serious computer searching tonight. We can compare what we find tomorrow."

Kenzie gathered her gear. "Okay."

"Don't forget this." He hoisted the cast net onto the dock.

"Thanks. I'll try not to kill myself."

Angelo held onto the dock's edge. "I'll run the bag issue by a couple of the guys at the fish house. Don't expect much sympathy. Turtles tear up fishermen's traps to get their catch." He pushed off and put the engine in gear. "Talk to you later," he said and swung the skiff around.

As she rinsed off her mask and fins, Kenzie

wished Angelo could have stayed to research with her. They were good at bouncing ideas off each other, but he had to get to the fish house to record the fishermen's daily catch. Another one of his mother's many responsibilities—now his.

Losing his mom was worse than horrible for Angelo. But at least his mother didn't choose to leave, as Kenzie's dad had. She trudged up the back stairs to her room. From the bottom bookshelf, she picked up a framed picture of her father. Since his defection, he'd done at least one good thing. He'd helped her invest the reward money she earned from the Key deer killer case. Did she have enough to buy a night camera? She woke up her computer to check.

Her mailbox flashed an urgent message from Ana. She'd attached four photos. The thief's bike. This could be the break they needed.

The first photo showed a dark, maybe black, bicycle jammed handlebars-first into the trees. Details were lost in shadow. A black cloth seemed to be caught in the branches above the bike.

In the second shot, the rag appeared to be tied on the rear of the bike.

The third shot opened. A tight, clear shot taken at the moment a breeze caught the dark cloth. *No way.* She magnified the screen. The state flag of Alaska? Here in the Keys? That's what it was all right. She'd learned about that flag in sixth grade. A thirteen-year-old orphan boy had designed the flag for a contest decades before Alaska was even a state. There was no mistaking the flag's dark blue color and subtle image of the Big Dipper and North Star in this clear shot.

Ana's fourth photo seemed a happy accident. She'd captured a shot of the rear bumper. The bumper itself was not clear. The tire was another story. In sharp focus, it revealed a deep and obvious tread pattern. Angelo's bicycle tire receipt. This bike and that receipt had to be connected.

Kenzie phoned Ana. "You did it. Your shots are great. This is solid evidence. I bet when we find this bike *both* of its tires are new. I'll send your pictures to the gang."

"*Bueno*. It is good you can use the pictures. *Pero por favor* say nothing in front of my parents. They do not know I took them. When *Papi* and I got home, it was late."

"You're right. They'd freak if they knew you were out in the middle of the night. I won't tell anyone whose pictures they are."

As promised, Kenzie didn't disclose the photographer. She simply posted:

> *Find this bike.*
> *Find owner.*
> *Load your cameras.*
> *Ride!*

She sent Angelo an additional message:
> *Bike doesn't fit sheriff's theory.*
> *Caribbean poacher flying Alaska flag?*
> *Doesn't work.*
> *We go with our own theory.*

If only they *had* a decent theory. She considered the suspects.

221

One: Fisher, with one new tire—not two. *No way*. Fisher wasn't from Alaska. He'd lived in the Keys his whole life.

Two: Shalima. No one seemed to know where she came from. If it was Alaska, her skin weathered extreme climates well. She'd use that fact to market *Shalima's Secrets*, wouldn't she? Kenzie'd seen no promotional references like that.

Three: Edna. Kenzie so wanted it to be her. Angelo had seen two new tires on her bike. But Edna wasn't likely to ride a bike to raid a nest she could easily reach on foot. Unless she used the bike for a decoy... What connection could Edna have to Alaska?

Ana's flag clue was great. Unfortunately, the more clues they got, the less they knew. Adding to Kenzie's frustration, that teasing glimmer of an idea returned, sparking but refusing to catch. The first glint had appeared this morning while she and Fisher patrolled. It was snuffed out when Ana arrived with the nest news. How could Kenzie fan that flicker into a flame?

KENZIE WOKE WITH A START. She lifted her head off her arms and blinked away the sleep sand from the corners of her eyes. In the monitor's glow, she studied the deep indentations on the underside of her forearms. How long had she been in this position?

Had she ever begun the promised Internet research? No. She'd been running down the short list of suspects when exhaustion overwhelmed her. Sun, snorkeling, and war with the cast net had sapped the energy required for a surveillance camera search. Groggy, she stumbled from her desk chair and flopped into bed, rubbing her neck and wondering if Angelo's research had been more productive.

Come morning, her e-mail provided the answer.

Night cameras are way too expensive.
I'll be fishing all day.
Back after sunset.
You?

Me? Nothing...yet. Guilt launched her fingers into action. As she waded through details about infrared security systems, Mom's phone rang. Minutes later, Mom tapped on the doorframe, phone in hand. "It's Ana."

What? Kenzie glanced at her bedside table. *Bee boogers.* She'd forgotten to charge her cell.

"Ana asked if you could go over later."

"And?"

"It's fine with me. *If* you catch up on all those chores you've neglected, including the laundry."

Crud. It would take all day to get the yard, house, and laundry done.

"I'm off to work. Remember, it's a late night for me."

"No problem. I'll be at Ana's."

With a warning look, Mom held out the phone but retained her grip when Kenzie reached for it.

Don't do it, girl. Kenzie blinked, halting the eye roll. "I know, not until after I finish my work."

"All right then." Her mother handed over the phone.

"Hey, Ana." Kenzie waved goodbye to Mom and mouthed *thanks.* "I've been working on that problem we have. Hold on a sec." Kenzie peeked down the hall. Covert communication would be so much easier if she could text. But, no-ooo. Not until next year. The screen door *thwacked*, then the Jeep's engine cranked. "I'm back. All clear. The latest scheme is to set up a kind of security camera. Angelo and I are trying to find one online."

"This does not sound easy. I will help. When

you come we can use my computer. For now, while you complete chores, I will do summer reading. For later, there is pizza."

"It's a deal."

"*Papi* will bring you when you are ready. Also, he will take you home after his dinner meeting."

"Super. This will be a great chance to check nests."

"Oh. I almost forgot." Ana's voice rose. "This morning, far from shore, a houseboat is anchored. The wind is swinging it so I cannot see its name."

"It has to be *The Bard*," Kenzie said. "Our ocean access guard is on duty."

"Fisher is not there. With the big boat there is no little fishing boat."

"The important thing is, he'll be there at night. It's calm over here; he's probably working this side of the island." Salty nudged Kenzie's knee. "I better get to work too." She finger-combed the puppy's back, knocking loose hairs to the floor. "Will your dad mind a shedding dog in his van?"

"He has not cleaned his van of sand and fishing tackle. He will not notice dog hair."

"Great. Salty loves to play on the beach. I'll call you when I'm finished. Probably around four."

Hours later, Kenzie propped her elbows on the computer desk in the Muñoz's living room.

Already tired from a full day's work at home, her Internet search for spy equipment had put her in a worse mood. "I thought I'd found it. That deer camera was perfect. No flashing signal. Batteries, recorder, camera all together in one weatherproof box. I could even afford it." Her head, heavy with disappointment, slumped lower and lower onto her fists. "There's just no way to get it here in time. We have to stop this creep...like yesterday."

"You are right." Sighing, Ana rolled away from her computer. "*Es muy frustrante.*"

"Frustrating?"

Ana nodded.

"Yeah, it's all that and more. We need another plan." Kenzie lifted her head and looked outside. "Uh-oh. Look. Salty's trying to pull your father's net off the railing."

"Oh no. *Perrito mal.*" Ana giggled. "Such a cute, bad puppy."

Before Kenzie reached the screen door, Salty released the net, then raced to the gate at the top of the stairs. "He probably needs to pee." She slid the door open. "It's getting darker by the minute. I'd better take him down."

Kenzie snapped the leash on Salty's collar, expecting him to leap at the gate. Instead he stood statue-still—head up, nose twitching—and stared into the mangroves. *Woof.* Kenzie flinched. Salty leaped at the rail—*Whomp*—growling and snarling his big-dog sounds.

"Ana, somebody's out there. I'm going to see who it is."

"*¡No! No vayas.*" Ana called through the

screen. "It is dangerous. *Por favor.* Please, do not go."

"It could be the thief. This could be our only chance." Kenzie opened the screen. She unhooked and shoved Salty toward Ana, closing him inside. "Stay here, puppy. I don't want you to scare them off. I need to see who it is."

"Oh, Kenzita... If you must go,"—Ana rolled to the door carrying a flashlight—"take this." Inching open the screen, she handed it to Kenzie. "Be careful. I will go down with my camera and see if that bicycle is again near the road."

"Good idea." Kenzie grabbed the flashlight, then closed the screen. She flung Salty's leash over the rail beside the cast net. *The net.* Bundling it onto her shoulder, she raced down the stairs. Ana's protests and warnings followed her all the way to the ground.

Kenzie chose the sandy path for its silent footing. A few yards into the woods, she stopped to listen. Silence. Except for the soft swish of palm fronds in the light breeze. Maybe no one was out here. Salty could have sensed browsing deer. Still, she wanted to be sure the remaining nests were safe.

The path led her away from the palms, yet the swishing grew louder. That didn't make sense. Kenzie switched off her flashlight. Her eyes adjusted to the last bit of daylight, and she crept toward the closest nest.

Swishing ended. Scraping began. Kenzie stopped. Her heart nearly did the same. Ahead in a clearing. A lantern. Its dim glow backlighting a dark form—the shape of someone hunching over the sand. Kenzie inched forward. The shadowed figure wore a wide-brimmed hat, long pants, and a long-sleeved shirt—dark-colored. *Purple?*

Scrape. Swish. Shovels of sand flew. The thief! In action. Who? *Move toward the light, you jerk. Turn your head.*

Wait. What if the creep had a gun? She should leave. Call the police. Ana was right. This was dangerous.

More digging.

No one could get here fast enough.

Sand flew. The poacher hadn't reached the eggs. They were still safe—for a few more minutes.

No one could stop this horror.

Another shovel.

No one but her.

Another shovel.

No choice. No other way.

Another shovel.

I have to do it. Before it's totally dark. Before it's too late.

Kenzie eased forward. Stopped.

No change. No problem.

Closer. *Snap.* She'd stepped on a twig.

The thief froze. Shovel in midair.

Every muscle in Kenzie's body locked. *I'm dead. I am so dead.*

In delicate slow motion, shoveling resumed. Silent, but no less deadly.

She dared to breathe again. Mingling with the rush of oxygen and boosting her courage, Old Turtle's image emerged. *Right.* Saving sea turtles. That's what she was doing. *So, get on with it, girl.*

Kenzie judged the distance to the nest, then crept forward a few more light steps. No crunches. No snaps. No more excuses.

She placed the flashlight on the ground. Easy now. She lifted the cast net from her shoulder, gripped it with her teeth. One step. *Wait for the clearing.* Two steps. *Almost there.* Three steps.

The crook changed position.

Kenzie stifled a scream. Bit the weights.

Digging resumed.

So did her heartbeat. She gathered the net into folds. Stretched an arm. Wound up. *Whoosh.* Missed the thief. *Clunk.* Hit the lantern. Knocking it over and out.

The thief dove on the net. Whirled. Plopped it over Kenzie's head and spun her, locking her arms at her sides.

No. No. No.

From behind her, furious hands wound the long line from her chest down to her knees. Cursing and spitting, Kenzie was knocked blindly to the ground. Shoved and rolled into the trees, screeching monstrous words. Trapped in the growing darkness like a fly in a spider's web.

She screamed with rage—until something snatched and sliced at the nylon mesh over her face—and crammed a bag into her mouth.

A filthy, suffocating plastic bag.

Bleah. The gritty bag tasted of chemicals, fish, and salt. *Gack.* Was this some fisherman's idea of a joke? *Here's what I think of your ban-the-bag idea.* Had she stumbled upon the hidden motive? Fishermen stealing loggerhead eggs to reduce the population of shellfish eaters? To slash the competition? Kenzie gagged and choked—on that idea as much as the bag. *Breathe through your nose. Don't panic. You won't swallow it. You are not a sea turtle.*

Kenzie kicked and struggled furiously. No use. *Bee boogers.* She folded her legs until her feet were underneath her hips. Pushed off the ground. No way. *Bumblebee boogers.* Maybe she could scoot on her back until she bumped into a tree. Edge upward inchworm-like against its trunk until she stood. After that, scraped bloody and raw, she'd stagger—where? No way. No how. *Big, black, bumblebee boogers.*

She'd almost nailed the creep. So close. Had he dug up the eggs after he tied her? She hadn't heard any more digging sounds. If only she hadn't knocked out the lantern. She never saw the poacher's face. Never heard a word. And yet, what if she had seen the creep, recognized the voice? Then what? Things could be much worse than being snared in her own trap, pricked with sticks and stones, and sucked on by vampire mosquitoes.

Insects crawled all over her. *Insects. Insects break out of cocoons. Why not me?* Twisting and wiggling, she rocked side to side. *Ouch.* Her thigh hit a rock. *Wrong.* That was her phone. In her cargo pocket. Her only hope. Call Angelo. *Humiliating.* She'd never hear the end of it. *Ana?* Ana couldn't maneuver Doonie through this tangle of trees. She'd want to call the police. And no way Kenzie'd call Mom or Mike. It had to be Angelo.

Bit by bit, bending sideways and raising shoulder to ear, she worked her hand toward the pocket. Finally, she touched the flap. With each effort to unsnap it, her fingers or elbow snagged in the webbing. Over and over she inched her arm down to start again. Muscles cramped. Anger and frustration pooled into tears.

A rustling in the dark. What? Something bigger than bugs coming to chew on her? Every muscle trembled. She was losing it. So was her bladder. She squeezed her legs and begged. *No, please.*

A scamper. *Don't pee.*

Close. *Squeeze tighter.*

Closer. *Don't pee.*

Whomp. Salty. The puppy pounced on her, sniffing and licking her face. *Thank God.* "Rab uh ag," she mumbled. *The bag. Grab the bag.*

He bit and tugged the net instead. After a few minutes, he whined and ran in circles. *Woof.* He barked again. Louder. Nonstop. Pacing, he sounded alarms at her side, then from a short distance away. Soon he returned to sniff and reassure her.

Suddenly, he stopped. Chilling silence surrounded her.

Crack. Twigs snapped.

Woof. Yap. Yap, Yap. Woof.

A faint light appeared.

Grrrr. Salty rumbled.

Kenzie trembled. *The thief.* Returning to silence Salty. And finish her.

"What in tarnation?"

A gravelly voice. *No. No.*

The light grew brighter—*It can't be*—and brighter still.

Hackles raised, barking his big-dog bark, Salty challenged the advancing voice.

Ancient Angry Edna.

They were doomed.

"Hmpff, you again. Troublesome dog." Edna grumbled in her bulldozer voice. "Are you alone?"

Salty raced to the dog-hating woman. *Salty, no. Stay away from her.* His barks quieted to whimpers.

Edna clomped closer. Close enough for Kenzie to make out her dark, long-sleeved shirt and an uncovered pile of snow-white hair. *It's a trick. She came back. She expects me to think it was someone else.*

Wagging his tail, Salty turned and trotted

back to Kenzie. She quivered—from relief or fear?—while the light swept the ground nearer and brighter, nearer and brighter, nearer and— *yeow*—like a shot in the eye, it blinded her. Kenzie squeezed her eyes closed, waiting for the brain-blazing light behind them to dim and hoping this nightmare would go away.

"Good heavens," Edna said. "You do seem to have the worst luck, dear."

When the glare eased, Kenzie chanced a look. Edna was still there, Salty at her side.

Edna placed the lantern on the ground and messed with something on her belt. A knife. She was unsheathing a knife. If Kenzie hadn't been so tightly bound, her heart would have exploded through her chest.

"Tell you what's the truth." Edna approached. "I never find what I 'spect to when this dog's carrying on." Edna waggled the knife like a scolding finger. Lantern light glinted off its blade.

Kenzie's blood iced.

"Never do. Sure sounded like he was coon wrestling. Looks like it was you that tangled with a critter."

Mumbling to herself, Edna sliced the net. "Crazy kid." *Slash.* "Always gettin' into trouble." *Slash.* "Going where you shouldn't." *Slash.* "Like to get yourself killed. Good thing I came home when I did." *Slash. Slash.* "Might've stayed for the fish fry. Might've stayed after my delivery." *Slash, slash, slash.*

Delivery of what? The possibilities were chilling. Delivery where? Kenzie's phone rang.

Its familiarity calmed her. *Take the cruddy bag out of my mouth.*

With one last hack, Edna cut the line free and held her knife high.

Kenzie threw off the tattered net with one hand, pulled out the bag with the other, and spat. *Thipft.* Stuffing the bag in her pocket, she leaped over the turtle nest past Edna. More grit. *Blech.* Kenzie yanked her phone free, scooped up her flashlight, and sputtered. "Ana."

"Chica, are you all right? Almost an hour you have been gone. Salty was barking and barking. Did he find you?"

"Yes. Oh, Ana. You won't believe what happened."

Salty bolted toward Ana's house.

"We'll be there soon." Kenzie hung up and fled as Ancient Angry Edna muttered, "Kid's crazy, all right." Edna hollered at Kenzie's back, "Ungrateful too."

Kenzie burst up the steps and into the house. "Ana, the thief." Her voice quivered. "I caught—I mean, I saw—I tried to—But the creep—"

Ana grabbed Kenzie's hand. "*¡Dios mío!* Are you okay?"

Kenzie collapsed in the chair beside Ana. "I'm fine," she said, her tongue sweeping the salty-sickening grit in her mouth.

"*Gracias a Dios.*"

"I could use some water."

Kenzie followed Ana to the kitchen. "The

thief, did you recognize him?" Ana asked.

"I never saw his face. I couldn't tell who it was. Or if it was a man or a woman." She still wasn't ready to share the whole mortifying story. Even with Ana.

Ana retrieved a glass from the dishwasher. "Here. On the refrigerator door is water."

Kenzie filled her glass. "Be right back." She carried it down the hall to the bathroom sink. Sip, swish, spit. Sip, swish, spit. Again and again. When the sickening bag taste was gone, she returned to the kitchen and refilled her glass.

"Kenzita, I did not get to the road in time. I have no picture. But someone very fast rode away on the same bike."

Kenzie plopped her glass on the counter. She hugged Ana. "Awesome. Seeing the same bike is huge. There's no question now. That bike is important."

Ana peered up at Kenzie. "Is it because of Salty you did not see the thief?" Ana's brow wrinkled with concern, and her thoughts tumbled free in a waterfall of words. "When I returned to the house and opened the door, he escaped under my chair. He was so...?" Her fingers—as if striking a keyboard—rapidly tapped her knees. "Frantic? *Sí*, he was frantic. And you were so long gone. I worried. I could not help you, so I opened the stair gate for Salty. His bark..." She sighed heavily. "*Lo siento mucho*. I am sorry. Too soon he alerted the thief."

"No. No. His barking probably *saved* me." *And gave Edna an excuse to return and play nice.*

"*Bien*. Good." Ana released her brake. "I

must tell the KTC members how important that bike is." She headed for her computer.

Yes, that devious woman had returned. Yikes. She was still there when I left. She could have taken the eggs after I ran.

"Oh my gosh, Ana. The nest is exposed. I have to go back. I have to protect it."

"Wait, chica, think what happened."

"Won't happen again. There's been too much activity. Nobody's going to come back now. Don't worry. I'm taking my turtle dog with me." Kenzie flew down the stairs, hesitated at the bottom, and called up. "Oh, I owe your dad a new net. I'll explain later." She took off again.

Salty found the nest before Kenzie's light did. At least a dozen eggs were exposed. Hopefully, dozens more lay safely underneath. Little by little she brushed sand back into the hole, praying that the embryonic membranes Fisher had described as so delicate were not torn, and the babies would live. Then she found the marker stakes and worked them into the sand. "Come on, Salty. That's all we can do. Let's hope the jerk's been scared away from this nest for good."

When she came out of the woods, Kenzie glanced out to sea. Light shone through *The Bard's* windows. Fisher now lived as close to the beach as Edna. A fact Ted read all wrong. A friend to PAT and Kenzie, Fisher would never hurt baby turtles. Or her. Ancient Angry Edna would, though. In a heartbeat.

The bike with the flag was the key. Find it, find the poacher. Kenzie reviewed the facts related to the bike. Angelo had found a receipt for bicycle tires by a destroyed nest. A bike with new tires was seen at the locations—and within the time frame—of two raids. The dark, probably black, bike flies the state flag of Alaska on its rear bumper. Its rider sped away after the interruption of the last robbery.

One issue could weaken the bike's significance—if a boat had approached the beach before sundown. That would mean the thief could have come by boat, instead of bike. If that had happened though, wouldn't Fisher have let them know? No. How could he? Fisher didn't have a phone. She'd have to wait for that answer. No matter. The bike was key. She was absolutely, positively sure of it.

And yet...the bike/Edna connection continued to mess with her mind. Why ride a bike to a location so close to your house? To create a decoy. Any other reason? Absolutely. Edna could be plain lazy. *Or...* She could have an accomplice, a partner in crime. The bike wasn't getting Ancient Angry Edna off the hook. No way.

As if Salty were as tired of the whole darn puzzle as she was, he pulled on the leash. "Okay, puppy. Let's get back to Ana."

Kenzie'd finally had to unwind. Who better to tell than the one person she could trust with her deepest secrets? Her legs draped over the armchair, she frantically scratched the bites on both ankles and finished her disastrous story.

"Seriously, Ana. It was like being wrapped in a giant spider web while hordes of mosquitoes raced the spider to see who'd devour me first. If I'd been there much longer, I would be a skeleton."

Ana covered her choking cough with a hand. There was no way to hide her laughing eyes.

"It's not funny. Look at my legs. I'm a living pincushion. What if I'd been forced to call Angelo for help?"

"He will find out anyway." Ana dug into a bowl of peanuts, then offered the dish for Kenzie.

"Not if I can help it." Kenzie popped a handful of nuts into her mouth.

"I cannot believe Ancient Angry Edna freed you. Do you really think she can be the robber after that?"

"Well, she did get there pretty soon after I got... " She couldn't bring herself to say, *trapped.* "And she tried to get me to believe she'd been making deliveries or something."

Ana managed one *pobrecita*, before she broke into giggles again.

Kenzie tossed a peanut at Ana. "Cut it out. You're as bad as Angelo."

"I am sorry, Kenzita. But you have to admit—"

"I'm *sure* it was Edna." Except there had been that fleeting moment when the thought of an angry fisherman entered her head... "She came back with an alibi to throw me off the scent. It has to be her."

Kenzie didn't mention the conflict between

fishermen and turtles. What if that made its way back to Ted? It would further fuel his distrust of Fisher. Ted would have a great time with the fact that some turtles—in addition to eating lobsters and crabs—also eat sponges.

"Let's focus, Ana." Kenzie moved to Ana's computer. "I need your input. Yesterday I posted your best photo on the KTC site under 'Wanted.' Now anybody can see it. I want to add a caption. What should I say?"

"Okay." Ana exchanged her grin for a thoughtful expression. "Keep it simple. How about, 'If you've seen this bike, contact... then fill in your e-mail address."

Headlights brightened the room, and Mr. Muñoz's van pulled into the drive.

"Close the page, Kenzie. About this investigation my parents know nothing."

"I hope we solve this case before *any* of our parents learn about it and freak." Out of habit, Kenzie patted her pocket for Salty's leash and felt the hated bag. "Crap. What do I do with this thing?" She pulled the filthy plastic free. Wrinkling her nose, she held it up as if it were a reeking gym sock. "Did you come up with any ideas about how to reduce the use of these things yet?"

Ana seemed about to burst.

"Don't you dare laugh. I mean other than for shutting people up."

"Oh, chica. I am sorry. I know it was awful for you." As if erasing a white board, Ana slowly wiped both hands over her face. "I have only this thought: Before at the shopping center, store owners have let us post signs. We could try that again."

"Yeah. Reminder posters. Like: *Did you remember your reusable bags?* Or—Kenzie mimicked the goofy grin and wiggling eyebrows of a bad comedian—*Bags in your trunk don't carry your junk.*"

Ana groaned. "A poet you are not."

Beep. Beep.

"It sounds like *Papi* is not coming in."

Kenzie stood. "Guess I better get going then." She locked her hands behind her neck and stretched. "I sure hope we get a break soon."

"I will call Lakisha about the bag idea, and someone will recognize that bike. Do not worry."

"Right."

Kenzie's *what if* worries raced her to the van. What if fishermen really were to blame? What if Ancient Angry Edna really had returned just to play the heroine? What if Edna actually made deliveries, and what if she delivered *venison... and turtle eggs?*

24

KENZIE'S RING TONE dragged her out of a long-awaited sleep. Well into the early hours, thunderous storms had kept her busy piling pillows over her head. Blurry-eyed, she reached for her phone, grumbling at its display.

"Angelo, it's only six thirty."

"Get used to it, Red. School starts soon."

Kenzie moaned.

"Listen, about Ancient Angry Edna."

He couldn't know about last night already.

"You there? Wake up."

Hearing Edna's name was no way to wake up. "I'm here."

"Her last name's Jenkins, right?"

"Uh-huh."

"Thought so. Get dressed. We're going over there."

He must know. But how? "Quit messing with me." Kenzie closed her eyes. "I'm going back to sleep." She dropped the phone by her pillow.

"Earth to Red." She envisioned his hands funneling the sound. "We *are* going to Ancient

Angry Edna's house."

He *did* sound serious. She retrieved the phone. "You're not kidding, are you?"

"No joke. Dad's making a big delivery to a Ms. Jenkins on Turtle Beach."

"What? " She mentally replayed what he'd said. "Why does she need a bunch of seafood?"

"No idea. Doesn't matter. We're going."

The more Kenzie awakened, the more maddening her mosquito bites became. Their itch brought vivid images of last night's terror. "Fine, go. You don't need me." No way she'd say the real reason she didn't want to go. "Besides, what's your dad's delivery have to do with us?"

"It's our only chance to see what's in those buckets and freezers."

"Hmmm." Kenzie roused. That wasn't a bad idea. Still... Ancient Angry Edna? After last night?

In his kennel, Salty sounded his let-me-out-of-here morning message.

"In a minute, puppy." Kenzie rubbed her eyes. "Why would your dad take you or me on a delivery?"

"I told him we wanted to check the turtle nests."

"Not bad. That should work for Mom too."

"Great. Anyone recognize the bike photos?"

"Not as of late last night." Kenzie dragged herself to the computer. "I'll check again." She tapped the function key. "Wake up. Wake up." Quickly, she scrolled through her messages, stopping at Ana's. "This is interesting."

"What?" Excitement upped his volume.

"What happened?"

"There was a cast net on Ana's bottom step this morning."

"So?" She imagined him staring at his phone with that *What, are you stupid?* face of his. "Her dad probably went shrimping," he said.

Wake up yourself, Kenzie. Keep him from asking any more questions. "It's not a big deal." *Except that it's an unslashed, never-been-used net.* "Ana wanted me to know she had a net. She knew I wanted to practice and that I need to return yours." *Geesh, that's lame.* "You got Ana's message about last night's attempt, right?"

"Yeah. The same bike. Gotta be the poacher."

"You'd think. But no one knows whose bike it is." *Or whose net.* "It sure seemed like a good clue—the best we had—but I can't connect it to a single suspect."

Things were looking totally hopeless. Kenzie wanted to crawl back under her sheet and hide. For about a year. She didn't need Old Turtle to remind her; she couldn't give up. Not even if one single egg remained to hatch. She had made a promise. She had a mission to complete. And it started with facing the day.

"Red, you're in a funk, aren't you?"

"A little."

"I didn't see the back of Edna's bike. It could have a flag."

Not likely. But worth checking out.

"Come on, Red. Snap out of it. How soon can you be ready?"

Salty pawed his cage door.

Kenzie yawned. "As soon as I take care of

Salty."

"Hey, leave him home, okay?"

"Geesh, Angelo. We're going to dog-hater land. I'm sleepy, not stupid."

In less than an hour, they were rattling up US #1 in Mr. Sánchez's truck. Kenzie poked Angelo and raised her voice to speak over the music on the radio.

"Ana thinks we should hang posters in the shopping center to remind people to take their reusable bags to the stores. Do you think we could put some in the tackle shops too?"

"Fishermen aren't going to much care. I tried asking guys at the fish house what else they could carry their bait in. They grunted at me like I was nuts. Mostly I got ignored."

Kenzie leaned into him. "We have to try something with those guys."

"They're not going to budge." Angelo reached into the door pocket. He pulled out a couple fishing weights, then rolled them between his palms.

"Mr. Sánchez?" Kenzie asked. "What did you use to carry fish and bait before we had all these plastic bags?"

Angelo's father dialed down the radio's volume. "*Cubos...* Buckets. Our fish we took in buckets. In the back." He gestured at the back of the truck. "*Grandes cubos.* I use buckets today."

Kenzie peered through the small window behind her. "Fisher uses those buckets like saddlebags on his bike. They'd be great to carry bait. Where do you get your buckets, Mr. Sánchez?"

"Men who build. Many supplies come in buckets. These men give empty buckets to me."

"That's super recycling."

"Never work. Fishermen don't want to save turtles." Angelo shook his head. "Did you forget the ongoing battle between sea turtles and fishermen?"

Thanks for the reminder. She was trying hard to forget.

Mr. Sánchez turned the truck onto Turtle Beach Road. "*Ángel,*" he said. "Not so many men as you think have such anger."

Angelo popped the weights back into the door pocket, crossed his arms, and sank deep into the seat.

Mr. Sánchez glanced at Angelo and sighed.

Oh, Mr. Sánchez, Kenzie thought—not daring to say it out loud—*I hope you're right. Angelo wants the same thing. He just hates to be wrong.*

Except for the DJ on the radio, no one said another word until they arrived at the last place Kenzie wanted to be.

Mr. Sánchez parked next to Edna's fence. He beeped, got out, and lowered the tailgate. When he began to struggle with an oversized cooler, Kenzie jabbed an elbow in Angelo's side. "Do something."

"*Papá.*" He opened the passenger door. "Let me get that."

Mr. Sánchez rubbed his back. "*Gracias,*

Ángel."

Angelo pulled the cooler onto the tailgate. He and Kenzie each grabbed a handle. Lugging the cooler between them, they followed Angelo's dad.

After the familiar sound of a hammer banging the latch, the gate swung inward.

"Well, well..." Edna growled, looking past Angelo's father. Straight at Kenzie. "This is a surprise."

"Surprise?" Mr. Sánchez removed his hat and stepped backward. "Señora Jenkins, you tell me to come this morning, no?" He ran his fingers through his thick, gray hair and looked up at the imposing woman.

Angelo and Kenzie set the cooler down. Hands in his pockets, Angelo concentrated on digging his heel into the ground.

Edna caught Kenzie's eye before shifting her attention to Angelo. "This your boy? Hard to believe. He was a little tyke when I last laid eyes on him."

What? Kenzie twisted her ponytail.

Edna focused on Kenzie next. "You got one of your crew's youngins working for you now too?"

"*Sí, es*— I mean no, no." Mr. Sánchez replaced his hat, then rested his hand on Angelo's shoulder. "*Ángel es mi hijo*, my son." He urged Kenzie forward. "*Y una amiga*, Kenzie." A friend.

Weirdness beyond belief. Edna didn't seem to want Angelo's father to know about their previous encounters. Kenzie searched her brain for a reason. At the moment it didn't matter. Freaky as it was, Kenzie was in total agreement with the lady. She'd rather die than have Angelo find out about last night's humiliation.

Edna muttered, "Such helpful kids." She gave them a meaningful glance. "Go on, you two. Take the cooler." Something in her expression reminded Kenzie of Red Riding Hood's wolf. "You'll have no trouble finding the freezers." True, and what else would they find?

They placed the cooler under the stilt house between the empty animal pen and the freezer chests. The deer were nowhere in sight. What had happened to them? Edna's bike—with no sign of a flag on it—leaned against the pen gate. Angelo quickly withdrew the tread sketch from his pocket, unfolded it, and compared it to each tire. "No match." He tucked it away seconds before his dad and Edna appeared.

"Señora Jenkins, the dinner of fish for *los niños* make already two thousand dollars. Father Murphy is much pleased." Mr. Sánchez opened a freezer and began to add his fresh catch to a pile of frozen fish.

Crap. The freezer held nothing illegal.

"Sunday will be a big day, señora. Already, many boats pay to catch fish for fund raiser. *Mucho dinero.* The children will go."

Go where? Kenzie wondered. She really should read the church newsletter.

"Glad to hear it." Edna screwed the lid off a bucket filled to the top with small fish packed in neat self-lock bags.

Double crap. The buckets are as clean as the freezer.

"Got a couple of new nets," Edna said. "Tried out one this morning. You know, if too many big fish"—she glanced at Kenzie—"get tangled up in those things, they get torn up so you can't catch a thing. Nothin' to do then except replace 'em. New one worked mighty fine."

Torn up nets? New ones?

A grin tugged the corner of Edna's mouth as she handed the bucket to Mr. Sánchez. "You take these. Freeze them for the tournament too."

Unbelievable. Ana's mystery net. A gift from Edna.

"*Muchas gracias, señora.* Always, you give us many buckets of bait for our fishermen." Mr. Sánchez stacked the bait fish in his now-empty ice chest. "For using your freezers, we are most thankful. Father Murphy's tournament will fill them with many more fish to fry. To deliver fish for church dinner you will need help, yes?"

Kenzie didn't listen to Edna's response. She struggled with the facts: Edna wasn't hiding or delivering one single illegal thing. She pulled Angelo aside. "Do you believe this?"

"No." He rubbed his forehead like he needed an aspirin.

Mr. Sánchez closed the freezer lid. "*Ángel,* you want to check the turtle nests, yes? We must soon go. Today is Saturday, but fishermen fish, and customers buy."

"Right," Angelo said. "Let's move, Kenzie."

"Mr. Sánchez and I will have a cup of coffee while you're gone." Edna raised an eyebrow. "Be careful, you two. Protecting sea turtles can be dangerous work." She started up the steps.

Great. Now she's a comedian. Or was that a threat? Kenzie walked away, her stomach curdling.

His arm outstretched, Angelo stopped her. He smacked his forehead and announced as if he'd boated a fifty-pound grouper, "Rome."

"Rome? What are you talking about?"

"Rome—as in the Vatican. Dad often helps Father Murphy sponsor fish dinners and tournaments. I knew the confirmation class wanted to go to Rome. Just hadn't put it all together. But Ancient Angry Edna helping? Whoa."

Yeah, this was a big whoa. Whoa to a lot of suspicions. Like a defeated soldier, Kenzie slogged behind him as they checked the three remaining nests. More than the battle was lost. The entire war was going down. She sank to the sand near the final one. "I was positive Edna was the thief. Turns out she's kind-hearted and a great secret-keeper. She keeps fish in the freezer and bait in the buckets. She doesn't seem much like a turtle egg thief anymore."

"She's lookin' clean all right. Her bike's dark green, not black. No flag. And no tire tread match."

"What do we do now?" Kenzie stared at the ripples on the water. "We're never going to catch the thief."

Angelo stooped beside her, his finger drawing circles in the sand. "Nothing happened to the nests *today*. That's good, right?"

Kenzie allowed herself a small smile as she pulled her ringing phone from her pocket.

"Hey Lakisha. What's up? Hold on. Angelo's here. I'll put you on speaker." Kenzie rested the phone on a piece of driftwood.

Lakisha's voice came through loud and clear. "There's a beach cleanup article in today's *Keys Weekly* and a picture of Ted and his mom."

"Was he stuffing his face?" Angelo asked.

Lakisha laughed. "He couldn't. He had two big garbage bags in his hands. But guess what's in the woods behind him?"

"Tell us." Kenzie waved a mosquito out of her face. "We're not in a guessing mood."

"A bike—with the Alaska flag on it."

Kenzie scooted closer to the phone. "No way."

"Honest. My aunt hung the picture on Winn Dixie's bulletin board. Some balding guy with a greasy ponytail tore it up."

"Why would anyone do that?" Kenzie asked.

"Who knows? Anyway, it didn't work. There's a pile of newspapers in the store rack, and Aunt Joan hung another picture. Since that bike was there on cleanup day, it must belong to a member of KTC. Why do you think no one told us?"

Kenzie wrapped her arms around her knees and hung her head. "I don't know what to think any more."

The truck horn beeped, and Angelo aimed his thumb at Edna's house.

"Well," Lakisha said, "I wanted to make sure you knew about the photo. See ya, Sunday."

"Kish, wait. Did you hear from Ana? Could your aunt get plastic bags banned at the grocery store?"

"You're swimming upstream, Red," Angelo mumbled.

"Yes, Ana called, and Aunt Joan spoke to the manager. He was sympathetic, but can't do anything."

"Did she tell him about the Key West store?"

"He said that's an independent, so they can make their own rules. It's a corporate decision for Big Pine Grocery."

"Bee boogers. Think he'll let us hang bring-your-own-bag posters in the windows?"

"I'll run that idea by Aunt Joan."

"Thanks for asking, Kish. And thanks for the news...I guess."

Kenzie disconnected and sat in a frozen funk. Each bit of news she'd heard blasted another hole in her theory. "All this time I thought that bike was the major clue. Now, that's as wrong as thinking Edna was the poacher because she poisoned Salty."

Angelo stood and held out his hand, offering to pull Kenzie to her feet. "Are you sure she poisoned him, Red?"

Kenzie focused on the nest beside her. "The only thing I'm really sure of is that I'm getting more and more confused."

"HOW ARE WE EVER GOING TO STOP this horror?" Kenzie massaged her temples. The nest she'd been staring at swirled, then dissolved into Old Turtle's pleading face. Kenzie's eyes filled—for herself or the turtles? She wiped her tears on her sleeve, then blinked. Old Turtle vanished. The nest reappeared. Shaking off the illusion's lingering effects, she raised her face to Angelo. "I may be confused, but there's no way I'm quitting."

"Who said you were?" Angelo pulled her up. "Lakisha's wrong. That bike can't belong to a KTC kid. You sent the picture to all the KTC members, right?"

"Yeah, I did."

"If it belonged to one of them, someone would have told you."

"I haven't heard from all of them." Kenzie dusted the sand off her shorts. "But other people helped that day. It could belong to one of them. We have to figure out who else showed up."

"What about the signup sheet?"

"Good thinking. I'll check it, and we'll go from there."

On the drive home, while Mr. Sánchez and Angelo discussed the business day ahead, Kenzie dissected what Lakisha had told them. That newspaper story was connected with someone or something —a fleeting thought she'd been trying to catch since Thursday. *Who?* Edna, Shalima, Fisher...Zilch. Nothing. *What?* Bike, the color purple, Surf Sandals...Total blank. *Quit trying so hard. It'll come.*

When Kenzie entered the house, Salty yipped and leaped. "Time for a run, puppy?" He scrambled to his leash and back to her again. "Guess that's a yes." She hooked him to the leash and called, "Mom, we're going for a run." Two blocks later, her ponytail flopped free. "Hold it, Salty." She tightened her scrunchy.

Ponytail. That's it. Bald on top. Ponytail below. Jake. The guy who claimed to be counting eggs, yet didn't bother to record his data. Finally. The connection to the nagging suspicion she'd been trying to reel in. Jake tore down the picture. Jake was at the beach on cleanup day. The bike could be—had to be—his. Melissa should know how to reach him by now.

"We're going home, Salty. Now."

The Turtle Hospital line rang eight times before Melissa answered. "Melissa, it's Kenzie Ryan. I'm fine. Just out of breath. Did you find out how I can reach Jake?"

"No way. When?" Kenzie slumped at her desk. Another dead end. "Did anyone say why he's leaving? Salmon fishing? Where?" Kenzie

253

leaped like an Olympic winner. "Actually, it's perfect news. Thanks a million." *Skip the signup sheet. I've got something better.*

Kenzie left the news on Angelo's phone, then called Ana. No answer, so she left a message: "Ana, I think we've got him." She hung up as Mom came into the kitchen.

"Sweetie, have a bite with me before I go to the hairdresser." Mom pulled two salads out of the refrigerator, placed them on the counter, and handed Kenzie the *Keys Weekly.* "Mike came by with it. That's a great shot of Ted and his mom, don't you think?"

The color photo was three columns wide. *A purple plaid shirt on the bike's basket. Yes.* She slapped the paper on the counter.

"What's wrong? I think it's a good photo. It's certainly clear."

"It's awesome, Mom." *More awesome than you know.*

"It's wonderful coverage for you kids." Mom handed Kenzie the salad dressing. "Oh, don't forget, Fisher will be here long before I get home. His pay's in the silverware drawer."

"I'll give it to him." *After he explains why he called Jake a "frequent defender" of sea turtles. That's looking seriously bogus.*

On her way out, Mom said, "Think about whether you want to go to the movies with Mike and me this evening. I'm going to run a few errands and go to the grocery after my appointment. I'll be back around 6:30."

Kenzie checked messages—for the fourth time. Still nothing on the bike. While waiting for Fisher, she skimmed a novel. Chapters flew by. She couldn't remember one scene. She turned on the TV. Flipped a dozen channels. Each one boring. Picked up her iPod. Put it down. No way she'd hear Fisher arrive.

With excess energy and no target for her frustration, she went outside to pull weeds. "I'm not afraid of you." She grabbed a prickly sandspur and yanked. "Take that." She pulled another. "It's over for you." A huge clump ripped loose. "Your nasty friends too." As the pile of garbage bags grew higher, her frustration eased, but she'd worked all afternoon with no sign of Fisher. It was nearly 5:30. Where was he?

She'd dragged the first bag onto the street and was returning for the next when Salty barked. Fisher cycled toward them. His basket overflowed with junk, and two heavy-duty contractor buckets were mounted over his back tire, hanging like saddlebags. That explained it. He'd been making recycling runs.

Fisher swooped from his bike. He propped it against a telephone pole, taking care not to spill his treasured discards.

"Allow me." He rushed to her side. One by one, he piled the bags by the roadside. "How else may I be of service?"

"Thanks." Kenzie wiped her hands on her shorts. "You can help me figure out a mystery. Come on up. I've got your money, and I want to ask you some questions."

The laugh lines around Fisher's eyes crinkled. "Indeed, I would expect nothing less from such an inquisitive maiden."

The minute Fisher sat at the breakfast bar, Salty rolled on his back begging for a belly rub. "Patience, faithful comrade. Your mistress requires assistance."

Kenzie poured Fisher a glass of tea. "Did you see any boats at Turtle Beach yesterday?" She handed him his pay.

He folded the cash, then placed it deep in his worn leather knapsack. "I spent the day seeking the elusive sponge and returned before the sun retired. I marked no vessels thereafter."

So, the thief had come by land—on the mystery bike. "Fisher, remember me telling you about the PAT guy, Jake, who didn't write down his egg counts? You called him a 'frequent defender.'"

He nodded.

"What else do you know about him?"

"Of his countenance I know naught, only his reputation as one of this season's most enthusiastic and reliable guardians."

"Well, there goes that idea. You were my last hope."

Fisher stoked his beard. "This is of great import to you?"

Kenzie propped her elbows on the counter "Yeah, it is." She sank her chin into her fists.

"Nobody seems to know him. Wait. You said *this* season. He wasn't a PAT member before?"

"He was not."

"Oh my gosh. Joining Protect-A-Turtle is the perfect cover up."

"Alas, I do not follow."

"This is the first season turtle nests have been robbed, right?"

"I believe that to be true."

Kenzie twirled a strand of hair on her finger. "Melissa said Jake's leaving the Keys tomorrow. I think he's the one robbing sea turtle nests."

Fisher rubbed one calloused hand with the other. His gnarled fingers clinched, as if itching to strangle someone. "What brings you to this conclusion?"

"I met him on the day of the beach cleanup. I told you he didn't write anything down. Remember? What if he fakes his reports? He could steal eggs from nests no one ever knows about. What if that's the reason he joined PAT? And why he volunteers so often?"

"Treachery." Fisher's eyes narrowed. "Continue."

"The newspaper did a story on the beach cleanup. It included a photo of a bike with the Alaska state flag on its back fender. A nest was robbed the day of the cleanup, and that's the same day I met Jake. On the beach."

Fisher nodded thoughtfully.

"A guy matching Jake's description ripped that bike photo off the Winn-Dixie bulletin board. I think it's his bike in the picture. That same bike was seen at Turtle Beach when other nests were robbed."

"Intriguing tale, indeed." Fisher sipped his tea. "However, it lacks a link twixt Jake and Alaska."

"Oh? Wait 'til you hear why Jake's leaving." She smacked her palm on the countertop. "He's taking a new job: salmon fishing...in *Alaska*."

"The plot thickens. Salmon, the king of cold-water fish. Seasonal fishermen have long traveled between Alaska and the Keys. As the season in Alaska is winding down now, this decision does seem suspicious."

"Exactly. We have to prove Jake's the crook. And we only have one day to do it."

Fisher picked up his knapsack. "Perhaps the time is ripe for my reading lesson."

"Fisher, not now. *I* need help. I need to concentrate on trapping Jake."

"Patience, my dear." Fisher rummaged in his bag and withdrew several bits of damp, bright yellow paper. He placed them on the counter and fit the damaged pieces together, forming a puzzle smeared with purple ink. He slid two legible pieces toward Kenzie. "I comprehend enough to find these intriguing. In light of your tale, I trust you will find them more so."

Fisher tapped the first scrap. "This word I know: *stop*. What sayeth this word?"

"*Delivery*. It says 'Stop delivery.'" Great, another mysterious delivery. *First Edna's, now whose?* Kenzie pointed. "What's on that piece?"

Fisher pushed the other yellow, smeary scrap closer. It was written in the same flowery style.

Kenzie examined it closely. "The only words I can make out are *too late*. Where did you find these papers?"

Fisher took a purple bag from his knapsack. From it, he pulled out a tattered white note. "Exactly where I found this."

"Fisher, is that bag what I think it is?"

"All in good time." He framed a small section of the white, ragged paper with his weathered hands. "Herein lies the intrigue."

Kenzie stood for a better view of what Fisher wanted her to read. In black ink and block letters, were written the words *salmon fishing*.

"Fisher, move your hands. Show me the rest."

He uncovered the four-line note.

"The first line says something about *last chance*. The only clear word in the second line is *know*, like you *know* because you've learned something. I can't make out any more words in the third line than what you already read, *salmon fishing*. The last line says *Pay up or else*.

Fisher raised his eyebrows. "What thinkest thou?"

She dropped to her stool. "Blackmail."

"Indeed."

"The mention of salmon fishing can't be a coincidence." Kenzie flipped over the purple satin bag. "I knew it. It's a *Shalima's Secrets* bag. Now, will you tell me where you found all this? And, please, just the facts."

"How I love an intricate tale." Fisher finished his tea. "Alas, as you wish." No question. A pout lurked somewhere in all his facial hair.

"As I was on this side of the island today, I visited my favorite treasure trove."

"Junkyard, right?"

"All in the eyes of the beholder, my dear. I noticed the open door on an old stove. Envisioning newfound riches, I investigated, finding only this sodden purple bag."

"Was the white note inside the bag when you found it?"

"It was."

"What about the yellow papers?"

"Strewn hither and yon. Aftermath of a festival for masked brigands."

"Fisher, please. Just the facts."

"Ah, the impatience of youth. I shall explain." He picked up one of the yellow scraps and pointed. "Tooth marks." Then he waved it in circles. "Fragments were scattered about the stove in a muddle of raccoon tracks, scat, and—"

"Scat?"

"If you prefer, poop."

"Ew."

"As I was saying, shredded paper, tracks, scat, and food scraps were unmistakable signs. Signs that the masked marauders were browsing and feasting." He touched Kenzie's hand. "My dear, the creatures were dining on sea turtle eggs."

RACCOONS. TURTLE EGGS. JUNKYARD. *How did these new pieces fit in the puzzle?* Kenzie chewed on her ponytail. "Fisher, how would turtle eggs get in a junkyard?"

"Perchance within a plastic bag, the remnants of which were in close proximity."

"Ugh. Those things are everywhere."

Salty scampered to the back door.

Fisher lifted a hand to his ear. "Hark," he said, as the puttering of an outboard motor grew louder.

Kenzie glanced at the wall clock. "Six o'clock. I bet that's Angelo. I sent him a message about Jake. Wait till he hears your news."

A short while later, Angelo perched on the stool beside Kenzie. He wore a silent mask of intensity as Fisher retold his story.

"I pray my tale has proven significant to you both. I have naught else to offer." Fisher gripped the counter's edge and creaked to a stand. "Though I wish it otherwise, I must tarry no longer. I prefer to traverse the island before night falls." He slung his knapsack over his shoulder. "Kenzie, though you are wise beyond your years, it would be a grave error in judgment should you not reveal your suspicion to our esteemed wildlife officer."

"Don't worry. I'll tell Mike." *But not until I can prove it.*

"Farewell, young sleuths. I bid you good hunting."

Fisher was barely off the front porch when Angelo said, "Spill, Red." He shifted the tattered notes around on the counter like a magician practicing sleight of hand. "Why'd Fisher bring these to *you?*"

Kenzie hesitated. *Would Fisher want Angelo to know about their reading lessons?*

"You're teachin' him to read, aren't you?" His elbows thudded on the countertop. Covering his face, he ground his palms into his forehead. Minutes passed. His shoulders rose, then fell, again and again. Each time with a sigh. Finally, he groaned, sounding more like a wounded animal than a regretful boy. "I should've done that for Mom."

I knew it. He feels guilty. Angelo honestly thought if he'd taught his mother to read English, she would have understood the directions—understood how dangerous her medications could be. That she'd be alive. He was finally opening up.

Oh, Angelo. He so needed a hug, and Kenzie was beyond ready to hug him. Facing him, she reached for his shoulder, smacked into his invisible force field, and backed off. So much for opening up. *Don't set him off. Give him time.*

She gathered and stacked the paper scraps. Yellow pile. White pile. Rearranged them. Small pieces. Large pieces. Over and over. When it seemed he'd never look up, she braved ending the silence. "Your mother was super sick, wasn't she?" If she hadn't already known the answer, she wouldn't have understood his garbled response.

"Cancer. Terminal."

"Angelo, you couldn't have helped that."

His feet fidgeted. "Could've tried."

"Just because you try doesn't make it work." How could she pull him out of this? Connect with him? "I used to think I could have done something to make Dad stick around."

Angelo's head jerked up. "Yeah?" His eyes accused.

Uh-oh. Nice job of not setting him off.

"You've still got a dad, though. Don't you?"

She'd pushed him away. *Again.* Was she ever going to learn?

Beep. Beeeep. The insistent Jeep horn blasted her idiotic comment out of the air, rescuing them from the awkward moment.

After dividing the bits of paper again into a yellow pile and a white pile, Angelo peered calmly across the counter at Kenzie. His mood was fickle as the wind. "Fisher's right, you know." Propping his feet on the cabinets under the counter, he leaned back and asked, "When are you going to tell Mike?"

Another successful deflection. He should be on the football team.

"Soon. Mom's been shopping. She must need me to carry bags. After I help her, let's go over what we know."

"I'll be workin' on the boat. Got some loose bolts."

Kenzie hung the empty green carryall bags on a hook, and Mom put the last can in the cabinet. "Sweetie, thanks for helping me carry these up. What did you decide? Do you want to go to that pirate movie in Key West with Mike and me? We're going to the late show."

"Can Angelo come? He's out back working on his boat."

"Of course."

From the bottom step, she called, "Angelo, want to go to the pirate movie?"

"Snapper are spawning. I'm fishin'."

Kenzie crossed the yard to the dock. "It'll probably be on DVD soon anyway." She climbed into the stern, shoved Angelo's tackle box out of the way, and sat facing him. "Okay, what do we know so far?"

Angelo began to rig a fishing rod. "You saw a suspicious person run away on the beach the day you—" He stopped for emphasis. "*Borrowed* my boat."

"Old history." Kenzie shot him a get-over-it look. "Right. A person wearing a purple plaid shirt. That started the purple curse. Ancient Edna wore purple, too, the first day I ran into her."

"Forget her. She's ruled out."

"But the plaid shirt's not." Kenzie showed him the newspaper. "Look in the basket of the bike."

"So, the shirt connects the person on the beach last Thursday and the person who owns the bike. Let's follow the bike."

"We have a connection between the bike and Jake now." Kenzie waved an imaginary flag. "He's going salmon fishing in Alaska."

Pulling the line on his rod, Angelo tested its drag. "Same bike was at Turtle Beach when someone messed with two nests. And Fisher's discovery of that note with eggshells ties whoever's going salmon fishing with turtle eggs."

Kenzie counted evidence on her fingers. "If the Alaska bike's connected with the wrecked nests, and Jake's connected with both the bike and salmon fishing, which is tied to Alaska, and salmon fishing is tied by the note with the turtle eggs in the junkyard..." Kenzie folded her fingers into fists and rubbed her temples. "Geesh. Mike will think I'm crazy if I try to explain this. We're missing something. Why was that block-lettered note in one of Shalima's bags?"

Angelo dropped the rod in its holder. "The salmon fishing note? It's a threat, right?"

"That's what I think." She unwrapped a stick of gum and put it in her mouth.

"What if the salmon fishing guy... Say it's Jake. What if Jake delivered eggs to the stove in the junkyard?"

"Yeah, the drop-off spot." Kenzie twisted her ponytail. "But the pick up person never got the eggs because the raccoons ate them."

"Right, so the pick-up dude didn't pay up. What if Jake wasn't supposed to know who gets the eggs, but he found out?"

"Maybe that's what the note meant. 'I *know* who you are.' He could have put the note in the Secrets bag as proof that he *did* know—to threaten Shalima."

Angelo slid another rod from under the seat. "We gotta figure out the other note. The yellow one that was all chewed up. Why would Shalima want the eggs?"

"That's the question. With all those chickens, it's not like she doesn't have plenty of eggs already."

"Kenzie," Mom called out the kitchen window. "Ana's on the phone. She's been trying to call you."

"Oops. I must have turned it off. Tell her to try again, Mom."

Kenzie answered on the first ring. "Hey, Ana. Big news—it's that PAT guy, Jake. He might be on to us, though, because he's moving to Alaska. That would explain the flag on the bike."

Kenzie poked Angelo with her bare foot to get his attention. "Wait a second." She punched the speaker button on her phone. "Angelo's here. What'd you say about Ted?"

"Also Ted tried to call you. A few minutes ago he saw the bike on Mango Lane."

"Did he give you the address?"

"He said only that it is a purple-and-yellow house."

"Shalima's house. Ana, stay on the line." She

lowered the phone. "Angelo, we've got to get over there. Now."

Angelo rested his hand on the fishing rod he'd positioned in the rod holder. "Boat's the fastest way, but—"

"Ana, listen. We're going to Shalima's. If you don't hear from me by 8:30, call Mike." Kenzie recited Mike's number. "Fill him in. He'll know what to do."

"*Chica*, this man, if he is the poacher, he is dangerous. Please, do not do this. Tell Mike."

"Not until we have proof." Kenzie hung up before Ana raised more doubts in her mind.

"Red, Ana's right, you know."

"I want all the pieces before I talk to Mike. If we catch Jake at Shalima's, I think we'll get them. We've got to get over there. The question is what do I tell *Mom*?"

"Want to go snapper fishin'? Beats a movie."

"I'll try it." She clambered out of the boat, dashed up the steps, and burst into the kitchen. "Angelo doesn't want to—" Mom was on the phone. "Oops. Sorry."

"Hold on, Mike." Mom turned to face her. "Okay. We'll take him some other time then, sweetie."

"He's going snapper fishing because they're spawning. I don't really get it, but it sounds like a big deal." Kenzie remembered a frequent phrase of Angelo's. "He's kind of in a hurry to 'catch the bite.' Can I go with him? We won't go far out."

"I'm sorry, Mike. What did you say?" Mom's brow wrinkled. "Are you certain?" She kept a hand on Kenzie's arm while she listened to Mike.

Then she lowered the phone. "I have reservations about this, but Mike says it's a great chance, and he knows Angelo is a safe boater. I want you here long before we return from the movie. "Sorry, Mike. I didn't get that." Mom tightened her grip on Kenzie's arm while she listened, then she looked into Kenzie's eyes. "Sweetie, Mike has a good idea. You can go *if* you promise to call me from the house phone as soon as you get home."

"Deal." Kenzie hugged Mom and spoke into the receiver. "Thanks, Mike. See you after the movie." She sped to her room to change into her bathing suit, emptied a lidded plastic box, and sealed her cargo shorts and phone inside it. She hesitated. What if she had to take photos in the dark? She tossed in her camera as well.

She flew out the back door before Mom could change her mind. Salty scampered ahead and had leaped on the boat before she made it to the bottom step.

Shutting down the engine, Angelo quietly rowed into Shalima's canal. Unlike the canal Kenzie lived on, there were few docks built along this one. In many places, its coral rock walls were topped with tangled weeds, mangrove and buttonwood trees, nearly camouflaging some of the homes beyond them.

"How come these houses aren't on stilts?"

"Built before the code required it."

Somewhere a dog barked, startling a great blue heron.

"What if Salty barks?" Angelo asked.

"He's staying in the boat."

"As if he knows what *stay* means."

"We'll tie him to a cleat with one of your lines."

"We can try." Angelo glanced to the west. "Sun's sinking fast. That's good for us."

Shalima's property, though thick with vegetation in front, was clear of undergrowth along the canal and easily recognized. Angelo rowed past, looking for a place to dock out of sight. "We'll tie up at the third light down and swim back."

"Perfect. Shalima's dock ladder can't be seen from her house. The shed's in the way. We'll have cover climbing up."

As the dark deepened, houselights along the canal provided spotty illumination. Angelo cut the running lights, then tied the boat to a piling. When he pulled off his T-shirt Kenzie did her best to ignore his bare chest. He'd always kept it on when the sun blazed. *Focus, girl. We have a crime to solve.*

Kenzie double-checked the seal on the plastic box. "Want to put your phone in here?"

"Nope." Angelo patted his tackle box. "Insurance. Keep one on board and take one on shore."

"Backup plan. I like it." Kenzie untied her sneakers.

"No bare feet."Angelo dragged his gear bag from under his seat. "Wanted to be prepared in case I had to wade in or out of a tight spot tonight." He rummaged in it, then pulled out two pairs of dive boots. "Good. Thought I still had my old ones." He handed her a pair. " These should fit you." He tugged on the others. "We don't know what we're getting into."

No kidding. More than the terrain worried her. If Jake was part of a gang, how many sickos might be in there? What if they had guns? What if they used them—on kids. She shivered. Temperature drop or rising fear?

"Angelo," she whispered, "are we crazy?"

"Probably." Silent as a snake, he slipped into the water.

Kenzie gripped the box. No second guessing. This was what she'd been waiting for. The fulfillment of her promise. She slid into the canal after Angelo and swam beside him, nosing the floating container forward until they reached Shalima's property.

Once on shore, Kenzie stepped into her cargo shorts. She envied Angelo his multipurpose fishing pants. He wore them to fish or swim, and they dried fast. Hers would soon be soggy, but she needed the pockets. She stowed the camera and phone, then set the box on the canal bank.

What was that funky smell? Ammonia? They crept forward. "Ew! Good thing you gave me booties. I stepped in chicken—"

"Shh. Follow me."

They crept past the shed, source of the odor, then across the backyard. The back of the house was closed and dark. After squeezing through the surrounding jungle, they found an open side window and crouched below it.

"Listen," Kenzie whispered. "Somebody isn't happy."

Through the small, cluttered living room, they zeroed in on the open front door. Shalima— back straight and one hand on her hip—stood silhouetted by the porch light. "I'm sorry. I can't help you." She shifted to one side.

"That's him. That's Jake."

Angelo elbowed her. "Shh."

"I'm closed for the day." Head held high, she sounded like an empress scolding her minions. "In any case, I'm certain I don't carry anything you want. Whatever it may be."

"Restoration." Jake patted his bald spot. "Maybe I want to restore my hair."

Shalima's hand moved to the doorknob. "The entire inventory of my restoration products can't solve your problem." She pushed the door toward him.

Jake kicked the door panel. "Don't play dumb." He wedged his foot against it like a doorstop. "You know who I am, and I know who you *really* are and what you're doing."

As if his words were darts, Shalima gripped the door and stepped back.

She's scared. Kenzie shot Angelo a look and mouthed, *We were right.*

"You got careless." Jake leaned into Shalima's face. "Careless when you stuffed cash in last week's payoff envelope." He jabbed her with his finger. "Lady, you owe me for last night's delivery. It came up short, but you're going to pay in full." He sneered. "Tonight."

Shalima backed further into the room. "I don't know what you're talking about."

"No? Then let me *restore* your memory." Jake

raised his fist to her face. "I got to thinking about where I'd seen this little beauty. Came to me it was on some crazy lady at the flea market."

Jake opened his hand. "Recognize this?"

Something in his palm gleamed. Shalima tried to snatch it. "Give me that ring, you fool."

Jake shoved the ring in his pocket. "I'm fool enough to call the sheriff and tell her what I know about my *employer*." Self-assured, he folded his arms. "You can count on it. I'll call the sheriff... unless you offer me a little bonus. Five hundred ought to do it."

"Get out," Shalima shrieked. "I'll call the sheriff myself." She reached for the phone on the table. "She's a customer of mine."

"Whoa." Palms up, Jake halted her. "I wouldn't do that if I was you." Rubbing his forefinger over his mouth like a windshield wiper, he sneered. "I spent some time in that shed of yours." He held up a key. "You really should pick a safer hiding spot."

Slow and cold as a glacier, Shalima lowered her hand.

"Lady, there's a lot more than chicken egg shells in that bucket out there."

Shalima sagged.

"Your sign says *Shalima's Secrets*. I'm thinking you got just *one* secret—a great big illegal secret."

So the chickens are nothing but a cover-up? Kenzie's stomach churned like the contents of a cement mixer.

"You don't—"

"Shut up," Jake roared. "The fun's over. This

business is getting dicey. I'm moving out of these lousy islands. After what happened last night, I deserve—"

"You deserve nothing. I told you to stop the deliveries. I left a message with the last..."

Pistol-like, he aimed his finger at her.

She backed further into the living room.

Jake followed.

"I told you *no more*. It's too late in the season. They're too developed."

Wide-eyed, Kenzie poked Angelo and mouthed, *That explains the yellow note.*

"I never got no message." Jake was inches from Shalima's face. "So you owe me for the last delivery."

Kenzie cringed at what his breath might smell like.

Shalima slumped into an easy chair like an empty canvas bag. "I don't have that much money here." She picked at the upholstery on the seat cushion.

Bumping Kenzie's shoulder with his, Angelo gestured to the canal.

"Not yet," she whispered.

A hand on each arm of her chair, Jake loomed over Shalima. "Well, lady, it's a new game now."

Shalima loosened and retied the ends of her head wrap. "I need time. Go. Now. You should never have come here. What if someone sees you?"

"What are you worried about? Nobody knows the real story—yet."

Shalima flattened against the chair. "But plenty of people know your bicycle. Those pesky kids put pictures of it all over the Internet."

"That's an easy problem to fix." Jake's words were menacing. "I can—"

Earsplitting screeches and yowls split the air.

"Cat fight." Angelo backed away from the window. "Time to go."

Warning barks joined the howls.

Jake stood. "You got a dog, lady?" He moved toward the door.

"No." Shalima followed him.

"Stay here." Jake shoved her away from the door. "Don't get any ideas. We're not finished. I'll be back, and I'll smash down this door if I have to."

"The canal." Angelo pulled Kenzie away from the window. "Now."

"No. The shed. I need pictures."

He sprinted ahead.

Had he heard her?

Splash. He was gone.

KENZIE RACED FOR THE SHED in her squishy dive boots. "Be open. Be open."

The padlock hung loose. She charged inside, startling the small flock of roosting chickens. Several flew past her head, escaping through the open door. She flinched. Something brushed her face. A chain. Kenzie yanked it. *Click*. Light washed over her—a spotlighted target. Bad idea. She yanked again. Turned toward the shelves. Snapped her picture. Flash.

Wham. The door slammed.

The padlock clicked.

Jake snarled. "I should've finished you the first time I had you trapped. Meddling brat. You're hard to get rid of. So's that mangy dog of yours."

Bam. Bam. Bam. Kenzie pounded the door. "*You* poisoned Salty!"

"Yeah. Same as those greedy coons. Trying to beat me to the goods."

"You're... you're..." No word was vile enough. She kicked the door. *Thud.*

"Treated that mutt to the goods twice—that I know of." He growled. "Still wasn't enough. Been nothin' but trouble. Both of you. I got you now, though. The mutt's next."

Thursday. On the beach. Salty chased Jake. Kenzie rested her head against the door. *Please, don't bark again, Salty. Please. Maybe he won't find you.*

"How'd those chickens get out?"

Shalima. Now they were both out there.

"Who's in there with my chickens?" Shalima fretted, clucking like a mother hen. "Tell me. Who?"

"That kid with the nosy mutt. She heard us."

He doesn't know about Angelo.

"A dog? No, no, no. A dog's in there with my chickens?"

"Take it easy, crazy lady. Just the girl."

"Now what?" Shalima whined, not sounding at all relieved. "My beautiful solutions. My treasured secrets. Everything's falling apart."

"Told you the fun was over, lady."

"Yes. Yes." Shalima switched into business gear. "What'll we do about her?" The queen of secrets was back.

"Leave it to me." Jake snorted. "Someone drowns around here every week."

Kenzie grabbed a shelf for support. Imagining the headline: *Star Swimmer Drowns*, she didn't catch Shalima's response to Jake's solution. His next words though came through loud and clear.

"Double the five hundred, and your problem will disappear. Back to the house, boss. I need my money up front."

Their voices faded. Kenzie pulled out her cell phone. Dead. Again. Double-crud dead. No problem. Angelo would call the sheriff. Would there be time for her to get here?

Kenzie's heart raced. What time was it? Would Ana call Mike? Fear gripped her chest. What if he turned his cell off in the movie? Could he do that? He was always on call. Wasn't he?

Relax. Breathe. Angelo's out there somewhere. He'll come up with something.

She pulled the light chain. No reason to hide now. She looked around for a way out of the flimsy place. On each wall, regularly spaced wire-covered holes opened high above the shelves—too small to climb through. Between many wallboards, wide gaps allowed the exchange of light and air. One gap provided a perfect view of the canal.

Several houses down, a dock light cast a glow on Angelo's boat. What was he doing? After checking the line that secured Salty's collar, he eased down into the canal with something under his arm. Her plastic box. He'd taken it back to the boat for some reason. He slid an oar out of the boat, then swam with an awkward breast stroke, floating the oar beside him and nudging the box ahead. Soon he disappeared in the shadows. On board, Salty alternated between chewing on the rope and barking at it.

If Salty made it to shore, Jake would kill him. She reached around, above, and between grumbling chickens, prodding and pulling each wallboard she could grasp. Unfortunately, gaps between boards didn't mean flimsy construction. Numerous hen pecks and splinters later, she collapsed—defeated—on an overturned bucket.

Nothing to do but wait. Wrong. Document the evidence. Turning in circles, she captured images of the walls from top to bottom and left to right. No detail would go unnoticed. She snapped pictures of egg buckets, close-ups of bottles and jars, unlabeled mixtures, charts and graphs, and a framed article from a beauty magazine dated this month.

What was that about? She lowered the camera and read the headline: *New Product Line Poised to Launch*. The story featured a young company, *Secrets in Paradise*, that promised *solutions guaranteed to produce luxurious hair and restore skin to flawless radiance*. Shalima's slogan. The article closed with a web address. Shalima was planning to sell online. *Crud. Crud. Crud*. This horror has to stop tonight. *Hurry, Angelo*.

Woof. Woof. With each bark, the chickens grew more restless. Bobbing their heads back and forth, up and down.

Yap. Yap.

Bruk bruk bukkaaaa.

Flap. Flap.

The birds hopped from perch to nest box and shelf to shelf.

Shalima's Secrets bottles crashed.

Eggs splattered.

Feathers flew.

Kenzie snapped pictures, dodged, ducked, and spit feathers.

"Red, you in there?"

Angelo. "Yes, but Salty's—"

"He's fine. Listen. I've strung a trip line across the yard. When I open the door, move along the shed wall. Head straight to the canal."

"Can you get the lock open?"

The padlock rattled. "No problem."

Woof. Woof. That was loud.

More rattling. "It's just a rusty old chicken shi...*ed* lock."

Woof. Woof. Loud and close.

"Salty's loose." Kenzie kicked and fist-hammered the door.

"Stand back, Red."

Bam. Bam. Metal clanked. The door shuddered. *Clang. Bam.* It burst open. A storm of chickens fluttered free. Angelo stood in the opening wielding his battering-ram oar.

"Salty. Where are you?" Kenzie turned one way, then the other.

"Canal." Angelo prodded her. "Go. Now!"

"Yikes." Her foot caught. In what—? Angelo's bait net. "No." She shook her foot free. "Not without you."

Woof. Woof. Salty raced by them. He dashed back and forth, scattering chickens, leaping and snapping at the crazed creatures.

Snap. Shalima's floodlights blazed. Jake roared around the side of the house, tripped over the fishing line, and crumpled. *Thump.*

Kenzie scooped up the net and sped toward him.

"Hey." Angelo whipped after her. "What are you doing?"

281

Jake struggled to his feet. His eyes met Kenzie's. "How? How'd you?" He staggered, then spun, attempting to take off.

Not this time, creep. Kenzie tossed the cast net. *Swish.* Bulls-eye.

Trapped, Jake flailed and squawked as much as the chickens. Entangling himself more, he stumbled, awkward as a monster from the deep.

Whoosh. Angelo swung his oar with lumberjack precision. *Smack.* Jake crashed like a rotten oak. *Thud.* Angelo straddled the thief, wrapped, and rolled him like a cigar. Then he rushed to cut each end of the trip line free. He returned to Jake and wound the filament around the packaged thief, securing his catch.

Salty scampered from Kenzie to Angelo. He pounced on them barking his aren't-you-proud-of-me puppy barks before returning to his joyful chicken chase.

Shalima rounded the corner and charged into the fray, long skirt whirling about her legs. "Oh, my darlings. My beautiful girls." Ignoring the cocooned Jake, she stumbled around the yard, trying to gather frantic chickens with her skirt. "Come to me. Here, chicky, chicky." Bending and scooping, round and round she went in a frenzy of cackling feathers.

Kenzie joined Angelo where he stood guard over the neatly bundled Jake.

"Nice toss. *This* time." He flashed a crooked grin. "You've been practicing."

"A little." If he only knew.

Shalima continued to dance and rave about the yard, waving her arms as if deranged. She ignored Jake, Angelo, and Kenzie too, focusing totally on the chickens. Her scrambled mind had cracked.

The more Salty yapped and chased, the louder Shalima shrieked and grabbed. She didn't catch a single bird until she reached into the red blossoms of a thorny bougainvillea. "Got you." Tucking the grumbling hen under her arm, she backed out of the shrub. Her scarf caught on a barb and came undone. "No. No. No." She fled, howling, one hand on her forehead, one arm grasping the chicken. The scarf unwound. Its loose end trailed on the ground.

Salty latched onto the fluttering cloth and ripped it free. Holding his head high, he pranced around the yard with Shalima's wrap flying banner-like behind him.

Shalima raced for the house and smacked into Sheriff Clark, just rounding the corner. The sheriff scowled. Her deputies stood googly-eyed.

"Did *you* call them?" Kenzie asked.

"Had to be Ana."

Kenzie's heart warmed. She could always count on Ana.

Wailing, Shalima tried to pass the police who blocked her path. "Ruined. All my research ruined." She lifted her long skirt and sobbed into its cloth.

Sheriff Clark, her deputies, Angelo, Kenzie, and even Jake, now alert and furious, stared. They stared at Shalima's long, poofy, polka-dot underwear. And they stared at Shalima's REALLY BIG secret: her hair. Not a silken, alluring halo to *drive men crazy*. A straggly, unsightly jumble of scrawny tufts. Tufts in tarnished shades of green and orange. Tufts that stuck out in all directions and lengths.

Sheriff Clark buried her face in her hands. Her upper body twitched rhythmically. *Was she laughing?* The sheriff mumbled, "Glad I didn't buy her conditioner." She shook her head. "I'm sure going to miss that face cream, though." She took a deep breath, straightened, and ordered, "Unwrap that idiot and cuff both of them." There was more chuckle than command in her voice.

Salty trotted up to Kenzie and Angelo with his prize, but it was bushes parting near the corner of the house that caught Kenzie's attention. *Uh-oh. Mom and Mike.* This scene would not amuse her mother. "Hey, Mom. Hi, Mike. Guess you got Ana's call."

Angelo sidled toward Sheriff Clark, gathering his gear along the way.

"Night fishing, huh?" Mike said. "These are the biggest snappers I've ever seen."

Mom approached Kenzie. Slow and deliberate.

Observing the move, Mike stayed in place. "Seems you kids ended one animal rescue and created the need for another," he said. "There are going to be a lot more homeless chickens."

A breath's space in front of Kenzie, Mom stopped and folded her arms. She slowly shook her head. "I should have known what you've been up to."

"We did it, Mom." Kenzie's voice quivered. "We caught the turtle egg thief. I mean *thieves*."

Mom closed her eyes. Calm before the storm.

Edging forward, Mike said, "Maggie." A gentle reality tweak. His gaze shifted to Kenzie, and his eyes flamed. He was not on Kenzie's side this time. She was in deep, double trouble. Without a life jacket.

"Mom?"

Mom winced. She opened her eyes, took a deep breath, and pulled Kenzie into her arms. Resting her head on Kenzie's wet hair, she asked, "What am I going to do with you?"

"Loan me your phone so I can call Ana?" Kenzie raised her chin. The ghost of a smile on her face. "Then, maybe you could take me to Turtle Beach? I have to know if we really stopped Jake in time."

Mom squeezed her. "Sounds safe enough. *Now*."

"I'm sorry you guys missed your movie."

"No problem," Mike said. "This was quite a show. And it was free." His attempt at humor didn't soften his gaze or halt his twitching jaw.

Mom and Kenzie stood arm-in-arm when Angelo returned. "Here's your box." He handed it to her. "I told Sheriff Clark everything. I'm out of here."

"In a second." Mike touched Angelo's shoulder. "Your father will be proud of what you did tonight."

"Maybe." Angelo draped the cast net around his neck. "If there's still fish out there to catch." Hands in his pockets, he headed toward the canal.

"Angelo," Mom called. "Your mother would also be proud."

Angelo stopped. He lowered his head as if inspecting the ground for something he'd lost. Moments passed before he turned to look at Kenzie's mom, his eyes searching long and deep.

Kenzie tried to go to him, but Mom held her in a hug. "Angelo, your mother would love that you protected Kenzie. It was heroic."

Like a cherished muffler, Angelo tugged his net tight on the back of his neck. He bunched its dangling weights in a fist.

"But, Angelo, you couldn't save her. There was nothing you could do." Mom's tone gripped him like glue. "It's important you know that." He studied the little weights in his hand, rubbing them against each other. A collection of mini worry stones.

Kenzie held her breath. He couldn't handle any conversation about his mom. *Listen to her, Angelo. Please.* She silently counted. At twelve Angelo raised his head. "I appreciate that, Ms. Ryan." He lifted the net off his shoulders. "I better get going."

"Wait." Kenzie broke away from Mom and caught up with him. "Angelo, remember when you called me the Lone Ranger?" She gripped his elbow. "I never wanted to go it alone. I can't. What would I have done if you weren't here?"

He spread his net over her shoulders and gently pulled her toward him. The box fell. Kenzie's heart flipped. Was he about to—?

He swallowed and stepped backwards, gazing over her shoulder. "You...uh...would have thought of something."

The moment dissolved. Kenzie sighed. Like it or not, she needed a new dream. One without Angelo in it.

Salty barked and bolted for the canal.

Fisher motored up in his flat-bottom work boat. Shifting into idle, he surveyed the scene. Seemingly satisfied, he tipped his hat and shifted to reverse.

"Fisher, wait." Angelo swept his net from Kenzie's back and the last bit of hope from her heart. He raced to the canal, net swinging freely. "I'm not up for another swim. Would you take me to my boat?"

On the drive to Turtle Beach, with Salty curled in her lap, Kenzie phoned Ana. Mike and Mom passed we'll-deal-with-this-later looks back and forth while Kenzie told Ana everything—from the moment Ana called with Ted's news to the moment Angelo left with Fisher.

"I'll fill everybody in tomorrow at church, Ana. I promise. Oh, one more thing: We need to visit Edna soon." Kenzie glanced at Mom. "Yes, I'm serious. We need to thank her, uh, for all the bait fish she gave Father Murphy—which she caught with a *brand-new* net. One she didn't *anonymously donate*. Like I said, I'll tell everyone everything tomorrow."

Mike parked his Key Deer Refuge truck along the beach, and Kenzie signed off. "Ana, you saved my life. For real."

"Edna?" Mike asked. "Ana's neighbor? The lady who lives right down the road?"

Mom opened the door. In the cab's light, Kenzie caught Mike's eye. *Don't, Mike. Don't go anywhere with this, please. I know I was wrong about her*. She nudged Mom. *Move. Let me out.*

"Have I met Edna?" Mom asked.

"Probably not." Mike rubbed a hand over his mouth. He seemed to be working things out in his head as he held them in with his hand. Holder of the winning card, last piece of the puzzle. The corners of his eyes crinkled. "She's a gruff old bird, but she's a softy at heart. Lonely, too. She doctors sick and injured deer until they're well enough to release. Everyone at the refuge knows. Not a single officer admits it though. It's nice you girls visit her."

Mike had just sealed the deal. *Mom, you got a keeper.* Kenzie wanted to hug him.

With a mysterious grin on her face, Mom squeezed Kenzie's hand. "There's something else nice you're doing."

"What?"

"When we left for Key West, Mike stopped to pick up his laundry, and we walked by the grocery." She paused, giving her grin growing time.

"No way." Had Kish moved that fast?

"Your friends have been busy. There was a poster in the grocery window reminding shoppers to bring reusable bags."

"Awesome. That's a start."

"I'm proud of you, sweetie, even though you worry me to death." Mom stepped down from the truck. "Do you want us to come with you?"

"Would you guys mind waiting?" Kenzie scooted out, set Salty on the ground, and hooked his leash to his collar. "I won't be long."

"Here, you'll need this." Mike handed her his

289

flashlight. "Take your time. We'll wait for your report."

Hiking a bit awkwardly in Angelo's dive boots, Kenzie meandered through the moonlit trees in search of the nest she'd saved last night. When the flashlight beam fell on it, she gasped. The sand was sinking in several places.

Behind her a twig snapped. *Footsteps.* Kenzie froze. It couldn't be. The horror was over. Wasn't it?

"Red, is that you?"

Kenzie's heart danced into action. Fast. Skip. Quick, quick. Skip. A spark of hope glimmered.

Salty leaped at Angelo, demanding attention and knocking something—a bucket?—out of his hand.

"Settle down, Salty." Kenzie yanked his leash. "What's in the— I thought you'd gone— How'd you get—?" *Settle down yourself, girl.*

"Thought you might need these." He pulled her sneakers and T-shirt out of the bucket. "Couldn't get out of the canal. Low tide. I can't pole across the sandbar like Fisher. My draft is too deep. Dad picked me up." Angelo tilted his head toward the road. "He's up there now getting the story from your mom and Mike."

"But how'd you know I'd be here?"

"I didn't."

"Oh." He hadn't come to be with her. Her heart sank with the sand. "Look." She shifted her flashlight beam to the nest. "Did you know they'd be hatching?"

"Not for sure. Looks like I got here at the right time."

It was freaky how often he showed up like this. "I was starting to shiver. You did get here at the right time." She slipped the shirt over her head. "Just like you did when I fell at Ancient Angry Edna's, and when you made it back to Shalima's and got me out of that chicken coop. Jake was about to kill me!"

"Come on, Red." He wrapped his arm around her neck and squeezed. "I wouldn't let anything happen to you."

Kenzie leaned her head on his shoulder. A leaf in an unpredictable breeze, her heart took off again. It soared, fluttered, then lurched. What was really going on between them? Living with jumping-bean nerves was exhausting. "Angelo, you and me? What's going on? Are we—?"

"Family, Red. We're family."

Salty pounced on Angelo. "You, too, Spiceman."

Kenzie raised her head even as her heart bottomed out. His answer wasn't a surprise. He'd said it before. It sure wasn't what she'd dreamed of hearing. Still, it was more than she'd once even hoped for.

Grasping Angelo's hand tightly, Kenzie lifted it from her shoulder. "Family's good." She faced him, managing a weak, but sincere smile. "No matter what happens... Family's forever."

A messy mix of joy and sadness bubbled, threatening to spill. She released Angelo's hand to switch off the flashlight, then knelt by the nest, hugging the excited puppy. Behind her, Angelo flipped the bucket upside down and sat on it.

"What's with the bucket?" she asked. A nice neutral subject.

"Thought you'd never ask. Dad's collecting them. Between Fisher and a couple of builders, he's already got a truck full."

"Seriously?" Wide-eyed, Kenzie asked, "For fishermen when they buy your bait?"

"No, for playing drums in the symphony." His you're-an-idiot tone was back, minus the old sharp edges. Playfully, with an awkward rhythm, he hand-thumped the bucket's side.

The nest erupted.

"Wow. You drummed them out."

Kenzie and Angelo burst into a giggling duet as he performed a drum roll. "Let the show begin." On his final beat, the turtles took off.

Kenzie sat and scooted backward against the bucket. Hugging her knees, enjoying the miracle. Salty lay at her feet. Angelo leaned forward. Arms encircling Kenzie, he rested his elbows on his knees and his head on hers. A watchful big brother. Not a bad thing to have, really.

A salty-soft breeze enveloped them, comforting as an heirloom quilt. Kenzie inhaled slowly and deeply. With every breath another muscle relaxed.

The hatchlings scrambled closer and closer to the sea, racing freely into their new life. *We did this. Angelo and I. We made sure these babies lived.* She shifted her gaze to the sky. There, in the moon's glowing circle, the face of Old Turtle beamed.

292

AUTHOR NOTES

Although all characters, events, and most locations in *Stakeout* are fictitious (including Turtle Beach), the island of Big Pine Key is real. The heart of Big Pine Key is about 17 miles from the real Turtle Hospital in Marathon, Florida. To reach the hospital, visitors travel east from Big Pine Key across the stunning Seven Mile Bridge. This famous 6.79 mile-long bridge rises *sky high*, as Kenzie describes it, above Moser Channel, providing one of the most breathtaking views in the Florida Keys.

Threats to Sea Turtle Nests and Hatchlings

All dangers to sea turtles in *Stakeout* from both nature and people are real. In the wild, raccoons are one of the most aggressive predators of eggs and hatchlings. Dogs, too, often destroy nests. (Salty, the turtle-protecting dog, is a product of my imagination.)

Stakeout focuses on egg poachers as a major danger. Luckily, poaching eggs is rare in the United States. But as recently as 2009, the Florida Fish and Wildlife Conservation Commission reported poaching in Palm Beach. At that time turtle eggs were selling on the black market for thirty-five dollars a dozen.

A greater danger to sea turtle nests is building homes and businesses near oceans. Construction pollutes water and causes beach erosion. Both destroy nesting habitats, so the sea turtle population decreases. Buildings also increase artificial lighting. As Ana's father discovered in the story, these lights can confuse hatchlings and throw them off course. Baby turtles may end up in dangerous territory or even die.

The Sea Turtle Conservancy website has a more complete list of threats to sea turtle survival at http://www.conserveturtles.org/ seaturtleinformation.php?page=threats.

History of the Turtle Hospital

The founding of the Turtle Hospital is a unique story. In 1980 a successful auto dealer, Richie Moretti, moved from the big city of Orlando to quiet Marathon Key, Florida. His dream? To retire peacefully—relax, fish and quietly bask in sand, salt water, and sun. Ever the businessman, Richie soon bought a small motel and went back to work.

Richie's Hidden Harbor Motel prided itself on a saltwater pool that soon went out of fashion. So Richie built a new freshwater pool. He transformed the old saltwater pool into an aquarium to entertain his guests, filling it with local fish such as snapper, barracuda, and tarpon.

During the 1980s Ninja-Turtle frenzy, a young Ninja fan wondered why the pool had no turtles. Richie's mental wheels spun into action.

By law sea turtles were highly protected. He could only capture turtles to rehabilitate them. Who could have imagined that humanoid Ninja Turtles would inspire a sea turtle hospital?

Richie bought the gas station next to the motel and turned it into a hospital with state-of-the-art equipment. He brought in veterinarians to treat the animals and paid for the hospital through motel income.

In September 1991 Monroe County Sheriff Rick Roth gave the hospital a confiscated burglar tool. Thieves had used this 14-inch-long, fiber-optic viewing scope to peer through small holes drilled into safes. (The hospital used this tool until they acquired the endoscope Dr. Lily uses in *Stakeout*.) Before the hospital had this new tool, doctors could only see tumors inside a turtle's body on fuzzy x-ray images. These pictures did not clearly show the difference between internal organs and tumors. With the new tool, hospital staff no longer released turtles with unseen tumors.

These tumors are caused by a disease called fibropapilloma. First seen in the 1930s, this disease is very widespread in Florida turtles. Little is known about its cause or cure. The Turtle Hospital uses surgery to remove any tumors from rescued sea turtles. Often these turtles successfully return to the wild. But surgery does not stop the disease.

The Turtle Hospital has been working with the University of Florida to research cures. Their mission has spread. Mote Marine Laboratory and Aquarium in Sarasota, Florida, and Clearwater Marine Aquarium, in Clearwater, Florida, both treat and research this disease. And in January 2010, Gumbo Limbo Nature Center in Boca Raton, Florida, received a state permit to treat fibropapilloma. Gumbo Limbo is also working hard to study this disease. Researchers at these sites hope to soon find a cure so turtles no longer have to suffer.

It's difficult to imagine a bright after-math of a hurricane. But in 2005 Hurricane Wilma wreaked havoc on the hospital and motel. No turtles were lost, but the property was badly damaged. Once again, Richie had a brilliant idea. He turned the hospital into a charity, offered educational tours, and opened a gift shop. He also restored the old motel to house hospital workers on site. As of 2010, admissions and donations provided total support for the Turtle Hospital.

Today the Turtle Hospital in Marathon, Florida, is a major tourist destination, unlike the quiet, private organization it was when Kenzie and Ana visited it. Though many visitors come to observe sea turtles in rehab, sadly they will not see the tarpon that once swam with the turtles. In the record-breaking cold winter of 2009–2010, while hospital staff and volunteers worked frantically to save nearly 200 sea turtles from death due to cold shock, the tarpon died.

Tours and outreach programs support the hospital's *Rescue, Rehab, Release* mission. As Richie and his assistant, Ryan Butts, told me, "Education is working." They shared the story of a young lobster fisherman who struggled to pull on board a 120-pound injured loggerhead that could or would not dive for food. (To preserve energy, sea turtles naturally stay afloat when they are ill.)

As mentioned in *Stakeout*, many lobster fishermen are not sea turtle fans because fishermen and turtles compete for the catch. But through outreach programs, this fisherman had learned how hard it is for sea turtles to survive. As a result, he delayed his fishing trip to rescue and deliver a sick turtle to the hospital.

Since it opened, the Turtle Hospital has treated and released more than 1,000 sea turtles—from its first two green turtle patients to hawksbills, loggerheads, and, the most endangered of all, Kemp's ridley.

Because of his passionate work to protect sea turtles and their habitat, Richie Moretti was awarded the prestigious 2007 International Fund for Animal Welfare (IFAW) Animal Action Award.

You can learn more about the amazing work of the Marathon Turtle Hospital by taking a virtual tour at http://www.turtlehospital.org/. There you can sign up for the hospital's free monthly newsletter full of rescue and release news. It also gives updates on the health and wellbeing of the resident turtles. The site and newsletter include stories and photos of individual turtles, the people who rescued them, the staff who treat them, and the schoolchildren and local organizations who support them.

The Turtle Hospital staff, volunteers, and members are true heroes. As we care for other living creatures on our planet, we also care for ourselves. You can be part of the effort by spreading the word, visiting the hospital online or in person, or joining the team with your donation.

Harvesting Sea Turtles and Their Eggs—Legally and Illegally

In many coastal towns outside the United States, in particular Central America and parts of Asia, people eat or sell sea turtle eggs. They do this even where harvesting, or taking, sea turtle eggs is banned. And, as mentioned in *Stakeout*, some communities value and harvest eggs as aphrodisiacs (love potions). Unfortunately, some people also harvest adult turtles. This sometimes happens even in the United States where it is a serious crime. People hunt green turtles for their meat and hawksbills for the beauty of their shells, which they make into jewelry and other fashion accessories.

Amazingly, eggs are harvested legally in some parts of the world because it helps sea turtles survive. A surprising, and often misunderstood, example of sea turtle conservation takes place in Ostional, Costa Rica, on the Pacific coast. During turtle nesting season, certain people are allowed to collect huge numbers of olive ridley sea turtle eggs. A *legal* harvest. Not only is eating eggs an ancient cultural practice, but the people also sell the eggs. Through education, residents of Ostional have learned that a controlled harvest allows thousands of olive ridley turtles to live that otherwise would never hatch.

Here's how this legal harvest came to be. In separate crawls known as *arribadas* (Spanish for *arrivals*), thousands of olive ridleys nest over a 2–5 day period on a beach much smaller than it used to be. *Arribadas* happen once or twice a month from July to December. Eggs laid by the first mass landing of turtles during each *arribada* are destroyed by the second arrival of turtles as they accidentally dig up the first nests while laying their eggs.

There is not enough habitat to relocate the first eggs, so the government permits a group of local natives to harvest these eggs. These villagers collect eggs only from the first layings of each *arribada*. Eggs that would otherwise be broken, decay, and poison the sand. This benefits the villagers, and the beach remains healthier for later nests. During the remaining days of each *arribada*, the same harvesters clean the beach and protect it from poachers.

This practice has turned former poachers into conservation leaders. A way of life has been saved, and people's lives have improved because they can buy legal and cheaper eggs. Demand for illegally poached eggs from other areas in Costa Rica has decreased. More turtles hatch. So Ostional's method of harvesting benefits both turtles and humans.

A different conservation approach is used on Costa Rica's east coast. The largest green turtle nesting site in the Western Hemisphere is located in the remote area of Tortuguero on the Caribbean coast. After scientists moved here to research this important turtle population, villagers learned the importance of saving the endangered green turtle. They also learned that eating turtles and their eggs poses a threat to sea turtle survival. Slowly, villagers realized that if they stopped eating sea turtles and instead protected them, they could make more money from tourists who would come to see the endangered species. Today Tortuguero has increased its number of nesting green turtles by 400% and is a model for other small communities.

However it is done, protecting sea turtle nests is critical, because only a small percentage of sea turtles live to reproduce, or have babies. Hawksbills may lay eggs as early as 3 years of age, but loggerheads do not reproduce before 12–30 years of age. Green turtles do not lay eggs before 20–50 years of age. Few eggs hatch, and many turtles do not survive to adulthood. Eggs are on the menu for many land predators. Raccoons, wild hogs, ants, coyotes, dogs, foxes, and ghost crabs devour turtle eggs. Sea birds and fish such as tarpon and jacks feed on hatchlings in the water.

Dangers to Adult Turtles

Once sea turtles are grown—except to lay eggs near the beach where they were born— they spend their lives in the ocean. There they have one major predator: the shark. Because sea turtles cannot pull their heads or fins into their shells, sharks often bite off fins, leaving turtles to die a slow death due to infection or blood loss.

Humans also threaten sea turtle survival in many ways. One major danger to turtles is trash—especially plastic bags. As Kenzie learned, plastic bags resemble jellyfish, a favorite food of many turtles. If not properly disposed of, garbage makes its way to the ocean, and feeding turtles often swallow it. In addition, boats injure many sea turtles.

Possibly the most serious worldwide threat to sea turtles is getting tangled in fishing gear, from simple fishing line to shrimp trawler nets. The good news is that in 1987 the United States passed laws requiring all U.S. shrimpers to use turtle exclusion devices (TEDs) on their trawlers. Since then, turtle deaths in U.S. waters have dramatically decreased. Even better, in 1989 the United States passed a law requiring the use of TEDs by all countries that export shrimp to U.S. markets.

Save-A-Turtle

Those who care about sea turtles can also join groups that protect them. In the story, Protect-A-Turtle (PAT) is based on an actual organization called Save-A-Turtle, Inc., of the Florida Keys. This group was formed in 1985. It is a volunteer, non-profit group that preserves and protects rare and endangered sea turtles as well as their habitats in the Keys and throughout the world.

Like PAT volunteers in *Stakeout*, Save-A-Turtle volunteers meet at the Turtle Hospital. They perform all the duties described in the story as well as many other important services. I promise there has never been a devious poacher among them.

Websites

Clearwater Marine Aquarium: http://www.seewinter.com/

Gumbo Limbo Nature Center: http://gumbolimbo.org/

Mote Marine Laboratory and Aquarium: http://www.mote.org/

Save-A-Turtle, Inc., of the Florida Keys: http://www.save-a-turtle.org/

The Sea Turtle Conservancy: http://www.conserveturtles.org/

Turtle Hospital, Marathon, Florida: http://www.turtlehospital.org/

For more information on fibropapilloma:

http://www.turtlehospital.org/fibropapilloma.htm

Other exciting YA novels from Leap Books...

**Island Sting
Bonnie J. Doerr
978-1-61603-002-5**

Kenzie didn't expect her first summer in the Florida Keys to be murder. She trades New York streets for life in a wildlife refuge and is soon tracking the poacher of the tiny Key deer.

Her new home does have some benefits --mainly Angelo, an island native, who teams up with her to nab the culprit.

But will they both survive when the killer turns from stalking deer to hunting humans?

Island Sting includes notes on the endangered Florida Key deer and National Key Deer refuge.

**For the Love of
Strangers
Jacqueline Horsfall
978-1-61603-003-2**

Philoxenia. When police call using this code word, 16-year-old Darya knows she will be sheltering strangers: women with missing teeth, dislocated jaws, black eyes, and stalking husands.

Other strangers--nonhuman--seek her protection, too, whispering from the depths of the forest in voices only she can hear. What if you discovered your birth fulfilled an ancient prophecy? What if you were destined to save an entire species?

Would you heed the call?

All her parents wanted was for Eryn to live a normal life...

Under My Skin
Judith Graves
ISBN-13 978-1-61603-000-1

Redgrave had its share of monsters before Eryn moved to town. Mauled pets, missing children. The Delacroix family is taking the blame, but Eryn knows the truth. Something stalks the night. Wade, the police chief 's son and Redgrave High's resident hottie, warns her the Delacroix are dangerous. But then so is Eryn--in fact, she's lethal. But she can't help falling for one of the Delacroix boys, dark, brooding--human Alec. And then her world falls apart.

Every woman in the Maxwell family has the gift of sight.

Freaksville
Kitty Keswick
ISBN-13 978-1-61603-001-8
ISBN-10 1-61603-001-1

A talent sixteen-year-old Kasey would gladly give up. Until Kasey has a vision about Josh Johnstone, the foreign exchange student from England. The vision leads her into deep waters...a lead in a play and into the arms of Josh. But Josh, too, has a secret. Something that could put them all in danger. To solve a mystery of a supernatural haunting, they must uncover the secrets of the haunted theater when they are trapped on the night of the full moon.

Thank you for purchasing this Leap Books publication. For other exciting teen novels, please visit our online bookstore at www.leapbks.com.

For questions or more information contact us at info@leapbks.com

CPSIA information can be obtained at www.ICGtesting.com
Printed in the USA
BVOW03s1226280714

360562BV00001B/2/P